Praise for *The Party Upstairs*

WINNER OF THE EDWARD LEWIS WALLANT AWARD

"Sharp and well-observed." —*New York Post*'s Best Books of the Year

"There's nothing like a great New York City novel, and praise be to the novelists who take us there: Think Cathleen Schine, Elinor Lipman, Emma Straub, Jennifer Egan, and now Lee Conell, whose exquisite debut gets to the heart of the city. . . . Like Kiley Reid's *Such a Fun Age*, *The Party Upstairs* will make you laugh even as you grapple with how money defines many of its characters' most significant choices. . . . An on-the-nose, of-the-moment dark comedy that delves deep into issues of wealth, gender, and privilege in the most iconic of American cities."
—*BookPage* (starred review)

"Masterful . . . A portrait of aspiration, class immobility, love, and rage, it's a gem." —*The Kenyon Review*

"Conell manifests a tension so tangible that we are left on edge, desperate for some cathartic return. But in a tale that is as poignant as it is funny, Conell's portrait of class division and privilege ultimately reminds us of the gaping disparities between our expectations and the harsh realities that often follow." —*ZYZZYVA*

"A portrait of social class in New York City, *The Party Upstairs* is at once witty, spooky, and lively, with several realities all performing themselves simultaneously. Lee Conell is a maestro." —Lorrie Moore

"Singularly suited to the specific times we're in . . . The novel's portrayal of class, the real and lasting effects that wealth, or lack thereof, can have on your mentality and outlook, is unparalleled." —*Literary Hub*

"A gripping tale of class and privilege . . . page-turning." —*The Economist*

"Lee Conell is already one of my favorite writers, and *The Party Upstairs* is a triumphant debut novel. She writes with such precision, utilizing a sharp sense of humor, that the cuts go deep, so expertly placed, and you find yourself irrevocably changed. Conell's voice is wholly original, unafraid to work with issues of class and gender and family. A wonder in every way."
—Kevin Wilson, author of *Nothing to See Here* and *The Family Fang*

"*The Party Upstairs* brings the Aristotelian unities to one Upper West Side apartment building in her debut, which follows a single day in the life of Ruby, the daughter of the super who oversees a gentrifying complex. What follows is Conell's perceptive observation of how class and politics plays out in the real world, behind the metal chain securing an apartment door."
—*The Millions*

"Conell, who won the Nelson Algren Literary Award for short fiction in 2016, ignites this suspenseful novel, taking place over a single day, with a passion, psychological insight, and a keen sensibility about class and economic difference." —*The National Book Review*

"The chapters alternate focus between Martin and Ruby, depicting their self-interrogations and flickering emotions with a nimble facility that recalls Virginia Woolf . . . sharp and affecting."
—*Chattanooga Times Free Press*

"*The Party Upstairs* is a nuanced, heartfelt novel that offers righteous anger spiked with enough good humor to keep the cocktail balanced, and a refreshing twist on an old genre: it doesn't try to disentangle character from class. The tangle, it suggests, is the point." —*Washington Square Review*

"Conell's smashing debut creates a vivacious microcosm of life inside a tony Manhattan co-op building. . . . Conell's talent for storytelling, wicked sense of humor, and compassion for her characters will leave readers eager for her next book." —*Publishers Weekly* (starred review)

"Conell's debut perfectly captures the co-op's ecosystem and the ways class informs every interaction, reaction, and relationship inside it. . . . Conell's writing remains clear-eyed, darkly funny, and deeply empathetic. A slow-burning debut that keenly dissects privilege, power, and the devastation of unfulfilled expectations." —*Kirkus Reviews*

"*The Party Upstairs* made my pulse race. It builds its tensions expertly, like a thriller, unearthing suspense from the daily struggle to earn and keep a paycheck, the never-ending threat of job loss and destitution. Lee Conell perceives everyone she writes about, rich and poor alike, with perfect clarity: on the one side those who gaze out on poverty as a kind of spectacle, on the other those who endure it as a kind of bombardment, and in the middle Martin and Ruby, the superintendent of an Upper West Side apartment building and his debt-ridden daughter, who pretend—but only pretend—that they're able to watch the bombs fall from afar."
—Kevin Brockmeier, author of *The Illumination*

"In *The Party Upstairs* Lee Conell follows Martin and Ruby, father and daughter, through a single day as they negotiate the exasperating occupants, living and dead, of the co-op where Martin works as the superintendent. Conell writes with wonderful wit and empathy about the importance of money, the longing for a larger life, and the confusions between a parent and an adult child. An irresistible novel."

—Margot Livesey, author of *The Flight of Gemma Hardy* and *The Boy in the Field*

"I savored every word of this funny, wise, and cool book. Ruby's post-college return to her parents' apartment in the basement of a building near the Museum of Natural History is hardly triumphal, yet on one March day and night she and her father—the building's super—manage to do and undo their best-laid plans and beliefs about who they are to each other and in the world. Lee Conell is profound, wise, and witty, and in *The Party Upstairs* has offered us all a manual for how to care for the spaces we inhabit and the people and events that upset our equilibrium in ways both good and bad—including ourselves. This novel will take its well-earned place among the enduring books about young women. It is serious-minded and relevant in the hardest times, and also offers the pleasures of a great party." —Alice Elliott Dark

"*The Party Upstairs* is a dazzling and dioramic novel—Lee Conell situates so much intricate life and energy inside of one day, one building. I'll be recommending this smart, funny, suspenseful, timely, and beautifully constructed book to friends and strangers."

—Chris Bachelder, author of *The Throwback Special*

"*The Party Upstairs* is thrilling—fiercely intelligent, meticulously crafted, and darkly, painfully funny. At every turn, on every page, Lee Conell offers rare insight and rewards her lucky readers' attention. This is a first-rate writer, unafraid and illuminating and vitally necessary."

—Bret Anthony Johnston, author of *Remember Me Like This*

PENGUIN BOOKS

THE PARTY UPSTAIRS

Lee Conell is the author of the story collection *Subcortical*, which was awarded The Story Prize's Spotlight Award. Her short fiction has received the *Chicago Tribune*'s Nelson Algren Award and appears in the *Oxford American*, *The Kenyon Review*, *Glimmer Train*, *American Short Fiction*, and elsewhere. She is a 2020 National Endowment for the Arts Fellow as well as the recipient of creative writing fellowships from the Japan–United States Friendship Commission, the Tennessee Arts Commission, and the Sewanee Writers' Conference.

ALSO BY LEE CONELL

Subcortical

THE
PARTY
UPSTAIRS

LEE CONELL

Penguin Books

PENGUIN BOOKS

An imprint of Penguin Random House LLC

penguinrandomhouse.com

First published in the United States of America by Penguin Press,
an imprint of Penguin Random House LLC, 2020
Published in Penguin Books 2021

ISBN 9781984880291 (paperback)

THE LIBRARY OF CONGRESS HAS CATALOGED THE HARDCOVER EDITION AS FOLLOWS:

Names: Conell, Lee, author.
Title: The party upstairs / Lee Conell.
Identifiers: LCCN 2019038097 (print) | LCCN 2019038098 (ebook) |
ISBN 9781984880277 (hardcover) | ISBN 9781984880284 (ebook)
Classification: LCC PS3603.O5329 P37 2020 (print) |
LCC PS3603.O5329 (ebook) | DDC 813/.6—dc23
LC record available at https://lccn.loc.gov/2019038097
LC ebook record available at https://lccn.loc.gov/2019038098

ISBN 9781984881892 (export)

Printed in the United States of America
1st Printing

BOOK DESIGN BY LUCIA BERNARD

CONTENTS

NIGHT

A LATER DAY

MORNING

1   THE INTRUDER

It was still dark out when Martin and his daughter, Ruby, sat down on opposite sides of the living room floor, closed their eyes, and tried to forget each other. Ruby, twenty-four, had moved back home only a week ago, and this was the first time she had agreed to meditate with her father. But instead of being present with his inhalations and exhalations, Martin found himself leaping into the future, stupidly hopeful that after they'd finished meditating, Ruby would hug him and say she could already feel her sense of wonder swelling and her anxiety ebbing and her inner light growing more numinous, and oh, even though her dad was just a building super he was smarter than any of her college professors, he was the smartest guy she knew, and she was so grateful to him. An embarrassingly needy fantasy. Martin's job often involved trafficking in the small embarrassments of others—in the last week alone, the corporate lawyer in 4D had called screaming with fear about a water bug in the hallway, the financial analyst in 9A had called about her tampon-clogged toilet, the hedge-fund-portfolio manager in 6C had admitted he'd drunkenly tossed his keys on the subway tracks—but he still never felt fully prepared for how humiliating his own thoughts could be, especially when they revealed his desire for the approval of his daughter.

Anyway, why seek her approval at all? Ruby was a mess—deep in debt, newly jobless, nervous about her interview today, and angry at finding herself back living with her parents in the basement apartment after years of steps toward some higher elevation. Martin should expect no hug from her, no declaration of gratitude. Of course, it would be nice if the meditation helped her a little. Maybe she would look up afterward and smile at him.

Only a few minutes in, Ruby coughed. Martin opened his eyes.

"So," Ruby said, "I'm not feeling happier yet."

"Meditation's actually not about feeling happier." He used the same gentle voice he had used on the couple in 7B when he told them they would have to pull up the blue Brazilian marble tile in their bathroom because of a leak. "Meditation's about looking inward. It's about increasing self-awareness."

"Oh, Dad," Ruby said, "if *you* were self-aware, you'd recognize this whole enlightened-guru thing is just your secular Judaism deteriorating into some half-baked New Age muck."

"That New Age muck helps lower my blood pressure." The gentle blue-tile-pulling voice was gone. "I need nice low blood pressure, Ruby, so I don't lose it when yuppie tenants scream at me about rats nibbling away at their cheese straws."

"God, the rats." She stood up from the floor. "Can we not talk about the rats again?"

"Lower your voice. Your mom's still asleep."

"Mom's always saying she never had the patience for meditation and you don't push it on her."

"She's not the one anxious and awake before the sun's even up."

Ruby plopped onto the couch. "Maybe I can try being mindful from over here? The floor is cold."

Of course the floor was cold. It was early March, the chill outside somehow made rawer by the nearness of spring, the hope for better weather. Still, Martin was pretty sure you were supposed to meditate on or close to the floor, no matter how cold it was. You could sit on a meditation bench, like Martin did, or a pillow, but you had to remain low to the ground. You definitely weren't supposed to go around seeking inner peace on couches, and especially not on *that* couch, which was an ugly couch, upholstered in a butterscotch-orange velour fabric with a print of an old mill and a couple of paunchy cows. Debra had forced him to drag it in from the courtyard's alleyway years ago ("It's not hideous, Martin, it's retro!"). The sad cow eyes repeated on the fabric behind his daughter somehow made him even more irritated with Ruby. "You know what happens if I *do* lose my cool in front of the tenants?" he asked her. "I lose this job."

"You've been the super here forever." She looked down at him. "They wouldn't fire you now. You're basically an Upper West Side institution."

An Upper West Side institution. Like the Museum of Natural History, where Ruby's job interview was today. Maybe she would mention Martin to the museum people. Maybe she would joke, "You should put my dad in a diorama." He felt the meditation bench digging into his thighs and said, "Actually, Ruby, the management company would fire me in a heartbeat if I shouted at a tenant. They want a younger guy. If I lose my cool, I lose this job. And if I lose this job, we lose our insurance and we lose this apartment." And if they lost this apartment, Martin and Debra would be homeless, at least for a little while. So much of their savings had gone to Ruby's college education. Leading to what? Now she sat there on the couch, wearing baggy jeans and a large T-shirt for a charity race Martin was sure she hadn't run, its front polka-dotted with the slogans of corporate sponsors. The shirt must have belonged to John, her exboyfriend, who had recently kicked her out of the apartment they'd shared in Brooklyn. Why was his unemployed daughter here in the basement wearing an oversize T-shirt covered with the names of massive banks?

"Wow, Dad. What a glare." Ruby sat straighter on the couch. "I'm not sure the meditation's working for you."

"Maybe don't be so snotty about my meditation practice while your mom and I let you stay here."

"Please." Ruby lifted her hands, as though the pink stretch of her palms should be enough to earn his compassion. "I feel pathetic already. Don't guilt me."

But his guilting must have possessed some power, because she hopped off the couch and sat down on the floor again, joining him once more in the muck of his spiritual practice. She bent her head and would not look at him. He closed his eyes, focused on his inhalation. At least Ruby was showing more signs of shame than she had last week. "I'm not your human daughter anymore," she had said to Martin and Debra as she moved back in, dragging old grocery bags full of clothes through the door. "It turns out you birthed a living, breathing think piece. The failure to launch millennial blah-deeblah." She had looked expectantly at her parents, but neither one of them had laughed. Her words had sounded rehearsed to Martin. Bravado paired with self-deprecation—was this all her education had taught her?

Ruby had graduated from college just after the 2008 recession hit and she was still mired in debt. Martin and Debra had contributed what they could spare. Stupidly, the specter of debt had been the least of Martin's worries when Ruby first moved away to attend her very expensive university on a partial scholarship. At the time, he had most feared that she would start to behave like the tenants in the building. When she called home to say that her dorm looked like a castle or to gush about some art history course ("Truly, Professor Sharondale's reconceptualized my understanding of dioramas as a creative force . . ."), part of him could only hear the call she might make after she hung up, a call to a maintenance man like him— some guy without a college degree—complaining about the appearance of mold in the dorm bathroom or about a dead light bulb.

"Cut the self-pity crap and just be proud of your daughter," sweet old Lily in 5A, his "building mom," used to tell him, with such sincerity that tiny veinlets surfaced on her wrinkled forehead. "It's not *Ruby's* fault the fever dream of free-market capitalism has corrupted the realm of higher education." Lily had always tried to cheer Martin up by blaming his parental angst on the free market. Several months ago Martin had gone to 5A when 4A complained about a leak, and found Lily slumped over on the toilet. She was dead from a hemorrhagic stroke. There was a leak in Lily's brain, it turned out, a blood vessel that had burst. She'd left the faucet on and when Martin saw her there, the running water had seemed to roar. Later that same day Kenneth in the penthouse had left five messages on Martin's answering machine about a giant bird ("An eagle or owl or whatever," Kenneth said, though Martin suspected a red-tailed hawk) dropping a decapitated and mangled pigeon carcass on his deck once again and could Martin clean the mess up?

It had felt almost sacrilegious to Martin, hearing Kenneth's voice so soon after seeing Lily's body. Lily had hated Kenneth. Before he moved into the penthouse, Kenneth had lived in 6A, the apartment above Lily's, with his wife and daughter. "I feel the creepiest laissez-faire vibes oozing through my ceiling," Lily had told Martin once back then, in the early nineties. "When Kenneth passes me in the lobby, he looks right through me. I'm an old woman, I'm rent-controlled, I'm invisible to him."

"Maybe he and his family will move out," Martin said. "Kenneth's always complaining that 6A's too small."

"He's waiting for me to die is what he's doing. He wants to buy my apartment and create a two-story duplex with 5A and 6A. I'm sure of it. He's got the Manifest Destiny glaze in his eyes. How can you let Ruby have playdates with his bratty daughter?"

"Ruby likes Caroline."

"Ruby likes Caroline's dolls."

Kenneth must have gotten tired of waiting for Lily to die. Once some of his portfolio investments had paid off, he received permission from the co-op board to build a penthouse on the roof. After he and his family had moved into the penthouse in the late nineties, Kenneth didn't sell their former apartment but rented it out to some sort of finance person. Time passed. Kenneth got stouter, Kenneth got divorced, Kenneth lost his hair. But he did not lose the Manifest Destiny glaze in his eyes. After Lily died, he did exactly what she had so often predicted. He politely kicked his renter out of 6A and then he bought 5A. Now he was in the process of constructing a two-story duplex, which he planned to keep for a while as an investment property. "My nest egg," he'd told Martin with a wink the other day in the elevator, and Martin had thought about the pair of pigeons nesting outside on the courtyard's ledge. Every morning, Martin fed those birds, hoping that one day he'd see their babies hatch. They were the closest thing he had to an investment property.

The opposite of mindful contemplation, probably, was contemplating another man's real estate. Martin's back had gone stiff, his knees creaked, and yet the older he got, the more nimbly his brain made wild leaps through time and space. He was supposed to be here, present, meditating next to his daughter, not thinking about Lily's death or Kenneth's apartments or the pigeons in the courtyard. He breathed in. He breathed out.

But then the heat pipe in the living room thumped and he remembered how the woman in 4B had recently complained about the thumping sound coming from 5B, which was caused by the private tango lessons the woman in 5B was taking with the woman in 2C, who had recently divorced the man who had once lived in 7D and who had lost his job in advertising just around the time Ruby graduated and was now in the process of selling his apartment to an heiress whose financial consultant lived in 6C and had complained recently about a leak caused by the attendant to the sick lady in 7C who poured grease down the kitchen sink, didn't know any better, and who rode the subway from the Bronx every morning with the nanny in 3A whose young charges tried to poison with cayenne-infused chocolate the pair of yipping Yorkies in 3D, an act of pure malice that didn't much bother anybody but especially not the attorney in 7A who had seen the dogs pissing directly onto the red-and-white impatiens she had asked to be planted in the tree pit outside the building, which were popular flowers with some in the building, yes, but others, like the real estate guy from Lyon in 6B and the financial consultant from Moscow in 8C, felt impatiens were tacky and populist and had tried to advocate for something more elegant, begonias, perhaps, and also wanted the green awning to be replaced with a burgundy one, but 9D had argued against both begonias and the burgundy color, mostly because he believed

8C was responsible for bringing in the new team of Russian elevator mechanics, who had, in the past, worked on missiles in what 7C was pretty sure these mechanics still called the motherland, and who 7C was also pretty sure were spies of some sort, a suspicion she had confided exclusively (she thought) to 3A, but 3A blabbered about it to the board members and her blabbering had backfired, so that now 7C was considered a paranoid woman, a possible isolationist bigot, and a *loose cannon*, which was probably true, since after the attacks on September 11, 7C had spent weeks in Westchester calling Martin about an oncoming toxic cloud headed for Manhattan and asking if he could double-check that the windows were all the way closed in the apartment, which was actually the same request made by 7B, who recently had maybe got bedbugs (they blamed the house cleaner) leading 4B (once the news got out) to panic and do laundry for six hours straight, which really pissed off 1D, because they had kids and the kids had soccer practice and 4B, whose child merely finger painted and did no competitive sports at all, was using all the machines, which 4B said was a necessary thing because didn't 1D hear about the bedbugs in 7B and 1D said the bedbugs were just a rumor, the bedbug dog from Queens had come in and sensed nothing, but still the paranoia reached such a pitch that many of 7B's belongings eventually wound up in the basement and Martin and Rafael, the porter, had had to drag armoires and mattresses and books and clothes out into the courtyard, and into the alley, and up the stairs for the garbage people to take away to waste transfer centers, to barges, to landfills, to landfills, to landfills.

Martin's heart, that dumb, flawed blood hauler, made sounds like a garbage truck in his chest.

He had fucked up mindfulness again.

Martin must concentrate on his breath, must forget the many

stories of complaint within this nine-story building. He must cool the hallways of his heart. No, not hallways. That was an apartment building sort of term. With the heart, you called them chambers. He knew all about the heart now. He'd googled "heart biological parts" after Lily's death had increased the constricted feeling around his chest. His own dad had died young of a heart attack. Over the last year or two, even before Lily's death, he'd begun to watch what he ate, gotten deeper into meditation, started bird-watching, all in the interest of lowering his resting heart rate. Of course, thinking too much about his resting heart rate seemed to heighten it again. He heard it now, his heartbeat quickening. He wanted to open his eyes, to stand up, to abandon his meditation bench.

But he needed to model for Ruby the soul-widening power of a single exhalation, the way it might make even their cramped, dark living room seem expansive, empty. Lily's apartment was empty now. A vision drifted into Martin's mind: Lily standing in 5A as a ghost. Her skin was as blue as when he'd found her, but her lined face had become a new smooth fabric. This Ghost Lily spun around inside what had been her apartment, her eyes widening as she registered the changes. Her home, 5A, all torn up, in the middle of a total renovation, a gut job. Her home, 5A, the victim of her despised free market. The furniture gone. The floorboards ripped away.

These days the apartments in this building were often gutted as soon as a long-term tenant moved out or died. The building was almost a hundred years old—prewar, the Realtors liked to say in hushed, incantatory tones. New tenants praised the character of the building's brick and limestone façade, lauded the attention to detail found in the scrollwork on the columns beneath the front awning. But they were increasingly eager to rip up the building's insides, the black-and-white bathroom tiles, the cramped kitchens. They usually preserved just enough original details to claim the apartment still had "prewar accents," which would help if they decided to sell the place down the line.

When Martin had first started out as a super in this building, a little over twenty-five years ago, the tenants had had more money than him, but the majority didn't have *that* much more. There were schoolteachers, musicians, pharmacists, guys with union jobs. That wasn't to say there weren't still assholes to contend with. Always in Manhattan, always everywhere, there were plenty of assholes to contend with. But over time, there'd been a kind of evolution in what an empty apartment meant to Martin. Once it had represented a potential home for a potential asshole. Now it represented a potential investment property for a sure-thing asshole.

Ruby wouldn't like that thought. She had told him, when she was still in college and deep in her literature classes, that he should never generalize, shouldn't call the tenants assholes in a group like that, they were individuals, each with their own history of loss and trauma, they had actual *names*, they weren't just their apartment numbers. Martin had tried to explain that she wasn't telling him anything he hadn't figured out for himself. He was aware that just as his full humanness didn't register with all the tenants, theirs didn't always register with him, despite the fact that he often had to deal with their anxious phone calls and their bags of garbage and sometimes, when the plumber was running late, their literal shit. But trying to think about what personal history of loss and trauma might cause a tenant to scream at him for failing to change a light bulb in the lobby right away was, frankly, beyond Martin's paygrade. Sometimes people just behaved badly because they had the power to behave badly. And every year, the tenants behaved worse, it seemed. When he first became the building super, a couple of guys in the building had always helped Martin shovel the sidewalk during blizzards, no questions asked. This past winter, though he had only gotten grayer and his back had only gotten worse, nobody had once offered to help him shovel when it snowed.

Still, why whine? The building had never been a utopia and things always changed. People, storefronts, cities. Even the dioramas and animal models in the Museum of Natural History changed, became more interactive or accurate or whatever—Ruby once told him the museum people had added a belly button to the blue whale. The only thing that didn't change were the old men like Martin whining about how things were always changing. That was why he should be focusing on meditation. In meditation, you created a home out of constant change. You lived in the moment, which meant there was no past and no future and, in a way, no death.

Yet only in a way. Because Lily was dead. It had been sad when the other rent-controlled tenants had died, but Martin hadn't been nearly as close to any of them as he had been to Lily. Which was maybe why he was having this vision now of Ghost Lily spinning around in her apartment, spinning faster and faster, and did Ghost Lily know that Martin had helped move out the furniture, his back stooped under the weight of her favorite sofa? Did she know that Martin himself had let in the demo crews?

The vision did not stop there. After surveying her destroyed apartment, Ghost Lily swooped vengefully from 5A down through a long-defunct dumbwaiter shaft, zooming her spirit self past strata of primordial linoleum, ancient concrete, steel beams, the wire mesh for plastered walls, the entrails of deteriorating doorbell cables, an abandoned gas main that had supplied the residents' lamps before the building got electric lights—until she reached the basement apartment and shouted at Martin's gray head, in her chirpiest tone, "And then the super woke up!"

And Martin woke up. He'd fallen asleep. Heat rose to his face. Had Ruby noticed his less-than-mindful dozing? Her wide forehead was a little sweaty, her hair a tangled whirl. Thankfully, her eyes were still closed.

This wasn't his first Lily-is-back moment. Over the past few days, Martin had begun to hear her voice in his head—commercial bubbliness with an edge of mockery. Yesterday when he was putting out rattraps, she had said, *Martin creeps toward the glue traps under the kitchen sink. Those suckers will catch a rat easy as one, two, three!* When she was still alive, any time Martin had gone to 5A to plunge the toilet or fix drains, Lily had narrated his actions. She used the same tone she had deployed as a voice-over actress to sell laundry detergent decades ago, in what she called the foreign country of her youth. "Martin leans over the drain and scoops out, *oh*, is that a sparkling clump of wet hair?" "The new rattrap Martin's installing snaps into place just like that! Those cute diseased critters won't know what hit 'em!" "Martin mops the Gatorade off the floor with not just the vim but the *vigor* required of a middle-aged man living in late-stage capitalism!"

For a full twenty years, he had lived with this, an old woman making fun of him. After Lily's death late last year, a silence descended.

But since Ruby had returned to the building, Lily was back in his head. Her voice didn't show up all the time, just once or twice over the course of a day, when, in quiet moments, he'd hear her saying things like, *Martin is marching forward into the chilly morning, he's sweeping up the mouse droppings like a man with a plan!* It made him feel a little crazy (why was his mind calling forth Lily's voice?), a little haunted (was this voice actually Lily, somehow, séancing in his brain, or was it all a big grief-fueled hallucination?), and also a little wonderful (because it was Lily, Lily who was dead, practically present again).

A few days earlier, Billy the Exterminator was at the building. Martin had asked him, "Do you ever have dreams about the animals you've seen dead at work? Or visions? Or, um, auditory hallucinations?"

"They're not animals," Billy the Exterminator said. He was a small tight-muscled Italian man from Sheepshead Bay, in his early fifties, just a few years younger than Martin. "You got that? They're not animals I've killed. They're *pests*."

"Okay, fine. You ever have bad dreams about pests?"

"No," Billy the Exterminator said. "I dream more about the chickens. I do feel bad about the chickens. The chickens and the cows. I grew up on fast food and I didn't think about it, but then I saw one of those animal cruelty documentaries. Made me rethink my whole childhood. A secret for you, Martin." Billy the Exterminator breathed in. "I'm vegan." He breathed out. "Don't tell any of the guys."

Martin had stared for so long that Billy the Exterminator added, "I'm kidding."

"Are you?" Martin asked.

Forget Billy and his fast food and all his pests. Forget the interlinked web of tenants' complaints he carried in his head like a map. Forget the blue whale's new belly button. Forget Lily and her voice and her death. Meditation was supposed to lift you out of harmful neural pathways, build up the brain's gray matter. What did that mean? Martin wasn't sure, but if his work as a super had taught him anything, it was that people always wanted to build something. If you didn't have the money to build a new apartment, why not build your gray matter? So: back to the breath.

Was Ruby's breathing kind of shallow? Normally, when he meditated alone, Martin wore noise-canceling headphones, but he wasn't wearing them now. He had wanted to get a sense of how mindful her meditation really was. Her breaths definitely weren't deep enough. She was stressed, probably. She kept calling the museum job she was interviewing for today her dream job. *Dream job.* One of those terms used by overeducated upper-class adults, that she'd picked up at college, or from Kenneth's daughter and her friend, Caroline, probably. The idea that a job was a cloud, a fantastical package of nine-to-five wish fulfillment. What would Martin's dream job be? He had never had one. He just had jobs for getting by. Like this one as a super, which was a *good* job, which required no college degree, which came with a rent-free apartment and health insurance and all of that, a fine job, but not a dream job; instead a job that often gave old dudes nightmares about dead tenants.

He looked over to the answering machine. No blinking red light. No urgent messages. Ruby still had her eyes closed, but she winced a little, like she'd finally heard Martin's thoughts running amok. Or maybe the floor really was too cold for her.

"You need a cushion?" Martin said.

Ruby's eyes opened. "What?"

"Might be more comfortable with a cushion, is all. Or if you want, next week, I could make you a meditation bench like mine."

"You made that yourself?"

"Yeah. I made it out of the floorboards in Lily's apartment. As kind of, you know, a memorial."

Oops. Not smart. Ruby's eyelids did their cry-prep crinkling thing that he knew so well from the weepy moments of her kidhood. She had loved Lily as Martin had, as a kind of family member, a grandmother figure. Lily, who had been estranged from her own family, often babysat Ruby, taking her to museums, the park, marathoning movies on VHS with her, or sometimes just reading to her from her many perpetually in-progress manuscripts—a treatise on capital in the new millennium, a Trotskyite rewriting of *Pride and Prejudice*, a novel about a Victorian factory worker who gets away with killing her overseer. All those childhood days spent with Lily had meant Ruby was wrecked when she'd heard of her death. She had called Debra and cried on the phone to her every day for two weeks. Now Martin waited for the tears. But Ruby only shook her head.

"Neilson in 3C told me something catchy the other day, during one of our meditation sessions," Martin said, once the threat of sobs passed. "He said a good movie, a good TV show, a good story almost always begins with action. But if you want a good day, that begins with inaction."

"Inaction, huh?" Ruby rubbed at her temples. "Well, I'm pretty skilled at inaction. I can't believe you meditate with that idiot."

"He's not an idiot," Martin said. "He's just a tenant."

"Same difference."

"Ruby," Martin said, but he was smiling, glad that Ruby's don't-generalize-about-the-tenants-empathy-for-all campaign had clearly ended. Ruby smiled back, encouraged. "I'll never forget when he left that message on the machine at two in the morning," she said.

"Right before I had to take the SAT. Totally hysterical because he'd seen a mouse."

"But you still did good."

"Imagine how brilliant I'd have done if 3C didn't wake me up with his fear of rodents. Well. It doesn't matter now." Before Martin could study her face, figure out if she were telling the truth, she yawned. Probably, instead of meditating, they should both be trying to sleep. Martin had only gotten a few hours. Ruby's voice had kept him from sleeping until one (even as Debra snored away). She had been on the phone with Caroline. The girls had been close friends as children—all the playdates and imaginary worlds, the molding of clay spoons and plates for their dolls, the classes at the Art Students League. But despite the time she'd spent with Caroline in her youth, Martin had never felt Ruby properly understood the differences between them. In the middle of their hushed conversation last night, Ruby laughed a triumphant hoot of a laugh, and he thought he heard her say, "Listen, Caroline, the thing about my dad is . . ." before lowering her voice again.

The way she'd laughed had put a feeling in Martin's chest like a stone. *The thing about my dad is.*

The thing about Martin's own dad was he'd been an angry man. The thing about Martin's own dad was sometimes he'd smack Martin if Martin so much as smiled at him funny. The thing about growing up with a dad like that was Martin would never have laughed about his father on the phone. So it was progress, really, that Ruby could laugh at him.

"Let's get back to meditation," Martin said. He closed his eyes, tried to feel the cold of the floor beneath him. He breathed in. For the sake of his own heart health, he must forget the barbed sound of Ruby's laugh.

Although Ruby was an only child, sometimes Martin felt he had dozens of daughters housed within her. There was the outer-daughter husk—tall, dark-haired, thick straight eyebrows often raised and face often pink—and then inside that? Not just the Ruby who stayed up late the night before a job interview, laughing about him on the phone, but also the one who had studied hard all through high school, peeling the dead skin around her cuticles, the girl her teachers had labeled (less like a student than like some scholastic specimen) "bright and creative," "determined to succeed." And also the Ruby who, in college, had asked that Martin and Debra buy her sculpting clay in lieu of the contributions they had insisted on making toward her tuition. And also the Ruby he had taken to the Museum of Natural History as a little girl, the hair-in-braids *Little House on the Prairie*–ish Ruby who had looked at a diorama of a wolf and said, "I want to go inside there, please." And when Martin said no, it wasn't allowed, you could look and learn, but not go inside the diorama groups—she had cried and then cried over her crying, wiping her running nose on the back of her hand until the skin gleamed like the wolf's glass eyes.

The older she got, the more Martin's task as a father seemed to be learning to differentiate all the Rubys in his memory from the present one. When he'd heard her on the phone after midnight, he wanted to ask her to quiet down, but couldn't think of a way to make the request without sounding as though he were treating her like a past Ruby, which Debra had told him they must avoid. "The goal is that she doesn't *revert* because of moving back here," Debra said one evening after they'd hurriedly made love, worried that Ruby would come home early from a dinner with Caroline. "It feels like we're the ones reverting," Martin said, as Debra buttoned her blouse with the rushed movements of an adolescent mindful of her curfew.

"We're not reverting, we're accommodating." Debra kissed him hard on the mouth. "Now put on your shirt, old man."

Debra had long served as peacemaker between Martin and Ruby. It wasn't supposed to be that way, to Martin's understanding. If anything, the mother and the daughter were supposed to fight, while the father played hero, showing up for dinner with an air of bewhiskered mystery, of important business too difficult to explain. But when Ruby was growing up, Debra had often been out of the apartment, working all day at the public library's Riverside branch and then taking night classes—first for her undergraduate degree, next for her master's degree in library science. Martin was the one who worked from home, or at least from the apartments and hallways and boiler rooms adjacent to home. Ruby saw him hauling other people's garbage, saw his fingernail beds turn black, saw him placate the worst of the whiniest tenants with a fake goofy smile on his face, like their submissive dog. Because Martin was responsible for making sure she got back safely from school, for making sure she did her homework, for yelling at her when she didn't return home when she said she would, he'd had to deal with more rebellion from Ruby than Debra ever had. Martin always assumed that their relationship would improve once Ruby moved out of the apartment. Once she had successfully launched herself into her life, she would turn into a new Ruby yet again, a new daughter filled with nothing but appreciation for him.

Only now she was back, and things were just like before. They sniped at each other, they argued. Debra was still doing her best to improve their relationship. When Martin had asked Ruby if she thought her degree excused her from having to wash her dishes, Debra pointed out that Ruby had cleaned the bathroom the day before. When Ruby called Martin's interest in bird-watching a prelude to a midlife crisis, Debra replied that if Ruby had a job like Martin's, she'd need to stare at some nonhuman creatures for a few hours, too. When Martin told Ruby she needed to cast a wider net for her job interviews and not just trust that the Museum of Natural History would work out, Debra told Martin that Ruby knew what she was doing, and couldn't they have some faith in their own kid? When Ruby stayed up late talking on the phone, Debra told Martin to wear his noise-canceling headphones to bed, because what else were the damn things good for.

But today Debra was going out of town, to Albany, to a conference for librarians where she would speak on a panel titled "Community Engagement and the Library: Mindful Outreach and In-Reach." Martin had gotten excited when he'd heard the title—maybe Debra was coming around on meditation. But no, she said she hadn't come up with the buzzwordy title, and anyway, "mindful outreach" in this context just meant not being racist or sexist or assuming incarcerated populations shouldn't have access to information.

Martin had first met Debra at a library downtown when she worked there as a clerk and he'd been studying for his pesticide-applicator certificate. One day he'd glanced around for a wall clock and his gaze went to the checkout desk, to Debra's face, which was clocklike, too pale and too wide. She was not beautiful. Still, something in Martin jolted. Before he left the library that evening, he asked her out for coffee. A few years after they'd had Ruby and managed to save some money, Debra began to take night classes to earn her college degree, but only so she could do more meaningful work at the library. She didn't want to just sit at a desk. She wanted to help people who truly needed the library's resources. It was the only way she felt like she was in the moment.

Maybe she had no patience for meditation, but Debra was mindful in her own way, and fearless in her own way, too. Now she worked as a correctional services librarian for the New York Public Library. She supervised the volunteers who answered reference questions from incarcerated populations, half of them seemingly idle musing ("How does eBay work?" "When did people first start to dance?" "Please tell me about clouds and what are they made of?"), half of them serious and sometimes time-consuming to answer ("How do I get a job when I leave here?" "How much are homes outside of New York City?"). She also helped manage satellite libraries on Rikers Island, going into the jails once or twice a week, setting up tables in the gym, checking books out by hand. But lately the work—the endless cycles of prisoners, of tragic stories, of angry guards—had begun to burn her out. "Do you feel that way, Martin?" she asked once. "You've been a super even longer than I've been a prison librarian."

"Yeah," Martin said. "I'm pretty burned out, too."

But he knew in a certain light he was lying to Debra. Some different kind of exhaustion was in his bones. It wasn't from pouring himself into his work like Debra did. It was from keeping himself so held back with the tenants every day, nodding exactly as he was supposed to nod, or keeping his face blank in a way that suggested only the most polite non-anger.

Ruby sighed loudly. "I don't think this is working, Dad," she said. "I keep going on anxiety spirals about my interview."

Martin frowns with concern, Lily voice-overed, *like a good dad not in the least aggravated or hurt by his daughter's failure to appreciate the shining promise of the present moment, and why should he care if his meditation idea was a bust, he is not bound by the false narratives*

*of his own ego, which is just a product of the consumerist society in
which he lives!*

"Bad energy today, that's all." Martin stood, trying to relax his
jaw. "We should try meditating again tomorrow, okay?"

"I don't know. I think I might actually feel *more* anxious now."

*But Martin is a man of many plots, he knows soon the sun will be
rising faster than one-two-three, which means the pigeons outside are up
and cheeping for food, Martin's a walking, talking self-help book of ways
to cope with one's own estrangement from labor due to the manner
by which consumerism consistently compromises our species-essence,
which—*

"Shh," Martin said. "Jeez. A goddamn monologue."

"Huh?" said Ruby.

He shook his head, tried out a smile. "I got another idea. Grab
some bread, okay? There's a few rolls on top of the fridge."

"Are you taking me to feed those pigeons in the courtyard?"

"Maybe."

"I forgot. Pigeons are like your therapy dog."

"They're not like dogs at all," Martin said. "They can fly."

They left the apartment and walked through the garbage room,
trash bags so full, they bulged over the edge of the plastic bins.
Martin was used to the stink, and maybe Ruby was, too—or maybe
she was pretending to be for his sake. She didn't crinkle her nose,
but she did dig her fingers into the old kaiser roll he'd given her.
When they passed the elevator-motor room and the smell dissi-
pated, she cleared her throat. "Caroline's having a party upstairs
tonight."

"Okay," Martin said.

"Kenneth just left on another vacation. She's house-sitting for him."

House-sitting seemed like a fancy term for staying at her dad's place while he was on vacation, but Martin didn't want to argue. "How's Caroline these days?" he asked.

"She's fine. Doing a lot more of her sculpture stuff." An edge in Ruby's voice. "And I guess throwing boring parties in her dad's penthouse. I'm not even sure I'm going tonight. I don't know most of the people she invites."

"You do what you want. Doesn't matter to me if you go to Caroline's party." Martin pushed open the fire exit door. "All Caroline's party means to me is that I'll have to spend tomorrow morning cleaning beer bottles off the roof."

"Caroline would clean up the bottles if you asked."

Martin laughed.

"She would. You're kind of an authority figure to her. Once she called you the Guardian Angel of the Basement."

The Guardian Angel of the Basement. Just a stupid name so Caroline could pretend he wasn't a human being employed by the building, but was rather some spirit watching over them, not out of the need for a paycheck but out of some higher celestial obligation. No way in hell Martin was an authority figure to her. Though yeah, Martin had often watched Caroline and Ruby on their playdates when they were small. He read them fairy tales or brought them to the Alice in Wonderland statue in Central Park. When the three of them were out together, Martin had imagined people thought the girls were siblings, that he was the father of both of them, and that nobody could tell one of them lived in the basement and one of them would live, once construction wrapped, in the penthouse.

It was even colder outside than he'd thought, but he was wearing a fleece vest and the air felt good, dignified, somehow, in its glacial bite. Too early for a lot of traffic or construction noises, for the roar of renovation. Although the sky was only just starting to lighten, his pair of pigeons made their alert thrumming throat sounds as soon as they saw him in the courtyard. He did not keep them caged up, of course, and they were not exactly his, even if he thought of them that way. Still, he was part of what sustained them, and that felt nice. Ruby handed Martin a roll. He tossed the bread at the birds and they left their perch to tear at it.

Martin had killed pigeons many times. People often spread pigeon-prevention gel on their windowsills, which would stick to the birds' wings. Then Martin would find wounded and disfigured pigeons flopping around the courtyard, too injured to be saved. There was nothing else to be done in those situations. The hawks and owls and falcons could only eat so much. When he wasn't killing pigeons, he was often chasing them away. They liked to nest in the stone scrollwork around the awning over the front entrance. At night he sometimes had to step outside the front of the building with a big stick—a sixteen-foot-aluminum-extension-pool-cleaning pole, the pole duct-taped to a paint-roller handle, the paint-roller handle duct-taped to a broomstick—and try to discern pigeon shapes among the shadows in the scrollwork. If the pigeons slept in the scrollwork, they would nest in the scrollwork, meaning they would shit on the scrollwork, and on the awning, and on the heads of tenants.

Luckily the pigeons on this ledge, the pigeons he fed, weren't technically nesting on the building's property but on the property of the Lutheran church next door. Martin could enjoy these birds the same way he could enjoy the birds in Central Park—as a specta-tor. In the time since Martin's interest in birds had begun to de-velop, a whole dimension of the city that had been invisible was now radiant. Trees once filled with chirping noises were now filled with distinct melodies, with names. Cedar waxwing. Baltimore ori-ole. Fox sparrow. Once, a summer tanager. Often, mourning doves. And cardinals, bloodred and bold. But the other bird-watchers he'd met didn't care for pigeons the way Martin did. Rats with wings, they called pigeons, as if the wings were not the essential differ-ence, marking what would otherwise be a plague-pissing pest as something nearly fantastical, or at least gravity-defying.

"How often do you feed this pair?" Ruby asked. She was shiver-ing a little under the thin coat she'd thrown on.

"Most days before the sun is up. They help me, sometimes, with the whole anxiety thing. I can tell them apart, too. See the one with the two black bars on its wings? That one's more aggressive."

"Watching the aggressive pigeon makes you feel calm?"

"I don't know." Martin looked away. "I just think they're cool. The patterns on their throats. They're beautiful."

If only they were not so beautiful, if only the plumage on their throats was not so iridescent. It would have made killing pigeons easier. A sudden rising anger in him. He had never told Ruby about those birds, their gel-weighted wings. But now he wanted to tell her what he had done to the birds in order to keep this job, for her, for her future stability, a stability she'd damaged with her academic choices. He wanted to tell her there were some kinds of debt she didn't even realize she owed, debts no dream job would pay back.

He hadn't always felt this way about Ruby's choices. He had been impressed she had gotten any significant scholarship money at all. But what had she done with it? Ruby had taken a mix of art history and literature classes, courses in American studies and creative writing and visual arts. She had to complete a final senior project, but the school had no majors or minors or any of that, part of their effort to encourage students, so said the pamphlets, to *become skilled at the challenges unique to the twenty-first century, to hone their minds to think outside of the box.* Somehow Ruby had been increasingly drawn to creating frozen moments *inside* boxes, culminating in her final college project: Four elaborate shoebox dioramas featuring the dumpsters behind the campus dining hall. Each diorama showed the dumpsters in a different season—a reference, Ruby said, to Monet's haystacks. She had sent Martin and Debra some photographs from the show and a copy of her artist statement. *I am interested in the way dioramas generate stories while sidestepping traditional narrative forms of rising action and conflict. Instead, the diorama form immobilizes and captures a moment we recognize as part of a story larger than the form itself.*

Well. Okay. The words were pretentious, but the dioramas Martin found inexplicably joyful. He loved the miniature Cheetos bag she had made for the spring dumpster, orange tinfoil peeking out of the dumpster lid, catching the equinoctial light. The fuddled footprints of frat boys and squirrels crisscrossing new patterns in the snow in the winter diorama. In the autumn diorama, piles of dried leaves with perfectly crafted teeny-tiny lobes.

Yes, he had been proud!

But in the end, his pride and the partial scholarship and years of out-of-the-box mind-honing had not made a big difference. Her return to the basement felt to Martin like a failure not only for Ruby, but for himself.

The pigeons gulped down the stale bread in big bites, their bobbling throats ballooned.

Ruby flexed her hands. "Lily would say the weather is cold as a financial adviser's heart."

Martin laughed.

"I miss her so much," Ruby said. "All those times she babysat me and read to me from her crazy manuscripts and ranted at me about the world."

"She liked to rant."

"We weren't even related to her. It's almost embarrassing, missing her this much. But she was just so *there*. You know?"

Later he would think about how different the day would have been if he'd been brave enough to admit his grief to Ruby in that moment. If he had told her that some Lily remnant narrated his movements as if he'd become a kind of figment in *her* mind. If only they'd stood out there in the early-morning light a little longer, talking about Lily, how she'd felt like family in a way that had astounded them both. If only they had mourned together.

But all Martin said was, "There's this great horned owl in Central Park the people on the birding e-group keep talking about. I haven't seen it yet."

"I'm not going bird-watching with you tonight, if that's where this is going," Ruby said. "I already tried meditation. My quota is one Quirky Dad Activity a week."

These important new forces of re-seeing in his life, reduced in Ruby's eyes to Quirky Dad Activities. What if he called her dioramas "quirky" in that dismissive tone? He wouldn't be completely wrong. But she would be completely devastated. His job, as Dad, was not to devastate her.

"I think we should go back inside," he said. "It's cold. You're shaking."

"So are you," Ruby said.

Just as Martin and Ruby kicked off their sneakers in the apartment, the landline telephone for work calls began to ring. Martin screened all the calls on that line, and he and Ruby both waited as the answering machine emitted its first long loud beep followed by the message itself.

"Hello? Hi, Martin? This is Neilson, Neilson from 3C, ha ha, well, you know that. I'm calling about a potential situation? Hope I'm not waking you up, my man. Wanted to check in and see if you could check out my shower today. It's clogging. Also, just returned from my early-morning jog and when I opened the foyer door, there were some blankets there? I mean, not *just* blankets but also a bundle of clothes and it looked like someone had been sleeping there. Do you maybe want to check on that?"

Certain tenants in the building had a way of commanding Martin not through assertive statements, but through questions. It was one of the services they were paying for: they could order him around and feel as if they were benevolently giving him choices. Tenants in the building sometimes also underestimated his intelligence. To his credit, Neilson in 3C didn't generally treat Martin like he was stupid, but he did treat Martin like he was extra-authentic, what Neilson sometimes called "a guy who does real work, with his hands." Which was exhausting in its own way.

Still, Martin was usually able to look past this, was able to feel grateful to Neilson for getting him back on a path of mindfulness,

on working to lower Martin's blood pressure. They had begun meditating together occasionally since shortly after Lily's death. Neilson, thankfully, was no Kenneth. There was never any Manifest
Destiny glaze to his eyes, only a slightly foggy look, which made his
mindfulness guru act very convincing. It was nice, the way Martin
and Neilson would sit on pillows together in 3C and breathe and
chant. They'd each spent their adolescence as transcendent hippie
white guys born in the mid-fifties, teenagers in the early seventies,
and for a time they shaped their lives around the same cultural
changes, dressed the same, maybe said some similar things about
the nature of the world or the subjective construction of reality.
The difference was that Neilson in 3C came from money and Martin in the basement did not. So Neilson had done his drugs and
joined his family business and kept his hair long. And Martin had
done his drugs and become a super and cut his hair short so plaster
and dust wouldn't get snarled up in it.

But whatever their differences, both of them were still looking
for transcendence. Neilson in 3C and Martin in the basement each
wanted to perceive every present moment as something burnished,
to see the radiant, radical, haloed beauty in right-nowness, whether
they were checking their e-mails or washing their hands or descending into the subway. Before he began meditating with Neilson,
Martin had tried taking a free evening meditation class at the neighborhood JCC. Neilson was there when he walked in, sitting with
his eyes closed, a small smile on his face. Martin was the only guy
in the room wearing cargo pants. Mid-meditation, he farted right
into his pillow. A couple of people grimaced, but nobody in the
class opened their eyes and nobody in the class laughed. If somebody had laughed, he might have laughed, too, might have stayed.
But he stood up right in the middle of the silent meditation. His

knees cracked. He left. After that day, he cut down on his gluten, which seemed like a yuppie-tenant thing to do, but what could he say, it had helped. Still, the idea of meditating in a group again made his stomach hurt with the force of a thousand buttered rolls. He'd been shocked when a few days after the JCC incident, Neilson approached him and asked Martin if he wanted to meditate in 3C sometimes, on afternoons when he had a break from work. "I don't blame you for leaving the class early," Neilson said, not bringing up the bodily function. "Sometimes it's a tad overwhelming in there for me, too. I can even lead us in the meditation sometimes, if you want. I have a pretty nonjudgmental approach."

Of course Neilson in 3C's voice as he left the message on the answering machine was the opposite of nonjudgmental. Was high-pitched, nasal, tinged with real alarm masquerading as deep irritation.

Martin called Neilson back and, while Ruby listened, thanked him for letting him know about the blankets in the foyer and told him he'd see about the clogged shower drain later today. The call woke Debra, who wandered out into the living room, squinting at the overhead light. "Did Neilson see another mouse?" she said when Martin hung up the phone. "I heard his voice."

"No mouse," Ruby said. "Only a human being. A homeless person in the foyer."

"Just some blankets," he said. "Go back to sleep, Deb." Martin kissed Debra on the temple. "Save your energy for your panel." Then he went into the kitchen to drink down cold coffee that smelled like mulch. Ruby and Debra followed him. "Dad," Ruby said as he poured his coffee. "Do you think you need help in the foyer?"

"You're not going up there, Ruby," Debra said.

Ruby touched Martin's wrist. "I could go with you and see if anyone is there."

"Nope," Martin said.

"What if the person's violent?" Ruby said.

Debra smoothed down her hair, which had frizzed around her face. "I did hear a story at work last week from Alice? About how a super tried to kick out someone sleeping in front of the building. And the person *stabbed* him." Debra eyes narrowed into what Martin thought of as her secret-sociologist look, a pained, almost Lily-like expression that appeared anytime she was suppressing some kind of observation on institutional failings.

"He got stabbed?" Ruby said.

Martin felt his heart speed up. Debra smoothed her hair again. "They think the stabbing person had a heroin problem. Some young kid around Ruby's age."

"Why would you compare me to the stabbing person with the heroin problem?"

"Not comparing!" Debra patted Ruby's back. "Just saying. Not a fun situation for anyone."

"I won't get stabbed," Martin said. "You know that. I had to ask some guy to leave the foyer just a couple weeks ago and he went right away. It's always fine. Nobody wants trouble."

"You're right," Debra said. "They're just tired."

"Except for that stabbing guy," Ruby said. "He seemed plenty awake. There should be a doorman. The people in this building are rich enough that there should be a doorman."

Martin swallowed his coffee, the cool of it thickening in his throat. A couple of people on the co-op board had recently brought up the possibility of hiring a doorman, but the idea had been shot down. Where would a doorman go? When you pushed open the front doors, you stepped into a small foyer with an intercom panel. There was room for someone to curl up on the ground, but no room for a desk and chair in the foyer. And the lobby beyond the foyer door was simply a long hallway, wood-paneled and beautiful, but too narrow. Expanding its size would mean decreasing the apartment size for everyone on the first floor.

"The building's not big enough," was all Martin said to Ruby. Then he stepped back into his sneakers, old New Balances jury-rigged with orthopedic foam insoles.

Debra took Ruby's arm. "We'll watch through the intercom and if your dad needs help, if there's a violent person up there, we'll know." Debra pushed a button on the wall and the camera on the intercom in the kitchen came to life. Right now the grainy black-and-white screen showed nothing but one of the foyer's mirrors. Everything seemed quiet through the camera, but its scope was limited—it did not show the floor, so if someone were lying there, that person would still be invisible. "We'll be watching and listening," Debra said. "If anyone tries to stab you, babe, just give a shout!"

"I'll be sure to shout if someone stabs me." Martin moved past them and out the door. Before he hopped into the elevator, he stood for a moment in the laundry room, which was closed to tenants at this hour, and breathed in the detergent smell. He hadn't been nervous when he'd received Neilson's call, but now he worried: What if someone violent *was* up there, and Ruby and Debra heard him get stabbed? Even with the static of the intercom, a stabbing sound would be a bad sound, a *spurty* sound. Not only would he be dying, he'd know his wife and daughter would be witnesses, traumatized for life, and Ruby already with so much debt—the therapy bills on top of that?

Sometimes, in moments of great distress, Martin half believed his chest had turned translucent. He feared that if he took off his shirt, instead of old-man flab, there would just be a glass window, and behind the window a cage of ribs and inside the cage of ribs, a heart that everybody could watch sputter and clog and fail, like a dying animal at a zoo. As he rose up in the elevator, he could feel it happening. His chest becoming glass. Everything becoming fragile, brittle.

When Martin enters the lobby, nothing seems in the least out of the ordinary!

Shh, Lily, Jesus, you old lovely croaking girl.

But yeah, she was right. Nothing *in-the-least* out of the ordinary. Though it was always a little weird, going from the scuffed floors of the basement to the terrazzo tile of the lobby, the gilded mirrors and cherrywood paneling that lined the hall. Nobody, as far as he could tell, had broken into the lobby. He went down the lobby hall. Through the locked glass door leading to the foyer, he saw not just a bundle of blankets but a woman, asleep, a gray gust of hair around her pallid face. Her worn puffy winter coat was the same pink color as the pack of tissues in her hand. Each time she breathed out, the trickle of snot caught in the groove under her nose moved closer to her upper lip.

"Excuse me." Martin pushed the glass door open, so it pressed gently against the woman's arm. "Excuse me, ma'am, but you'll need to leave."

The woman cracked open one eye. She lifted the pack of tissues and rubbed the plastic packaging against her nose. "I have family upstairs I'm waiting for," she said.

Martin glanced toward the intercom. Debra and Ruby would be able to see him but not the woman, who was still on the floor.

"I'm here for Lily," the woman said.

His jaw felt too soft, as if the roof of his mouth might cave in. "Lily?" he said.

"Yeah. I'm her cousin. I tried to buzz 5A and nobody answered. I'm waiting for her to get home."

Her voice sounded a little like Lily's. For a moment, he wanted to let her in. He wanted to open the door to her. To lead her up to what had been Lily's apartment. But of course that was impossible. "Ma'am," he said, "I'm going to have to ask you to—"

Her face was reddening. "I *told* you I *know Lily*, Lily in 5A, I'm related to Lily in 5A, I'm Lily's cousin."

"Lily is. Well." Martin paused. "Passed."

"Passed? As in dead? You mean dead?"

"Well," Martin said. He swallowed. "Yeah."

The woman stood up, her legs wobbling. "I need to get in the apartment."

"You need to leave, ma'am."

"Your breath stinks." She put a hand on Martin's shoulder as if to push him aside. Her grip was very strong. "Give me the fucking keys." She was yelling now. "Let me in."

"We're going to call the police, ma'am," Martin said. "My wife's watching." He pointed to the intercom.

"I *am* watching." Debra's voice. Over the intercom, she was all sternness and crackle.

"You're trespassing," Martin said. "We'll call the police right now if you don't leave."

The woman's eyes moved to the intercom. She locked her gaze

with the hole in its metal interface that contained the tiny camera. Martin listened for the long soliloquizing rage of Lily's ghost voice. But nothing. Instead, the woman muttered a few curses under her breath.

And then she stumbled out the door into the early light that shone so softly on her she seemed a little like a ghost herself.

When Martin had found Lily dead, first he had called 911. Next he had turned off the faucet she'd left running. The floor was soaked. Lily's cat, Mel Blanc, liked to sit in the sink, shedding her hair into the drain. "Keep Mel Blanc out of there before she clogs it up," Martin once told Lily, and Lily said, "If I wanted something that would listen to me, I would have a dog." The sink was still full of water and cat hair. He threw up into it.

For a few days, the usual parade of complaints from tenants stopped. 4B adopted Mel Blanc. 7C left a long message on Martin's machine about how Lily had been the only one to really listen to and not judge her theory about the elevator mechanics being spies. 2D said, "She always held the door for me, Martin, even when I could tell it was so much work for her."

In the immediate aftermath of Lily's death, the building felt sad, but also more humane. People held doors and each other's gaze, took the time to scratch 3D's Yorkies behind the ears, lowered their voices and spoke almost melodiously about what was gone. In those moments, the building was not a seething mass of wants and demands. There was no pecking order. There were just souls. Souls sitting on sofas and inside apartments and souls fixing elevators and unclogging drains and souls holding doors for other souls. A kind of vision of the building in which, yes, Martin's chest was translucent but it wasn't a big deal because so was everybody's. Everybody was a bit more see-through.

Then the paperwork began. Kenneth bought Lily's apartment, 5A, and hired an architectural firm to determine ways to combine 6A and 5A into one massive two-floor apartment linked by a glass staircase. Before the official demo crew arrived, Martin was tasked with removing Lily's fridge.

As Martin had rolled the fridge to the freight elevator, he tried not to think about the large quantities of oranges Lily kept in there, or the ice cream she had always offered him when he was upstairs for a job ("Mint mint mint!" she would sing), or the intimidatingly large bowls of sugary puddings she made, or the slabs of brie that she would not spread on anything, but would scratch at with her nails, eating whatever got stuck to her hands. Just a few months ago, she had held out the remaining cheese block to Martin, saying, "Do the fancy ladies in this building offer you cheese like this when you fix their sinks?" Then she had laughed and thrown the bric back in the fridge, where it stayed and got old, unwanted mold sneaking in. All over the cheese a host of flatulent microbes had clustered, farting more and more, until the smell escaped even the fridge, and Kenneth had breathed it in when he was showing some contractors around 5A and said, "No more!" and called Martin.

"Martin?"

Debra's voice at the intercom.

"Martin, are you okay? Is the intruder gone?"

The intruder. Yes, that was the right way to think of her if he wanted to get through the day. Not Lily's cousin. Not a woman he'd kicked out.

"She's gone," he said to the intercom. "I'll be down in a minute."

He stepped outside the building and breathed in the cold air.

The intruder was still in sight, walking slowly west, toward the river. The clouds hung around like wet wrung socks illuminated by a burning yolk of sun, and he had kicked the intruder out, he had done his job.

When he returned to the basement apartment, Debra, exhausted, had already gone back to bed. But Ruby was still huddled by the intercom, glaring at him. Martin's skin felt stung, like his daughter's glare was made out of bees. Once there had been bees living in the water tower on the roof. They must have been attracted by the garden Kenneth had hired someone to plant around one of the penthouse's decks. Martin hadn't known about the bees, of course. He had climbed up to the top of the water tower, thrown his leg over the ladder so he wouldn't fall, lifted a small hatch in the roof. He was about to climb in to check on the float switch when bees coated and stung his face and his hands.

Now his daughter took his hands in hers, as though a kind gesture might distract him from the way she was glaring. "She's Lily's family," Ruby said. "Why did you and Mom think it was okay to kick her out?"

"She's not the first person who I've had to ask to leave the foyer," Martin said. "And you never complained so loud before. Think about that. You're only upset because this woman looks like Lily."

"She doesn't just look like Lily. She's *related* to Lily." Which daughter peered up at him now from the outer-daughter husk? One of the littlest Rubys? No, it was still just his current daughter, a grown woman trying to manipulate him into feeling guilty by summoning his memories of a younger Ruby, by trying to make him think he'd disappointed the purest kid side of her.

"I kicked her out because that's my job," Martin said. He removed his hands from Ruby's grip. "If I don't do my job, I lose my job. Your mother gets that. Why don't you?"

"She wasn't just coincidentally here. She was at our foyer, waiting for Lily."

"It's not our foyer."

"Huh?"

"You said she was at *our* foyer. But that's not right." He scratched at his beard. "The foyer doesn't belong to us."

"It kind of does."

"Maybe you're getting this household mixed up with your ex-boyfriend's."

"John. You know his name."

"*John* owns a foyer, maybe," Martin said. "But not you. Not me. We are a foyerless family."

"John didn't own any foyer. His family home in Connecticut has a foyer maybe, but—"

"*Foyer,*" Martin said. "Such a hoity-toity word. Is it French, do you think?"

Ruby closed her eyes. "I never took French."

"What *did* you learn at that school?"

She opened her eyes again. Ah. There was twelve-year-old Ruby. The sanctimonious and the sulky side emerging in tandem, a sure-fire sign of her adolescent self. "We could have brought her to the apartment for a little bit, at least," she said.

"Oh, yeah? And what would we do with her here? Keep her, like a pet?"

"We would figure it out. We would find her some resources. Isn't meditation supposed to help with compassion?"

"I don't need a lecture on compassion, Ruby."

"I'm not lecturing. I'm just saying—"

"Shh." He held up a hand. "Your mother's trying to sleep again."

"You're being inhuman. So is Mom. If you really cared about Lily, if you were actually sad, you wouldn't have made her leave."

"Shut up," he said. A long silence between them. "You have to be quiet because your mother's trying to sleep. She's nervous about her panel. Think about someone other than yourself. Okay?"

She stood there, watching him like he had turned into a muted TV, a commercial she didn't want to hear.

Well, fine. He could mute her, too. He put on his noise-canceling headphones. He went to his meditation bench to watch his breath alone. He closed his eyes and their apartment disappeared entirely, and his daughter did, too. His heartbeat slowed. His face cooled. His breath was the only sound. It was like he was alone in a vast single-story building, or an echoing hallway, or a familiar chamber, dark, with its own steady pulse.

2   RUBY AND THE TRUE DISGRACE

When Ruby had worked as a barista, the line of customers in the morning often stretched out the door. At least once every single day, she would have no idea how she would be able to process the personalized beverage demands of so many people, the lattes and the cortados, the almond milk and the soy. Dizziness would overtake her, and for several breaths she could not see individuals before her, just a multifaced blob of early-morning want.

The anger Ruby felt for her father after he'd kicked out Lily's cousin was like that long line of customers, it had so many faces. It was dizzying, her rage; it seemed to portend a wide range of specific demands. Some part of her was angry because of how her father had dismissed the woman in the foyer, and some part of her was angry because of how he'd then dismissed Ruby's own feelings, and some part of her was angry because her father always seemed to view any inkling of moral certitude she had as the misguided product of an expensive liberal arts education. How would she deal with each face of her anger right now? How would she give each component of her own rage the attention it needed? It would feel good to rip off the headphones her father wore, to scream into his face, which, unlike her anger, was singular, basically immutable. All her life, her father's face had seemed unchanging to Ruby, even as the logical part of her brain acknowledged that his beard was now streaked with white and his wrinkles had begun to set.

It was especially difficult to notice the wrinkles now, since he was acting like a little kid—moping on his meditation bench, playing pretend enlightenment the way some five-year-old would play pretend in the Kingdom of Make-Believe. Her father had pointed out that she had never been so upset at him for kicking someone out of the building before. And he was right about that. He had received calls about homeless people in the foyer quite a few times during Ruby's childhood. A man would call and report that someone was sleeping downstairs, his voice suggesting that Ruby's father had failed at his job. Or a woman would call, say she was sorry*so*sorry to leave a message at such an early hour, but there was somebody just outside the locked lobby door, and wasn't that a security concern? Not only had Ruby grown up acclimated to such calls, she'd also grown up acclimated to the queasy guilt that followed them—thanks largely to Caroline, who not only had more toys, but also, seemingly, a stronger moral compass. Once, during a childhood playdate up in 6A, when they were in the middle of Holocaust-orphans-sisters-survivors and pretending to run away from the Nazi guards, Caroline abruptly stopped wheeling her arms around as if a new idea had occurred to her. She had plucked at the lacy white collar on her new denim dress and said, "My mom told me your dad kicks homeless people out of the building."

Ruby looked down at her own frayed jeans. She was near the end of second grade and something about all the emphasis on place value in math had made her newly aware of loose threads.

"That's very mean of him. Homeless people need our help. They have no place to go."

Ruby had said he was just doing what the people in the building told him to do, and Caroline had said that you couldn't just follow orders or you got World War II. "*My* mom helps homeless people," Caroline said. "She donates clothes that they can wear at job interviews."

It was time to change the subject. "Look!" Ruby said, pointing at a large stuffed animal. "A Nazi! A really big one! Run!"

"A Naziiii!" echoed Caroline. "Run to the forest!" At peak drama in their games, the beauty mark on Caroline's cheek seemed to throb. "Run run run to the forest, the Nazis don't know about the forest there!" She gripped the cloth arm of her newest doll.

Caroline's parents gave her new dolls all the time. She owned dolls that could say "Mama" and dolls that could say "Hungry" and dolls that could piss right in your arms, and she had all the American Girl dolls, except for Addy, the black one, and Molly, the one with glasses. During their playdates, they sometimes made monogrammed pottery for the dolls using Caroline's clay. If Ruby didn't have clay on her hands, Caroline would let her not only hold the dolls, but also cover the doll bodies with her own to protect them from Nazis. Caroline was better at playing Holocaust-orphans-sisters-survivors than Ruby was. Even when they were pretending the Nazis were threatening to gas them, Ruby was always sort of smiling. Whereas Caroline could quickly turn stormy, sad. There was something fantastical about the scope of Caroline's solemnity. Ruby loved watching her face. Even Caroline's laugh possessed a keening at its core, a sense of rhythmic lamentation underneath her "ha ha ha!"

Caroline's grandmother had survived Dachau, but her grandmother's parents had not. Ruby's own maternal and paternal great-grandparents, who were also Jewish, had come over to New York alone, without family, from somewhere in Eastern Europe, but nobody was sure where exactly because of shifting borders. Her parents knew next to nothing about them. Maybe because Caroline could recite her grandmother's dark history—give actual dates and names to the places where atrocities happened—she seemed more sophisticated to Ruby, more grown-up, even though Caroline was physically much smaller than Ruby. As a child, Ruby had often imagined that if they had actually been in a concentration camp together, she would have given Caroline some of her rations to keep her from getting too feeble to work. When she became jealous of Caroline, she enjoyed contemplating how she would save her from the death camps in an alternate universe. She thought about how she would shield Caroline's body with her own whenever Caroline would hold up some new gorgeous jewel-eyed doll and say, "This is Samantha and she's a lawyer. Okay, Ruby? She's a very special lawyer for very sick kids and their parents." A few minutes after she accused Ruby's father of meanness against the homeless, she held out Jasmina. "Jasmina is a princess, but also she is a journalist. She writes about politics, and she tries to expose evildoing by using her words. Ruby, have you heard of Watergate?"

Ruby had not heard of Watergate.

"Well," Caroline said, "Jasmina fixed it. She fixes all the things in the world that are *a true disgrace*."

A true disgrace. Caroline said those words just like she had said *Watergate*, as if they were the name of a special, powerful doll Ruby would never have met without Caroline as her conduit. Ruby's dolls did not pee, did not talk, did not come with their own career trajectories or historical backstories. Ruby must have unconsciously adopted a tragic air of deprivation, because later on during their playdate, Caroline had adjusted her lace collar again, and said, "I'm sorry I told you that your dad was mean for kicking people out."

"It's okay."

"I know he can't help it."

"It's his job," Ruby said.

Then Caroline had given Ruby one of her American Girl dolls, the Colonial Williamsburg–era redhead. "You can watch Felicity until our next playdate, if you want."

Ruby was always leaving 6A with borrowed stuff. Caroline's parents would give her educational books on animals and ecosystems and history and famous artists, then ask her if she felt properly stimulated in school, if she was being presented with educational opportunities. But now she had something better than an educational opportunity. She had one of Caroline's fanciest dolls.

Back in the basement apartment, Ruby had gone to her father and, clutching Felicity to her chest, said, "It's very mean, what you're doing. Homeless people have no place to go."

He laughed in her face. Her father had never laughed at her like that before, had always laughed *with* her. She'd been so stunned, she'd let go of the doll, which hit the ground with a smack. Ruby picked the doll back up, turned her around and around, looking for signs of damage. The doll was fine. But Ruby's limbs tingled. Had it actually been thrilling, for a second, thinking she had harmed Caroline's doll? No, that made no sense. Caroline was her kind, generous friend. And this doll was a total plastic innocent.

Her father said, "You shouldn't be borrowing stuff from tenants, anyway. If you damage their dolls, who do you think gets in big trouble?"

"You," Ruby said.

"That's right."

Ruby looked down into Felicity's glassy eyes. If her father were fired, they would lose their apartment. Ruby, her father, and her mother would wander the streets of the Upper West Side together, sleeping in Central Park by the ducks, huddling together by a campfire near Bow Bridge, waking up every day in some outdoor place filled with all the natural light the basement apartment didn't receive. They'd wear rags like the orphans in *Annie* (which she'd just watched with Lily, who had lectured the whole time about how the ridiculously rich Daddy Warbucks was the real villain even if he adopted children, because hadn't his own wealth generated the systems that created and forgot orphans in the first place; did Ruby understand?). Rag-wearing Ruby would pass Caroline in Strawberry Fields, and Caroline would look away, deeply ashamed. Ruby would be the girl who was at last poor enough to be truly noble and sympathetic and orphan-like, instead of a regular girl with a home and nice enough parents. If she smashed this doll somehow, if she dropped her from a great height, or burned her beautiful doll hair—then the role Ruby played in Caroline's life might change.

But of course she didn't do any of that. She took good care of Felicity, read to her every night, and returned her to Caroline unharmed.

A few weeks after Caroline accused Ruby's father of being very mean, something bad happened to Ruby and Caroline when nobody was watching. The girls had just graduated from second grade and were not supposed to be alone. Ruby's father was meant to babysit them during their playdate. But there had been a waste-pipe leak in 2D, damaging 1D's ceiling. Something in one of the apartment units was always breaking, everything always on the verge of flood or fire. Back then Ruby saw her father as a kind of magician, preventing the building from succumbing to a range of biblical afflictions: infernos, deluges, pestilence. He was the one to call the firemen, the plumbers, the bedbug guy. He was responsible for saving them all from disaster. On top of that, their apartment was rent-free! Ruby was proud of this fact—she felt like they were getting away with something, especially knowing Caroline's parents had paid a lot of money to buy their apartment. Ruby and Caroline never discussed this difference.

If the leak had not occurred, the girls would never have been alone in the building to begin with. They would have been at the Museum of Natural History, one of Ruby's favorite places in the world, especially during summer vacation when the air-conditioning was a welcome relief. While Caroline's parents and Ruby's mother all had to work that day, Ruby's father's week had been slower than usual, the calls to his answering machine almost nonexistent, as many residents were away on vacation. He had promised to take her and Caroline to see the largest-ever scientific reconstruction of a dinosaur. "The paleontologists looked at all these bone fragments," he'd said to Ruby the night before. Even though they were eating dinner, he still wore a baseball hat streaked with plaster, which he liked to call "the guts of good real estate." His beard was dark then, his back still very straight. "They looked at all these tiny bone pieces. And they guessed at where the muscles might be."

Ruby had gazed at her plate. Her mother was taking night classes, and dinner without her always meant boneless fish sticks, corn, and rice. With the right amount of salt, it tasted okay.

"You know what a paleontologist is, Ruby? A paleontologist is like a plumber of the prehistoric. A paleontologist is trying to figure out how the insides of something huge and ancient are meant to flow together. When we go see that dinosaur tomorrow, it'll be like seeing the oldest pipes in the oldest building in the world."

But the next day, just as they all were about to leave the building to head to the museum, there was a panicked call from 1D. Ruby's father called Ruby's mother and told her about the leak, but she was at work and couldn't get away. So he called Lily in 5A, to see if she might babysit Ruby and Caroline while he managed the issue.

Lily often watched Ruby for free, taking her to the playground, to the park, to the Met. "It's good for me to have a reason to get out," she said. Other times Ruby hung out in 5A, an apartment even more fun than Caroline's because not only did it have a cat slinking around, it was also full of all the best non-doll stuff: art supplies from Lily's "I'll be an artist" phase, gems from Lily's "I believe in the power of healing crystals" phase, videocassettes from Lily's "I'll write a neo-Marxist critique of Hollywood" phase. It was like a mini-museum dedicated to Lily's shifting obsessions. Plus, any time Ruby was there, Lily gave her a bowl of ice cream and provided her with drawing pencils.

While Ruby drew, Lily talked. Sometimes she read from one of her many in-progress manuscripts, but often she simply reminisced. She went on about her history with voice acting ("What I hated in the end was how the work made it seem like I was totally void of a body"), and her cat ("An undiagnosed manic-depressive"), and her parents ("Drunken louts, not in a nice way, why do you think I de- cided not to have kids, because god, what if I became my parents,

Rubes?"), and the art that she loved, especially the paintings of Alice Neel ("They're realistic, but distorted, Ruby, and nobody else will ever so perfectly capture the beauty and vulnerability of belly rolls"). Sometimes she railed against those in the building she called "Big Money Folks," people she said were just waiting for an excuse to kick her out of her rent-controlled apartment, and other times she talked to Ruby about how she was happy to watch her while her mother worked at the library because libraries were the last true public spaces in a democracy gone to the wolves. Occasionally, while Lily ranted, Ruby would look up at her from her sketch pad and try to draw her. Lily was the most beautiful old person Ruby had ever seen. She had a large, soft body, blue eyes made huge behind her glasses, long pale earlobes that resembled blanched Swedish Fish, and hair dyed a dark brown. She smelled like litter-box deodorizer, tangy sweat, and citrus—along her windowsills were gnarled orange peels curling into the fetal position. She claimed the peels kept away cockroaches. In her drawings of Lily, Ruby always made sure she was surrounded by orange peels that looked like smiling mouths.

Everything would have been fine that day if Ruby and Caroline had been able to go to Lily's apartment while Martin dealt with the leak. But Caroline was allergic to cats ("Not to cats, technically," she liked to say, "but to the protein pests in their dander"). And so Lily lumbered downstairs to babysit Ruby and Caroline in the basement. She smiled at Ruby, frowned at Caroline, and immediately reclined on the couch and turned on the TV once Ruby's father left. "Long night," she said to the TV. "Hardly slept. Back pain. What a comfy couch."

"It's got cows on it," Ruby said, in case Lily hadn't noticed.

"These kinds of rustic prints were popular postwar," Lily said. "Mass-produced couches referencing the artisanal. Everyone wanted to pretend they could just go back to the happy days on the farm. Utter delusion."

"If the farm was so happy, why do the cows look so sad?"

"It's a good question, my Ruby. If you didn't love ice cream so much, I'd tell you."

"Can you take us to the museum?" Caroline asked.

"I told your dad we'd stay here. Let's watch TV."

"Don't babysitters usually have *activities*?" Caroline said.

"Not this one," Lily said.

"Come on." Ruby took Caroline's hand and led her to her room. Her stomach hurt a little. Usually their playdates occurred in Caroline's apartment, with all its light and toys, and the fantastic off-white leather swivel club chair they used for interrogation scenes during Holocaust-orphans-sisters-survivors. But Ruby's room had just a bed, a small chair, a gaggle of worn-out bears and dolls. Caroline picked up a baby doll with its eyes stuck wide open in an expression of pure terror.

"That's Joan," Ruby said quickly. "She's a journalist."

Which was a lie. The doll was named Cindy Baby and she'd never had a job in her life. Caroline put Cindy Baby down again and sighed, but very quietly, like she wanted Ruby to believe she was nobly repressing the weighty oomph of her disappointment.

"I'm sorry we're not looking up at the big whale right now," Ruby said.

"Do you know the biggest heart in the known universe is the blue whale's?"

Do you know do you know do you know. Caroline was always starting sentences this way, as if she was not content just to own and share spectacular dolls, but must own and share, too, the spectacular and strange facts of the universe. The protein pests in cat dander, the big hearts of whales, which Olsen twin had been born first, the name of the most recent glacier to glide across and cover Central Park twelve thousand years ago. She knew all these things.

The steam pipe in Ruby's bedroom gurgled and hissed. Ruby would have liked nothing more in that moment than to kick Caroline out, the way her father had kicked out homeless people. *Leave,* she wanted to tell Caroline, *or I'll call the police.*

She said instead, "We could draw."

"I just came from art class."

"Maybe we could play hide-and-seek?"

"How? The room's so tiny."

She was right. Ruby's room was too small for hide-and-seek. And yet she never wanted to trade her room for Caroline's. Because while Ruby's room was small, in some ways the whole basement felt like hers. The laundry room, the boiler room, the storage room. All a part of her father's kingdom, something to which Caroline had no claim.

That gave her the idea: There were other places in the basement they could go. They did not need to stay in this tiny space. "Follow me," Ruby said.

Lily was still on the couch, her knuckles white from clutching the remote. When she saw Ruby and Caroline emerge, she pointed at a girl on TV advertising pills to make a person less sad. The girl stood in a meadow filled with wildflowers. "Are you searching for a sense of purpose?" the girl asked.

"Do you hear the gurgle in that voice?" Lily said. "Goddamn, like her larynx is giving birth to llama babies. How do they let these people's voices on TV?" Although Lily's voice now sounded a little croaky, she often told Ruby that during her time as a voice-over actress, her voice flowed like honey and her larynx was lauded for its flexible ligaments. She had been especially skilled at declaring, in a bubbly but sassy-girl voice, one detergent's superiority over the other when it came to making stains, grime, and unseemly streaks vanish just like *that*.

"It is very difficult to get on television," Caroline said, looking at the sincere TV girl. "She's probably trying very hard, Lily."

"It's not about trying, kiddo," Lily said. "It's about sounding."

"I'm not a kiddo," Caroline said. "I'm a kid."

"I think that lady on TV sounds awful," Ruby said. Then she told Lily that she and Caroline wanted to play a game of hide-and-seek in the laundry room, which was just down the hall from the apartment.

"Your dad lets you do that?" Lily asked.

"Uh-huh."

"Okay, okay." Lily waved her hand. "It's like the way kids in suburbs play in the yard, I guess. You basement kids play in the laundry room."

"Exactly," Ruby said. "It's like the suburbs but for basements."

"Just don't stay out there too long." Lily reached into her pocket for a tissue and blew her nose hard. Then she kissed Ruby on the top of the head. She did not kiss Caroline on the top of the head. "I want to be the hider," Caroline said quietly. Her face had become a hardened shell, like one of her dolls.

"I want to be the hider, too," Ruby said.

"You're *always* the hider, Ruby. You never seek."

"Lily," Ruby said, "could you be the seeker?"

"I want to watch TV, sweetie."

"Please?"

"Okay, okay, yes, yeah, sure, I'll count to, what is it, ten?"

"Five hundred," Ruby said.

Lily looked doubtful, but she closed her eyes. "One," she said. "Two. Three." Her breathing got a little more regular. Ruby put her finger over her lips, grabbed Caroline's hand. On the way out of the apartment, she shut the door as quietly as she could.

Then she took Caroline past the laundry room, past the garbage room, to the door of the elevator-motor room—the ultimate hiding spot. Caroline shoved it with her shoulder. It was locked. "It's okay," Ruby whispered. "I have the best memory ever."

"No, you don't," Caroline said.

"Yes, I do. And I know the code. Eight-eight-eight."

Ruby's father had shown her this room a few weeks before when she had asked him how the elevators worked. There were two elevators in the building: the main passenger elevator, mahogany-paneled and brass-buttoned, and the freight elevator, which was only for Ruby's father and maintenance people. The freight elevator had bars instead of walls. Its single bulb cast its light on peeling plaster in the elevator shaft. There were still abandoned dumb-waiter shafts that had traveled alongside kitchens, near where the maids' rooms were, and for a long time in the building, food had been ferried up and down that way. "Before either one of us was alive," her father had said, and Ruby tried to grasp the magnificent oldness of her own home.

In the motor room, her father showed her the big generators that turned the alternating current into direct current. It was a place of pendulation, of sudden rotations, of machines that seemed like gear-brained bodies. "There are invisible forces all around us," said her father. "Currents, magnets, ions, waves in the air." He waved his arms in the air like a bird trying to take off. Ruby's head rushed with the sound of her blood. These wheels turned and lifted people to their homes, or lowered them back to the city streets, where they might go to the playground or learn about dinosaurs in a museum or find groceries. It was some sort of an enchantment.

There were two big machines, one of which had a wheel on it, long steel cables going around and around. That big machine was for the passenger elevator, Ruby's father told her. The other elevator machine in the room, for the freight elevator, was a smaller barrel machine that had been in the motor room since 1911. "It's illegal to install something like this now," her father said. There were even more ropes around the barrel machine. "Always reminded me of something on a whaling ship."

Ruby thought about the blue whale hanging from the ceiling at the Museum of Natural History, imagined its innards as this motor room, its giant heart a primordial turbine.

"The barrel machine is dangerous, dangerous, dangerous," her father went on. "You get near that one, you get even a little bit near, you could lose your arm. The wheel starts spinning when you don't expect it to spin. Boom. George in the building next door, he knew a guy who lost his arm. You know what that means you should do, Ruby?"

"What?"

Her father had smiled and said, in a voice rich with sarcasm, "You should definitely touch those cables."

Wow. Wow. Wow. Her own father had not only brought her to this previously unseen space, but had used sarcasm, trusting her to hear the nuances. Ruby felt taller, wiser, *ancient*. She had laughed. And of course she had not touched the cables.

Ruby did not tell Caroline any of this after she put in the code that let them into the motor room. This was Ruby's kingdom, and she was the one who controlled what Caroline did and did not know about its courtiers and nobles, its magnificent machines. All she told Caroline was, "Wait, just wait."

When the door clicked open, nobody came running after them. Lily, on the couch, was still counting to five hundred, or else she had fallen asleep. The girls stepped inside. The door clicked closed. Caroline gasped. She turned around, her mouth moving as though trying to form words about all she saw: the baffling machines, the spinning cables, the sense of mysterious movement.

"My dad knows all the names for all these machines," Ruby said. "Isn't that amazing?"

Caroline said, "Let's pretend this was where they gassed them."

"Huh?"

Caroline began to chant. "We are orphans, they have locked us up. We are orphans, they have locked us up."

"But we're already playing hide-and-seek," Ruby said. "You can't play two games at once."

"At *my* school," Caroline said, "anything's allowed as long as you're following your real passion."

"Your real passion?"

"Yes," Caroline said. "There are no rules except for 'Use your words.' Anybody at my school can play two games at once, easy."

Ruby blushed. She felt like a baby. She had shown Caroline the motor room, shown her the secrets of the basement, the secrets of *Ruby's* home, she had resourcefully remembered the code, and still Caroline was commanding their games. "They won't be able to keep us here for long," Caroline said. "The Americans are coming. They've hidden a key inside one of these machines to free us. We just have to find it."

Then Caroline reached out toward the barrel machine. She paused, looked back at Ruby. Asking, with her eyes, *Is this safe?*

And Ruby said, in an attempt to mimic her father's sarcasm, "You should definitely touch those cables."

But Caroline was deep in the Holocaust-orphans-sisters-survivors game and their Holocaust-orphans-sisters-survivors games were always powerfully earnest. She took Ruby at her word. She reached out to touch the cables.

Ruby screamed. A whole zoo of animals roared their roars in her voice. There were baby llamas in Ruby's voice, and howler monkeys, and angry mama bears, and full-grown lions, and wolves, wolves, wolves. She leaped forward, between Caroline and the machine, and grabbed her, and Caroline howled and hit Ruby on the side of her head, and then the cables started to spin, they started to go round and round and round, and Ruby started to pee.

The pee was so hot that she thought for a second a gash had opened up in her right inner thigh. Everything inside her was panicked, burning.

But she had stopped her. Ruby had stopped Caroline from hurting herself. She had been a good friend.

Not that it mattered much. Caroline shrieked: "You tried to kill me!" She rushed to the door, attempted to open it, couldn't. "You're trying to kill me!" she hollered at the door. Which was when Ruby realized the door had automatically locked behind them. They were trapped.

Soon both girls were sitting on the cold concrete floor, their faces wet with sweat and tears. Caroline wanted to know why Ruby had told her to reach for those ropes if they were dangerous. Ruby explained that she'd been trying to be sarcastic. Caroline told Ruby she hated her, she hated her so, *so* much, and she wasn't being sarcastic, either.

"You even peed your pants, you stupid baby," Caroline said when Ruby was silent. "Ruby Ru-pee. Do you even know what a rupee is? Do you even know you're a stupid baby and you even peed your pants? You're a *kiddo*. That's what you are. *Kiddo*. Do you know that's what you are?"

Ruby started to cry again, and she told Caroline yes, she knew. When Ruby's sobs got louder, Caroline's face softened. She said, "I'm sorry I yelled. I'm sorry you peed your pants, Ruby."

"I didn't pee them that much."

"Yes, you did. Do you want mine? We could swap."

Ruby shook her head. Caroline's pants would be too small for Ruby, which was a shame, because Caroline's pants flared out at the ankles in a way that made Ruby think of fancy ball gowns. Ruby hiccuped, looked up at Caroline again, looked hard at her beauty mark until the beauty mark seemed like a piece of snot that Ruby could, if she reached for it, wipe away.

"Maybe we should sing 'I Am the Cute One'?" Caroline said. "Maybe that would make us feel better."

Caroline had a cassette of songs by the Olsen twins, who were just a little older than Ruby and Caroline. Sometimes Caroline would play the tape and she and Ruby would sing together, each pretending to be one of the Olsens, two only children turned twins.

"I don't feel like singing," Ruby said.

"Do you know the Olsens aren't identical twins?" Caroline said. "They're fraternal. That means they each came from their own egg. Even though they look the same."

"I know that," Ruby said. "You told me before."

"Do you think the Olsen twins are true friends?" Caroline said. "Or false friends?"

"What?"

"My grandmother told me she survived the war because she didn't have false friends like most people."

"Oh," Ruby said.

"She said she had some real true friends." Caroline looked seriously at Ruby. "I'm sorry I called you stupid."

"It's okay."

"*We* are real true friends."

"Yes," Ruby said.

"And that is how we will survive."

"Yes," Ruby said, not entirely sure if they were playing Holocaust-orphans-sisters-survivors again, or if this was Caroline being Caroline. The barrel machine was again whirring away. Somebody was operating the freight elevator. Her father, probably. Maybe that meant he had finished fixing the leak. Or maybe Lily had realized they were missing. She must have alerted Ruby's father and now he was in the freight elevator, searching for them.

Only still nobody came.

"What are the dolls doing now, do you think?" Caroline asked.

"I don't know," Ruby said.

"Here's what I think the dolls are doing. First of all, I think Jasmina's off saving the world. Maybe she's stopping Holocaust the Sequel."

Wrong. Ruby knew all about dolls. When you weren't in the room with them, when you weren't imagining hard on their behalf, they couldn't save you or anybody else. She said, "What's Holocaust the Sequel?"

"It's what comes after the Holocaust, kiddo," Caroline said.

"Did your grandmother tell you there would be a sequel?"

"No. I asked her about the Holocaust the other day for a school project. She told me the true-friend thing and then she told me she didn't remember much else. But she remembers everything! She's written books, she goes all over the country talking about what she remembers. Why does she lie to me and say she doesn't remember, if she loves me as much as she says?"

"Maybe she's lying about that, too," Ruby said, her pants piss-wet and rank.

Outside the motor room, Ruby learned later, everyone had become the seeker—not only Lily and Ruby's father, but also a contractor assessing damage to a tenant's ceiling, also some nannies pulled from the laundry room. They were all looking for the girls. Ruby's father (who would be the most blamed for the incident) was the one who heard their voices, singing rounds of "I Am the Cute One" as loudly as they could.

Shortly after the elevator-motor-room incident, Lily took Ruby to the Museum of Natural History. When they stood before the diorama of hunting dogs on the Serengeti Plain, she cleared her throat. Diorama displays had their origins in what were called cabinets of curiosities, she said, or sometimes cabinets of wonder. "Cabinets meant rooms back then," Lily added. The wealthy would go on hunting explorations. Then they needed a place to show off their kill. Exotic animals were originally killed in great numbers and displayed as trophies not for the public, but for other rich people. Now, sometimes, people painted beautiful landscapes into the background instead of just putting the animal up on the wall, and everyone was allowed to look at and learn from the posed dead. Some of the animals in this hall had been killed to convince humans that the landscape where these animals lived should be preserved and protected.

"Are you too young to comprehend the tension?" Lily asked. "The tension between an educational effort and a trophy? Do you understand?"

Ruby said she understood. But really she was thinking: How did Lily know all this history? She was very smart, Ruby decided. She was brilliant, maybe even more brilliant than Caroline's traumatized grandmother who gave lectures around the country. Hearing Lily go on in this way, Ruby felt like the voice-over actress inside Lily had truly begun to emerge. She was *selling* something. But what? The dioramas were not for sale, Ruby was pretty sure.

They stood in front of the Serengeti Plain a little longer, in silence. Ruby scrutinized the smallest of the hunting dogs. She said, "My dad wanted to look at the dinosaur."

"Huh?"

"When we were supposed to come here that day with Caroline." Ruby pulled her braid until her scalp prickled. "He's mad at me for sneaking into the motor room. He told me he was disappointed in me."

"The reality is it's one matter for just you to get into trouble," Lily said, reaching down and gently extricating Ruby's braid from her fist. "But when you drag Caroline into trouble, too . . . Do you know your dad almost lost his job because of what happened?"

Ruby did not know that. Her father had told her Caroline's mother had called and been "upset." But he had hidden from her that he almost lost his job. It no longer felt thrilling, the prospect of sleeping in the park, now that she knew how close it had come to happening. *A true disgrace*. She heard these words in Caroline's lark-voice, as if Caroline were right behind her. But nobody was there.

"The thing to know about you and Caroline," Lily said, "is you're not in the same class."

It was true. They went to different schools.

"I'm not saying you can't be friends with Caroline at all." She rocked back on her heels and her ankles creaked. "But there are certain things . . . Your dad says I shouldn't go on about this stuff because it might alienate you." Lily eyed the diorama like she wanted to reach through the glass divider there. "And he said it's not like we're eating coal. Well, I know that. I'm not saying we're eating coal. What I'm saying is nobody wants to voice this. Ruby. Do you recognize that nobody wants to voice this? The middle class in the city is on the verge of vanishing. Your pal Caroline's father came into my apartment the other day pretending to want to chat about our lives over tea, but no no no, he was measuring the door-ways with his eyes. They're waiting for me to kick the bucket so they can buy my apartment and combine it with 6A." Lily lifted Ruby's braid up so that it hovered like an exclamation point over her head. "They want to build not just a penthouse but a two-story dream palace, with a fancy staircase."

Ruby had heard Lily talk about this before, but she'd grown ac-customed to half tuning out her rants about the rich. She had never really listened until now. A dream palace. She imagined Caroline descending the staircase in a shiny dress with puffed sleeves, hold-ing an expensive historically significant doll from a time period Ruby had probably never known existed.

"I'm not afraid of them, is the thing," Lily said. "The key is not to be scared of the economically powerful, at least not if you're close enough to be smelled. People are animals. They smell fear and it starts a chain of reactions. It's a whole loopy soiree in the limbic system. But you control your fear, you control your dominance."

Ruby crossed her arms over her chest and looked at the floor.

"God, your father would say this is inappropriate." Lily dropped Ruby's braid. It fell down between her shoulder blades. "I'm not supposed to say any of this. Forget it, okay? Let's get out of here. You done looking at these dead things? You all good, sweetie?"

Ruby wanted to cry, but tears would allow Lily to smell her sadness. "I'm all good," she said.

She tried to be all good on the walk back to her building. She was supposed to forget what Lily had just told her, so she attempted to think of something else. She repeated in her mind, again and again, *Cabinet of curiosities. Cabinet of curiosities. Cabinet of curiosities*. It was a wonderful phrase.

Back in 5A, while Lily was in the bathroom, Ruby wandered over to a pile of library books. One of the books was on dioramas at the Museum of Natural History. *Behind the Glass: A Chronicle of Habitat Dioramas*. Lily had taken a book out before their trip, Ruby realized, so she could seem smart when she took Ruby to the museum. Lily had wanted to show off to Ruby!

A new and nearly unbearable love swelled in Ruby. It was not as if her heart had grown to the size of the heart of a giant whale, but more like a giant whale had burst inside her heart. It hurt so much. It felt so good. She was *all good*.

Ruby grabbed her backpack and placed the library book inside of it. When it was time to go to the basement again, she snuck the book out. Lily would have to pay for the book, and Ruby felt badly about that, but it would have felt worse to think about the strangers of the New York Public Library system smearing, without thought, the pages of an object that had brought the giant whale into Ruby's heart, that had made her feel full to bursting with love. She showed the book to nobody. Not her mother, who would lecture Ruby if she found out she'd stolen a library book. Not her father, who would shout at Ruby if he found out she'd robbed a tenant. She didn't even show the book to Caroline, whose justice-seeking dolls would never forgive Ruby. She kept it for herself, memorized its facts, and looked through it often, not just that year, but all through middle school, through high school, even sometimes in college. When she moved into an apartment, the one she shared with six other people, she took the book with her, and when she moved in with John, she took the book to John's place—their place now, he said—and showed it to him.

"I stole this when I was a kid," she told kind, strong-jawed John, who had made it his life's mission to ensure equal opportunities in the educational sphere, and who sometimes took Ruby's hand and declared that, despite all her debt, she represented the beginning of what he thought would be a success story that bravely defied systemic pressure. ("I hope you write that into our wedding vows," Ruby joked once, and John started to cough.) When she showed John the book, she was not wearing a shirt. She held the book up to her chest.

John smiled. He suffered from rosacea, which gave him a ruddy Bill Clinton–ish complexion, making his smiles seem so over-the-top genuine they began to feel political. Still, that wasn't his fault, so Ruby smiled back. John took the book and looked at the due date inside it. Then he reached for her hand and kissed the inside of her wrist. "You've had this thing so long," he said. "It's basically yours."

"It's not embarrassing that I still have it? Or, like, shameful?"

"Do you think it's shameful?"

"Well. I stole it from a rent-controlled tenant who took it out from the library. How is that not shameful?"

"You were a little girl," John said. "I think it's cute."

Ruby decided that one of two things happened to the shames adults carried from childhood: These shames became very cute, or they became very ugly.

"Did you steal much else when you were a kid?" John asked.

"No," she said. "I caused trouble in other ways." And then she told him about getting locked in the elevator-motor room with Caroline. She was smiling the whole time she told the story. Like that shame had become adorable. Like she was very far away from that basement and would never go back. She did not tell John that after that day in the elevator-motor room, Caroline was not allowed to have playdates in the basement again. They always met in 6A instead, under the eye of Caroline's mother or father or a certified babysitter. She did not tell John about how her father almost lost his job. She did not tell him that she had peed her pants. She lied. She said Caroline had been the one who'd peed.

"Seriously?" John laughed. "Caroline is so self-possessed. It's hard to imagine her peeing at all, like, ever, even into a toilet."

"Oh," Ruby said, "she peed. She definitely peed."

John poked her in the ribs. "You sound happy about it. You don't have a secret lady–hate boner for Caroline, do you?"

"Of course not!" She pushed his hand away. "I love Caroline. Anyway, I've never had a hate boner."

"They can feel good," John said. "But they're destructive. I always tell my kids at Hover Up, during our breakout sessions? I tell them you shouldn't waste energy on even a little anger."

And here Ruby was, back in the basement apartment, wasting all her energy on anger toward her father, who sat once again on a meditation bench, breathing in and out with such regularity, it was hard to believe he wasn't deliberately trying to infuriate her. She tried to take a deep breath herself. She knew in some way her father was aggravated that she was living at home again after the brouhaha about college, those high school teachers announcing to him at graduation that they were so proud of Ruby and all she'd go on to do. She had never told her father that at times college had been enormously isolating. She didn't want to sound like she was complaining, certainly not to her parents, who worked real and demanding jobs. And she didn't want to make it seem like she hadn't also loved college. Most days, even when she felt alone, she also felt thrilled to be there, bopping around campus with the sense that the world was fuller than she'd realized. Her art history professors lectured with a warmth and an eloquence and an intelligence that in itself felt like an art object.

But she also often felt, despite decent grades, like she herself was an intruder, about to be discovered and kicked out. The other students, most of whom came from homes with far more money, spoke with so much easy confidence, even (and sometimes especially) the ones who loved to talk about their anxiety issues. "Did you know," they'd say in class, like Caroline, and then would spout out some esoteric insight or fact. They wore brand-name clothes and the ones who didn't wear brand-name clothes made the choice look intentional and thoughtful and cool. Ruby took a few sculpture classes, a few painting classes, but couldn't shake her shyness around the kids who called themselves artists so effortlessly, as if they were simply sharing their first name. Whatever former boldness had made high school easy enough for her began to shut down. When she was in college, it was only on the phone with Caroline, for whatever reason, that she felt comfortable enough to talk about her love of dioramas, to talk about how she hoped to do something with the form some-day. It was only with Caroline that she could say "do something with the form" and not feel stupid. She even felt a little superior: At the time, Caroline's own art was limited to a series of sculptures she was making of her own hands. One of her male professors had told her that the hand sculptures were "self-indulgent and the outstretched fingers suggest, I hate to say, a most painful priapism."

"I had to look that one up," Caroline told Ruby on the phone in tears. "I think he's saying I made penis fingers."

"That's so sexist," Ruby said. "I'm pretty sure that's sexist."

"I'm going to take a break from the art classes, I guess."

And then, to make Caroline feel better about the penis fingers, Ruby had confessed to her how lonely she was at college, and Ruby also had begun to weep, and they'd both hung up a full hour later, thrilled by their shared near-synchronous sobbing.

Of course, Ruby wound up making a couple of decent friends at college, too. She had a work-study job at the campus coffee shop, and became close with the other student workers there. In between semesters, Ruby used the experience at the campus coffee shop to get a summer job at a far fancier coffee shop in SoHo, which paid better than the summer internships she found and which made her looming debt seem less daunting. She had assumed she would get some decent full-time job with benefits once she graduated. In the meantime, she had regular customers who tipped well. When she told Lily about her coffee shop job, Lily had been proud. She had said, "Your real education will be at that job."

"It's just temporary," Ruby had told Lily. "Just for when I'm in school."

"The school of life is eternal!" Lily sang.

When Ruby first graduated, she had avoided applying for jobs in the service industry. But she couldn't find anything other than part-time gigs or babysitting or internships with tiny stipends. At last she had found a low-paying office job nominally attached to a nonprofit that placed art therapists in hospitals and seniors' centers. The job paid almost nothing. She stayed there a year and then went back to the coffee shop where she'd worked summers, figuring she'd make some sort of a lateral move or go to graduate school soon. Or maybe she'd get a job at a fancier coffee shop still. Or maybe she'd learn to make drinks at an upscale bar where drunk people tipped even better.

John had been concerned she was getting stuck in the wrong direction. "I see this with the Hover Up kids all the time," he said. "They stay where they feel safe. You should apply to some places with an actual career path. The coffee shop's cute, but it's not totally real."

And then even the cute coffee shop had shut down when the owner sold the building and rent skyrocketed. Once she was unemployed, John decided Ruby, too, was not as cute as she had seemed. She'd realized over the last couple of weeks how easily she herself could wind up like the woman in the foyer, trying to get a moment's rest. How easily some man like her father—now meditating in front of her so serenely—might show up and tell her to leave, please, ma'am. Only a few months ago, she had dropped a dollar into the cup of a man sitting outside the coffee shop and had joked to another barista, Jane, "I'm not being charitable. I'm networking in case this place goes under." She'd thought she was just being funny.

Her throat had gone dry. She went to the kitchen for a glass of water, but stopped at the intercom that hung just to the right of the sink. It had felt so strange, watching her father and Lily's cousin inside that video screen. For a moment, the woman had stared at the camera and Ruby's father had stared at the woman. A frozen instant, which had produced in Ruby the same tenderness the Museum of Natural History's dioramas often did. Like she was simultaneously gazing at a private moment and invading a biome that soon would cease to exist. That tenderness was much better than the fury she felt now as her father sat in the next room breathing in and out mindfully, after being so mindless with Lily's relative, so small-hearted.

She leaned into the intercom and pressed a button so that the camera would go on again. The foyer, translated by the crappy camera into black-and-white, did not look so glamorous as it appeared in person. There were the mirrors, yes, but their gilt frames looked gray. There was the wood paneling, but it could have been bare drywall. There was the—

There was the woman.

Lily's cousin. In the building again. Right there, right *there*, on camera. She had come back, must have guessed Ruby's father would be gone by now. She was still trying to get inside the building. She came right up to the intercom and jabbed her finger at the button that must have connected to apartment 5A. Her eyes darted around the small space. She then blew her nose into a fistful of tissues.

On impulse, Ruby picked up the receiver, which rattled against the intercom's tiny microphone. The woman jumped and dropped her tissues. "Hello?" the woman called into the emptiness of the entranceway. "Is someone there?" She jammed her finger at the button again.

Ruby should call out to her father. *The woman's here again*, she should say. *Dad? The woman who yelled at you, she's back.*

But he wouldn't hear her. Not through his headphones.

"Hello?" the woman said. She lifted up her tissue packet, blew her nose, then said again, "Hello?"

Ruby could have said anything into the receiver. Like: *What can I do for you?* Or: *Never yell at my father again.* Or: *I'm sorry my father kicked you out.* Or: *I'm calling the police.* Or: *I loved Lily, too.* Her mind wobbled among these options.

But all she wound up saying was: "Hi." She said the word very softly, like *Hi* was a curse she was too young to utter.

The woman's head jerked up. "Who's there?" Her voice now low. "Lily, is that you?" She smiled. "I knew that asshole was lying to me about you. They said you were dead just to get me to leave! These vile fucks. Let me in. Hello?"

Her voice was what did it. Her voice was exactly like Lily's.

They have no place to go.

"Lily, let me in. Do you know what I've been through? You were right about Hal. Look, I'm sorry about the money." Her voice softening again. "Let me in. Please. *Let me in.*"

Ruby pressed down on the button with the key icon. The woman heard the buzzer and started. Looked around.

Then she opened the door between the foyer and the lobby hall.

Ruby had done it. She had buzzed the woman into the building. She stepped away from the intercom and got a glass of tap water. She drank it all down standing right there by the sink. Then she walked by her meditating father, into her own room, where a few of her dolls still lived, halfway hidden behind old textbooks. They smiled at her while the exposed heating pipe hissed out warmth.

3   YOU WILL FEED HER FISH

Martin's second meditation session of the day was more constructive. This time, he got into a zone, existing almost solely in his breath for over an hour. Lily's voice remained silent. Every now and then the image of Ruby glaring at him would surface. When that happened, he tried to do what Neilson called, during their meditation sessions, "dropping the storyline." He would simply let the image of his glaring daughter exist in his mind, without attaching any feelings to it, and then Ruby would melt away. Eventually, he felt relaxed and centered. He and Ruby both wanted the same thing: respect from the other. He decided he was not angry at his daughter at all. Just eager, once more, to help her, to earn back her respect.

But how? Meditation had not seemed to calm her down. Neither had feeding the pigeons. Maybe the problem was both those activities fell into the whimsical New Age Quirky Dad territory. What he needed to do was provide her with some kind of practical task that would make her feel valued in their family, but that wouldn't require much effort on either of their ends. What task? He waited for a light bulb to go off in his head, like he was a cartoon character, and then remembered that yesterday 7B had left a message about a dead light bulb at the building entrance.

He rose from the meditation bench, went through their bedroom—Debra, snoring—and knocked on Ruby's door, seeing the thin line of light filtered beneath it. When he walked in, she was sitting at the desk, which, since she'd gone away for college, had become Martin's reading territory. His books—mostly tomes on meditation, rodent extermination, and North American birds—were piled all over. But Ruby had made room for her sketchbook. He looked at the piece of paper beneath her right arm and saw only a few rectangles with a human-shaped blob in the center. Ruby quickly covered the paper with her hands. "It's a plan for a diorama about Lily," she said to Martin. "I'm going to start making my dioramas again. As soon as I get money for materials, I'm going to present her old apartment as sort of an endangered habitat. I think she'd like that. Right?"

Ruby didn't seem interested in resuming their former argument about the intruder, which was a good sign. In fact, she looked a little guilty. She must regret what she'd said to him earlier. "Lily would love the diorama idea," Martin said, brimming with fatherly forgiveness that made him feel not old so much as sage. Then he cleared his throat. "There's a building problem I thought you should know about."

Her face went pale.

"Nothing serious. Just a light bulb out in the entranceway."

"A light bulb."

"I've been meaning to fix it. You want to help?"

"You want me to change a light bulb?"

"It's a specialty bulb. It's good for you to learn how to change stuff like that. Those dioramas at the museum? They use all sorts of specialty light bulbs."

Ruby looked up at the overhead light. She had not yet changed for her interview. She was still wearing the baggy jeans and the charity run T-shirt.

"Changing these bulbs, it's a useful skill," Martin continued. "And I always feel less nervous when I learn a good useful skill. But maybe you have better things to be doing with your time." He tried to say the words not defensively, but like they might be a simple fact that he'd forgotten.

She stood. "I don't have anything better to do with my time. Let's go change a bulb."

When he and Ruby walked into the foyer, Martin noticed that a bunch of the intruder's pink tissues were scattered on the floor like dirty flower petals. He'd missed them somehow, earlier, when he'd first asked her to leave. "Your new best friend left me a mess," he said. Ruby looked away. He didn't stop to pick up the tissues. Instead he walked through the front doors and Ruby followed. Outside, the sun had kept climbing the sky. They both blinked into the brightness of the day. It was supposed to rain later, but you wouldn't know it.

He put down his multitiered toolbox. The toolbox accordioned out and he ticked off a quick inventory for Ruby's benefit: A drop cloth, a breakaway knife, Channellock pliers, three screwdrivers, duct tape, fingerless gloves, latex gloves, a small bucket, a folded apron, power tools. And the specialty bulb.

"What's that?" Ruby said, pointing at two pieces of turquoise cloth scrunched up in the corner of the toolbox.

"Those are shoe covers," Martin said. "When I go into people's homes, I slip them on over my sneakers so I don't scuff the floors."

"God forbid."

"No, Ruby, listen. It's one of the most important things you can do. More important, sometimes, than fixing what's broken. It shows people you understand that you're in their home. It shows them you respect their space." He placed the ladder against the wall by the awning, where a black wrought-iron lantern hung. Inside the lantern were frosted incandescent candelabra bulbs meant to look like gas flames.

"Very Victorian," Ruby said.

"That's the idea," Martin said. "Climb up the ladder."

"And now I'm being forced into child labor! Even more Victorian. Lily would have a field day."

"You're not a child."

"I'm joking around, Dad," Ruby said.

The little kids from 3A and their nanny exited the building, the kids waving carrot sticks and screaming. 6B exited the building, nodded to Martin, then began to shout something in French into his cell phone as he walked toward the subway. Ruby mimed covering her ears and Martin smiled. Then she climbed the ladder. "Any more calls this morning?" she asked, with a lightness that convinced Martin she truly had forgiven him for their earlier fight. "Any more intruders?"

"No," Martin said. "Some people asking me to look out for their UPS packages. That's it." He handed her a screwdriver and tried to explain how she had to open the bottom half of the lantern to get at the burned-out bulb, but she had already figured it out on her own.

There was actually nothing very special about this specialty bulb. An extra swivel to get it screwed in right. Some specificity about securing the sconce again. But little he really needed to show Ruby. Why had he decided this was something for her to behold, then? This was not a true learning experience. This was just installing an expensive light bulb.

Right as Ruby screwed the bottom half of the fake lantern into place, a voice called out, "Oh, my! Is that Ruby?"

Heading out of the building was Christine, or, as Martin thought of her, 2D. She wore yoga pants that looked like a tropical-parrot pelt and a workout shirt with many straps. Martin tried to hide his dread of her by bellowing out, "Beautiful morning!"

"My gosh!" 2D said, looking not at Martin, but at Ruby, who climbed down the ladder. She pulled Ruby close to her and began to holler. "This one I've watched grow up! This one is like a niece to me! Ruby, you're exactly my height! How did I never notice? How are you? Visiting the family?"

Ruby's eyes darted toward Martin. "Actually, I lost my job," she said. "And broke up with my boyfriend. So I moved back in with my mom and dad."

"Wow!"

"It's kind of embarrassing, I know."

"It's not embarrassing! The key to success is saying 'heck no' to shame. Life is full of ups and downs, highs and lows. Your dad got you doing his job for him now?" She pointed to the ladder and then laughed before either Ruby or Martin could respond. "Look," 2D said, "I have a seminar to go to for work today, but why don't we set up a consultation session for later this week, Ruby? The first ten minutes are free."

"A consultation session?"

"I'm a life coach now."

"I don't know if I need a life consultation. I just need a job."

"You need a life consultation, sweetie, to know *what* job you need. But look, okay, I do actually have some employment for you. Why don't you feed my clown fish? Could that be a nice micro-job?"

"Feed your clown fish?"

"Sure. Like I said, I have a seminar all day and then I'm spending the night at a friend's. I thought I'd have to run back here to feed them, but you can just step in instead. They're very relaxing. Your blood pressure, watching these fish? It plummets. Not in a dangerous way. In a very positive way. I've cut out caffeine and I've gotten these fish and I feel better than I ever have before!" 2D smiled. "Come by anytime this afternoon."

Martin knew what 2D was doing. Oh, he knew how this all worked. A favor for a favor. Entangling his daughter in the exchange. If Ruby fed 2D's fish, Martin in turn would owe 2D for the kind deed. Surely Ruby understood this.

"Well." Ruby looked at Martin. "Okay, I guess."

All those student loans, and still no awareness of the way traps of debt opened up in this world.

"Wonderful," 2D said. "You can get the key from your father. Right, Martin? And maybe while you're taking care of the fish, your father might take care of those birds on the ledge in the courtyard?" And there it came. 2D had perfected her glares so that they seemed not just like facial expressions, but like actual words, a torrent of finely articulated accusations. "Martin," she said. "I know you've seen them. They nest on the ledge right across from my apartment. Which means those birds are constantly flying over my terrace and dropping little presents behind. I've left you message after message. The birds—"

"The thing about the nest is—"

"It's a public-health hazard! Martin! There's pigeon shit all over my terrace and I? Listen. I cannot handle shit. I have people coming over on Sunday, I have my *sister* coming over, with her *child*, and there's flying-rat crap all over my terrace, they're bombing me every hour of every day, and I've got this seminar today, I mean, there's just a lot going on? Martin?"

"I'll take care of it," Martin said, conscious of Ruby next to him, watching.

"You said you'd take care of it before." 2D's eyebrows went up her forehead. Being around 2D and her fine raised eyebrows, Martin briefly became the sort of man aware of his own eyebrows, of the loose coils of eyebrow hair spiraling out in what Ruby, with her useless art history classes, might call wild rococo designs. *Oh yes, my father keeps his eyebrows in the rococo style*, she would say to that rich fucktard John when they got back together, because probably they'd get back together and all the practical skills Martin had tried to teach her in the meantime would be useless because they'd just hire someone, Ruby and that fucktard, they'd hire someone like Martin to replace their light bulbs.

He was very tired. He wanted to go to sleep on the floor, right where he'd found the intruder earlier. Had he mopped in there? He should mop up the foyer.

"Martin. I need you to promise. Today you'll take care of the nest. Today."

"Today. Yes. I'll do it."

"Perfect." 2D lifted her hand, waved a little. "I'll see you later. Amazing spying your sweet face again, Ruby. Thanks for all your help with the fishies."

She jogged away. A few cars passed. Ruby said to Martin, "She's a terror."

"But you're going to feed her fish."

"I don't have to."

"You already said you would. So you'll do it."

"I won't if it upsets you."

"You will feed her fish, Ruby," Martin said. "You said you'd do it, so now you'll do it. And I'll do what she said and destroy the pigeon nest because that's how the cycle of favors works in this place. Which you should know. Were your eyes shut the whole time you grew up here?"

"Dad."

"Let's head downstairs."

As they walked into the foyer, Ruby said, "You shouldn't have to destroy the pigeon nest."

"At least it's better than what the penthouse people make me do to pigeons."

"The penthouse people? You mean Caroline's dad?"

They stood unmoving in the foyer. Ruby looked at her shoes. Old running sneakers. Was she picturing the footprints she'd leave at their apartment's threshold without shoe covers, the film of dirt she'd bring in to the place where she'd grown up?

A part of him hoped so.

Ruby said, "You don't have to destroy that nest."

The pink tissues in the foyer seemed less like flower petals now than wet laughing mouths. He bent down and began to gather up the tissues. Ruby just stood there, arms at her sides. After a moment, Martin turned and looked at Ruby, and she, too, bent low and began to pick up the scattered tissues, to gather them quickly into her hands.

4 IN THE *BASEMENT*-BASEMENT

Before the intruder, the last person Ruby had let into the building without her father knowing was John. This was the previous July, shortly before she and John had moved in together. Her parents were out of town for their anniversary, a real triumph as it was hard for Martin to get away from the building. Her father had asked Ruby to spend the night in the apartment just to keep an eye out, in case something went wrong with the elevator, which had been finicky lately. He gave her the numbers of several elevator mechanics. As soon as he was out the door, she called John and asked him over.

John had gone to college with Caroline. Ruby had met him at one of Caroline's parties in the penthouse, but he had never been to the basement before. When she brought him downstairs, they had only been together a few months. Before their first date, she had feared he was the worst kind of nonprofit worker, the rich boy with family money who displayed his paltry do-gooder paycheck as a badge of integrity, one that read, *I could be a bro-cog working at a hedge fund, but instead I'm making a difference.* But he wasn't like that. He seemed to really care about the students he worked with at Hover Up. Sometimes when she slept over he would wake her in the middle of the night, unable to contain his worry that one kid wouldn't turn in her financial-aid form in time, or that another kid's scores might not make the cutoff for scholarship opportunities if he didn't get math tutoring like John suggested.

Their sex, so far, had been playful and sometimes even a little goofy. The idea that sex could make her feel younger, more childish, and not more adult, was revolutionary to her. Maybe the unexpected playfulness was what made room for her to become so unexpectedly serious about John so fast. What Ruby wanted that day in July, very much, was to show John the place where she grew up so that they could have sex in her childhood bed. What she told him, though, was that she wanted to show him her childhood home and did he want to spend the night? He'd said yes in his soft but deep voice that reminded Ruby of the man who narrated many of the books-on-tape she'd listened to when she was small—a child's version of *The Arabian Nights*, a whole series of Greek myths for kids. When John spoke to Ruby with his books-on-tape voice, he always left her feeling assured not only that he knew exactly what was going to happen next, but also that if something truly bizarre occurred in real life—if a goddess sprang out of a father's forehead or if a woman turned into a nightingale—John would take it in stride and help Ruby do the same. He would make it seem that the magical or horrendous twist was part of a larger and wiser authority's plan. Once, thinking of Lily, Ruby had even asked John if he'd ever done voice-over work. "Like, movie trailers?" he'd said.

"Or commercials."

"I mean, I try to sell the kids I work with on the idea that they have, like, a future," he'd said, and she'd said never mind.

When John arrived to see her childhood home, she'd met him upstairs, not just buzzing him in, but greeting him at the foyer like a doorman. She hoped she wouldn't run into Lily in the lobby—Lily hadn't met John, because Ruby worried that if she did, she'd look at him the same way she looked at Caroline, except worse. But no Lily in the lobby, nobody there at all. They took the elevator together to the basement. When the doors opened onto bright fluorescent lights and scuffed laminate flooring, John's eyebrows curved in. Ruby watched as he processed the peeling plaster walls, the maze of ceiling pipes. He ducked his head into the hallway filled with garbage cans and crinkled his nose. Then he walked to the wall with a bank of dozens of glass electric meters for the upstairs apartments. Under the glass, tiny wheels spun. He examined this spinning with his head tilted as if he were taking in important specimens that needed to be classified. "I didn't realize you grew up in the *basement*-basement," he said to the meters.

"It's not like I slept in the boiler room or whatever. I lived in an apartment. It's right down the hall." She pointed to the door labeled *B*.

"I guess I didn't imagine what 'basement' would actually mean."

Ruby had not yet been to John's childhood home, but she had not had to imagine it. He had shown her photographs the fifth time they'd slept together. The house had a wraparound porch and curvy shingles and a picket fence painted periwinkle blue ("My parents aren't white–picket fence people," John had said proudly, as if the periwinkle shade made his mom and dad countercultural revolutionaries). It looked like the kind of house that had gables, not that Ruby was entirely sure what a gable was. She had had no pictures to show John in return. The basement did not photograph well. There was not a lot of natural light. Would he make a comment about that when they stepped into the apartment? No, he'd just look around, process the lack of windows, and say nothing. She would have to pretend to notice neither his processing nor his careful silence.

"Maybe we should go back upstairs," she said. "This is a bad idea."

"What?" He stepped forward, took her hand. "You're being crazy."

"My parents don't know you're staying here. They're weird about things like that. They never even liked me having boys in my room when they were around."

"Just a few hours ago you were saying how much it meant for me to come to the place where you grew up."

"I don't know." Ruby squeezed her toes in her sneakers, listening for some kind of a snap of joint that didn't come. "I think you were picturing something fancier? Like Caroline's penthouse apartment?"

"You're projecting on me right now." John swung her hand back and forth, like they weren't in the basement at all but were about to frolic in a field. "I think it's really cool you grew up down here."

"You think this is cool."

"It's like you had your own underground lair. Way better than a backyard." He gestured to the electric meters. "Did you spend a lot of time watching these spin?"

"Not really. I just passed them every day. They were like lawn ornaments."

"Electric garden gnomes," John said. She laughed a little, and John pulled her to him.

Clearly, there was no going back upstairs. Anyway, to keep John out of the apartment where she grew up would in some way be to deny him access to a part of her she truly wanted him to see, to love. So she put on her most compelling crooked smile ("Your nineties rom-com girl-next-door look," Caroline called it), and took John into the apartment. "My favorite part is the ugly couch," she said, speaking a little too quickly. "With the windmills and the cows? Those kinds of prints were really popular after the war. People wanted to just go back to the farm."

"False nostalgia," said John.

"Exactly."

"Still," he said, "it looks amazingly comfy."

"It used to belong to some tenant who moved out. No new tenant would be caught dead with this couch now."

"I guess the building's changed since you were a kid, huh?"

"Actually," Ruby said, trying to sound offhand, "I had this idea where I'd do a Museum of Natural History sort of autobiographical diorama series of this building throughout the time I lived here? To show how it's changed?"

"Are you telling me there's been changes in New York City? I've *never* heard a native New Yorker address that before."

"Okay, point taken. Maybe let's look in another room?" They walked into the small kitchen with the new giant white oven. "We think that's Angelina Jolie's old oven," Ruby said. "The super at this building with all these celebrities hauled it over here just for us when Angelina dumped it."

"Amazing," John said. "Incredible." But his eyes seemed to drift to the wall behind the oven, to the tiny barred window that looked out onto the gray concrete of the courtyard.

The sex that night, in her childhood bed, was quiet. It definitely didn't construct some sort of coital bridge between past or future or do whatever transcendent, transformative thing she had hoped the fucking there would do. John stroked her hair for a while afterward. The steam pipe, in the summer, was as silent as they were. Eventually John said, "It must have been kind of painful, as a child, to grow up feeling like a second-class citizen in your own home. In your own apartment building."

"Well, it's not ours or anything." Ruby frowned. "We don't own the actual building. Or even this apartment."

"Don't be so literal. The way you reacted when I came downstairs. I can tell there's some deep-rooted emotional stuff there."

"No therapizing tonight, please." She tried to move back into that zone of playfulness, reaching toward John's arm to grab a wattle of loose elbow skin. "What do they call this part of the arm?" she asked. "It's like the scrotal elbow sack."

He pulled away. "I just mean, Ruby, it must have been hard. The basement of the building doesn't fit in with any of the other floors. You've got high-end real estate for a whole bunch of floors, and then you've got the garbage room. Right?"

She understood what he wanted now. If she couldn't own good Manhattan real estate, she could at least own some of the inequality she'd experienced. She could at least own a solid upstairs/downstairs story to be trotted out at the appropriate times, like she was some Dickensian dungeon-scrubber. But she'd seen the people sleeping in the doorway of the church next door. The inequities in the neighborhood went deeper than anything she herself had experienced. She wanted to tell him that as a child she hadn't felt as if the basement failed to fit in with the rest of the building. She had felt as if the basement made the building work and she was somehow part of all that working.

"I don't know," Ruby said at last. "When I was younger, at least, it was kind of entertaining living down here."

"Entertaining?"

She told him about how after ten at night, after the laundry room and the garbage room were closed to the other tenants, and elevator access to the basement was cut off, her mother and father would take turns rolling her around in the laundry cart. She'd close her eyes and pretend she was in outer space—a special cosmic corner where the stars smelled like detergent and Saturn's rings were thin sheets of fabric softener. She worried John would call her out on sentimentality. But instead he pulled her close. More silence. Eventually he said, "This bed is super–low down."

"It's made out of an old elevator box."

"An elevator box?"

"Yeah. For elevator doors."

"This bed we're on now?"

"The mechanics threw it out when they installed new elevator doors and my mom thought it'd make a good bed." Ruby laughed. She figured John would laugh, too, and then kiss her and then maybe they'd have sex again, better sex. But John only said, a few moments too late, "That's really amazing."

"Maybe not *really* amazing."

"So your mom saw this thing in the garbage room and she basically repurposed it?"

"I don't know if she'd put it that way. I was a little kid and I was getting too tall for my little-kid bed and, you know, she had just gone back to school, we didn't have much money then."

"She repurposed it," John said.

"She was only trying to save money." Ruby's voice was so sharp it surprised her.

Again, silence.

"I'm sorry," John said at last. "I feel like now I'm the one projecting something on you. God, I'm such a hypocrite."

"No," Ruby said. "Forget it."

"At the Hover Up training, we give volunteers this whole unit on not superimposing their privileged value systems on the kids. And yet here I am . . ."

"No, no," Ruby said. "It's fine. No superimposing happening."

"Ruby."

"You're right. In a way, she repurposed it."

She buried her face in the dip of John's chest, closed her eyes, breathed in and out slowly, hoping John would think she was asleep. He was not fooled. "Listen," he said. "I didn't mean to make you feel . . ."

"It's fine. I don't feel anything."

"Well, I don't want to make you feel *nothing*." He lifted her chin and kissed her. She opened her mouth obligingly. But instead of seeing John's purposeful red face, she was seeing the apartment where she'd grown up, really seeing it: the cluttered coffee table her mother had rescued from the garbage room, the sagging couch with its starving cows, the abraded aquamarine tiles leading to their front door with its variety of padlocks.

Then after she'd imagined the padlocks on the front door, her brain started to move *outside* that door, and she was seeing things beyond the apartment, traveling along the hallway that extended from the front door, into the environs of the basement at large. She felt a powerful whirring all through her, felt the boiler going, felt the elevator-motor room, the pulleys and furnaces that ran a building. Water mains, water meters, all kinds of valves, three backflow preventers, steam pipes for heat, other pipes carrying electric wires, gas pipes, sprinkler pipes. She saw the black laminate flooring of the hallway, the off-white walls, smelled the dry sweet perfume of laundry detergent tinged with the wet too-sweet smell of garbage.

Was this what her father, newly New Age, called a visualization? Or was this something bigger, an actual vision of some sort?

Her brain traveled upward, then, to the lobby, full of mirrors, through the foyer, outside the wrought-iron doors, the sidewalk splotchy with gum and dog pee and coffee sloshed out of over-full cups. Ruby saw—even though he was in Montauk with her mother—her father, hair white, back bent, sweeping the sidewalk, sweeping the candy bar wrappers and the crumbled tissues and the small leaves of the honey locust tree, and John moved toward her, his tongue on her neck.

Okay.

She was here.

Back here.

Back here and John's tongue was leaving long wet streaks of spit along her collarbone. She pushed him off her.

"You're mad," John said.

"No, no. I just feel a little funny."

He took a strand of her hair and twirled it around his index finger. "Ruby?" John's voice was low. "What if we explore the garbage room?"

"Explore the garbage room?"

"I mean, we might find stuff we want."

"Are you saying you want to dumpster dive? In my building?"

"Kind of. My roommate used to all the time in college. Once, Alex found basically two *tons* of unopened Fritos."

She took his hand and unwound her hair from his finger. "Weren't you on a meal plan?"

"Either way, that food would have gone to waste."

Ruby rolled over onto her back and looked up at the ceiling, at the steam pipe.

"Come on, Ruby. Please? Maybe we'll find something neat.

Something you might even use for art. You said you wanted to get into making, like, autobiographical dioramas, right? Maybe you'll find something you can put inside a diorama. Trash can be really inspiring."

He wasn't saying her name, but she knew he was thinking of Caroline, who had returned about half a year ago from a dad-sponsored trip to Europe with shorter hair and a new focus: She had begun making marble sculptures resembling disposable objects. *"Expendables,"* Caroline called the series. As far as Ruby could tell, Caroline had never tried especially hard to be part of any sort of art scene—"I'm interested in friendship, not subcultures," Caroline told Ruby once—but she had met some guy in Italy who encouraged her to think about incorporating a sustainability angle into her work, and something about this advice had set Caroline on a new, more dedicated path. She sent Ruby long e-mails about the Italian boy. *He creates sculptures out of found trash and they're beautiful but also I feel like they don't exactly SAY anything other than la la la look trash has texture too? I argued with him that I don't want to turn our waste into some other funny form. I want us to look hard at the integrity of the objects we throw away themselves. I guess something about all the cathedrals here made me realize also I'm interested in that fine line be-tween the parodic and the divine??? It feels almost terrifyingly parodic to write that sentence to you Ruby but it's really how I feel, I have this drive since I came here that I never had in college when I was making all those stupid sculptures of my own stupid hand and, well, you are my oldest friend and if I can't be earnest and pretentious and self-deprecating in a letter to you O THEN WHO. PS We went to a quarry with the same marble Michelangelo's Pieta itself is carved out of and I told my mom this and she asked if I was going to come back to NY a Catholic and was not even joking, ha ha, anyway I love you.*

When she'd returned to the States, Caroline had immediately set to work on a triptych of marble sculptures resembling paper plates. Ruby did not feel threatened by news of this series, which sounded to her like something that had been done before. But Caroline had managed to make *Paper Plate with Pizza Grease*, *Paper Plate with Leftover Pink Frosting*, and *Paper Plate with Pigeon Shit* look singular and gorgeous. *Paper Plate with Pigeon Shit* was Ruby's favorite. The hue of paint Caroline had found for the pigeon shit was breathtaking: the perfect purply milkiness.

She'd sculpted a marble Styrofoam cup that looked vividly pocked and a pair of marble maxi pads with wings (*the folds resembling the robes of the* Pietà, according to one art blog). Most recently Caroline had learned that her marble *Spork* series was going to have a small sidebar in an interior design magazine. "It's a little weird because obviously the works are supposed to critique mass consumerism," Caroline had said to Ruby. "They're not supposed to be interior design sort of pieces. But I guess I'm not at the place where I can complain. Exposure's exposure."

Ruby had tried to be happy. Caroline had worked hard, had been spending day and night in her studio. But it was difficult not to feel like it was unfair that Caroline was profiting off an artistic take on trash when Ruby was the one who had grown up right next to all that garbage. Shouldn't she be the one inspired by it, clever about it, making statements? Ever since she graduated college Ruby seemed unable to make or state anything, could barely articulate her urge to make or state. Now, of course, John wanted to inspire her, to be a kind of muse by asking her to traipse through the garbage room with him. And that was sweet, wasn't it? She tried not to think the darker thought, that John was encouraging her murky artistic ambitions not because he cared about *what* she would make, but because such ambitions would make her more like Caroline. Which would in turn make her less like someone who had grown up next to the garbage room. She would not think that, no, because that thought wasn't fair to John. He was just trying to help her feel self-actualized in some way.

So she clapped her hands like a self-actualized camp counselor, trying to rally herself. "Okay," she said, and rolled out of bed, pulled on her jeans. "Why not take advantage of the basement amenities?"

She yanked John's hand toward her and led him through the apartment, unlocked the many locks, shepherded him into the hall-way, tried to bring back that feeling she'd had in her vision earlier—a powerful whirring.

And here, now, the garbage room. Bulky black garbage bags among piles of cans and newspapers and purses with broken zip-pers. A giant air filter had been placed beside some broken folding chairs. In the corner of the room, just to the right of the paper recy-cling, sat a pile of nice cutting boards, sustainably harvested wal-nut, or something. On top of the cutting boards sat a teddy bear and a jean jacket.

"Jackpot." John went for the pile of cutting boards.

"No. Don't."

"What's wrong?"

"That's Rafael's pile."

"Rafael?"

"The porter. He helps my dad put out the garbage cans sometimes and he always gets first dibs on the trash. When people throw out paintings, if he likes them, he'll hang them up in the alley."

"Gosh," John said. "Even the porter has a curatorial side hustle."

"I'm just saying he'll probably take those cutting boards back to New Jersey tomorrow, along with the teddy bear for his daughter."

"So even though he's left the cutting boards here, they're his?"

"He gets first dibs. But all the other stuff outside of Rafael's pile is fair game."

"Okay. Fine. I will abide by the cryptic rules set forth by my beautiful tour guide to the basement."

The tour guide to the basement. Well, sort of. While she could show him these rooms, she could not show him what made this building run.

She could not tell him about the nannies from Ecuador and the Philippines who kept the kids they watched away from the glass recycling and broken bottles with serrated edges. She could not bring him into face-to-face contact with the plumber who had prostate cancer, or the pump mechanic from New Jersey who had just divorced his wife and lost the kids but kept the motorcycle. She could not introduce him to the elevator mechanics her father called in, the Russian guys who had trained on Soviet missile-guidance systems. Or Rafael, even, with his new baby and his parents and sisters far away, Rafael who Ruby had caught weeping over the garbage once and who hadn't looked her in the eye since.

These were the people who populated the basement in the daylight. Helping John know them, understand them, would be beyond her abilities to guide and beyond his desires as a guest. John and Ruby were simply touristing around the garbage room right now. Prismatic slicks of who-knows-what liquid on the floor. Eight pairs of compression socks in the bin meant for wet garbage. John began to dig up the socks, which luckily were completely dry, wedged between tied-up trash bags. He tossed two pairs to Ruby. After a few more minutes, he looked into another bin for wet garbage and found, at the very top, an unopened bottle of wine. "Unbelievable," he said, "right? But you know we have to drink this wine."

Ruby said, "I'll go get a bottle opener."

She went back into the apartment. The year before, as a birthday gift, she had bought her father a chrome-plated bottle opener in the shape of a sparrow, knowing that he was newly into bird-watching. Now she held the bird in her palm and looked into the dents of its eyes before bringing it to the garbage room. John opened the wine and took a deep gulp. He passed the bottle to Ruby and she swigged.

John gestured to Rafael's cutting boards again. "He doesn't really need *five* of these. Right?" He lifted up a cutting board. "I could give it to one of the Hover Up kids. Wendell's writing his essay on his dream to become a chef." John held the cutting board up a little higher.

"Take it," Ruby said, giving in. "Go ahead."

They returned to the apartment, drank the rest of the wine, and had much better sex.

John left around eight in the morning for work. Since Ruby's shift at Mellow Macchiato wasn't until three, she overslept until almost noon. Finally she got out of bed, got dressed, placed the used condoms in a CVS bag, and stepped out into the living room.

Her shoulders jumped.

There was her mother, peering at her over a newspaper. Her parents had returned from their trip and had tried not to wake her. Her father, who sat in front of the TV, didn't look her way. But he said, staring at the weather radar map on the screen, "Will you go upstairs with me, Ruby?"

Had they found out John stayed the night? Ruby's mother turned her gaze back to her newspaper too quickly.

"Am I in trouble for something?" Ruby asked.

"Let's go upstairs."

Ruby and her father took the elevator to the first floor, walked down the lobby hallway, stepped out under the awning. The sun was up and bright and hurt her head. She'd had far too much wine. She was still, she realized, holding the CVS bag.

Her father pointed to a patch of sidewalk. "See that?"

"What?"

"That spot. On the sidewalk where I'm pointing?"

"Uh-huh."

"That's where I put the recycling when I haul it up from the basement. When it's recycling day and I come up with the bags, no matter how late at night it is, Ruby, somebody is always waiting. Sometimes it's this white guy in his thirties. Sometimes it's these crews of women, mostly Hispanic, with empty baby strollers. They pile the strollers full of glass and plastic bottles and tie plastic bags to the strollers and fill those bags with glass and plastic bottles, too. Sometimes they have shopping carts, but the strollers are easier to maneuver. The women see me and go, 'Hello mister.' If it's the white guy in his thirties who makes it to that spot there first, he always tries to get me to talk to him, as a fellow white guy. He always goes, 'Oh, having a good day, buddy?' Meanwhile I'm sweating all over from hauling up the glass and the paper from the basement. If too many of the stroller women are here, or if the women and the white guy are both here, they get in fights over who gets a claim over what. Everybody wants the plastic, because it's cheap and light and nobody wants to carry the glass bottles back." Finally her father looked at her. "The point," he said, "is if you're going to dig through the recycling, Ruby, if you're going to dig through the plastic and paper and glass, you should wait up here, around that spot. You should wait your turn. Okay? That's how it's done in this city."

She said nothing.

He took her hand—the one not holding the CVS bag—and placed the sparrow bottle opener in her palm. "You left this in the garbage room." He began to walk back to the building. "Return that cutting board to Rafael, too, will you?" he called over his shoulder. "It was a present for his wife's sister. She's visiting all the way from Texas."

He walked through the entrance doors into the foyer. Ruby didn't follow. She didn't move at all. The spot on the pavement looked like all the other spots. Her head pounded. She walked to a garbage can at the end of the street and threw out the CVS bag and the sparrow bottle opener and called in sick to work and got on the subway and almost vomited about five times before she reached the apartment she shared with her slew of roommates. Back in her non–elevator box bed, she called John and said, "I almost hurled on the subway. The train was delayed and delayed. And when I got back to the apartment, Jordana had clogged the toilet." Then she began to sob. She did not mention that her father had noticed the missing cutting board. She didn't want John to associate his visit to her childhood home with guilt. Still, maybe he sensed she was shielding him from something. Or maybe he still felt sheepish about the way he'd said *repurposed*. He murmured to Ruby that she was wonderful and he was sorry about the roommates and the tampons and then John said, "You should just move in with me."

She had hauled her belongings—just a few boxes—into John's apartment, which was huge and full of light. He received help with rent from his parents every month. "I'm personally fine living in a less nice neighborhood with less space," he told Ruby, "but my mom sent me nonstop articles about bedbugs and robberies and insisted she'd have a heart attack if I *didn't* accept their help." He had helped her unpack, lifting each one of her shirts and dresses and spinning the garment around like he was dancing with an invisible Ruby.

They had settled into a routine. Takeout for dinner, a movie. Turn-taking with loading and unloading the dishwasher. Nights, she'd hold him when he panicked about some kid from Hover Up he couldn't help. He'd breathe into her hair and say, "You always smell like coffee."

Then the fights, slow at first, about dishes and then about smelling like coffee, how she was too old and too educated to always smell like coffee, and why wasn't she applying for other non–coffee shop things, new options? John, when he said the words *new options*, often pushed his hair back on his head, revealing a flush at the top of his forehead. Then Lily was dead, and when Ruby shook, he stroked her back, and the next day she told him he treated her like she was one of his kids from work, the high schoolers he was supposed to guide to college, and he said Ruby needed a guide, clearly, and she could learn a thing or two from the ambitious students he mentored, the students who came from way more difficult backgrounds than she had, by the way, and turned into real success stories.

"They don't turn into stories," Ruby said. "They're people. They'll just keep on being people."

They'd had an especially bad fight right after the coffee shop closed down, when Ruby told John she planned to apply to other, more stable coffee shops, as well as a few waitressing gigs. She didn't necessarily dream about working in these places, but she didn't hate the work, and it would allow her to start earning money again— otherwise she'd be dependent on John's grocery money on top of a place to stay. But John had said, "You have a college degree. You're

selling yourself short." The problem was not the words or the sentiment, exactly, so much as the tone. He still spoke to Ruby the way
she'd heard him speak to his Hover Up students, as though she
were a teenager and his belief in her abilities was part of his job
description. "We probably should break up," she told John, and began to cry. John did not look as surprised as she would have guessed.
In fact, he looked a little bit relieved. He told her he'd need her to
move out very soon in that case. He said, "No matter what, Ruby, I
will always believe in you," and handed her a tissue. She dropped it
on the floor, hoping it would plummet fast, but it only drifted, very
slowly, and John, misunderstanding, handed her another.

Now, Ruby gathered up tissues in the foyer of her father's building.

Was this why her father meditated, working so hard to stay in
the moment? Did it keep snot-streaked objects from becoming
mystical portals to other times? She glanced up at her father, waiting for him to sense what she'd done, to accuse her of letting the
woman into the building today. But he was distracted, it seemed,
lost in his own head. After a minute, he took the tissues from her
hands and said, "You shouldn't be picking those up. I'm sorry."

"I don't mind."

"You go back to the basement. I'll take care of the tissues and I'll
take care of the pigeons like 2D asked. You go get ready for the interview."

When Ruby returned to the apartment to change into her interview
outfit, it was a little after eight. She went into her parents' bedroom
first to see if her mother had any last-minute interview advice, and

found her removing a black dress for the conference banquet from the closet. Ruby imagined her mother zipping the dress into a garment bag and riding to Port Authority on the subway with the dress over her lap like a tired child. "I can't believe you're going to be gone all weekend, Mom," she said.

"You've turned sweet again," her mother said. "I figured you'd be mad at me about the whole intruder thing."

"I still think you guys were cruel. But it's over now. And if you're gone, who's going to make sure Dad and I don't kill each other?"

"Don't hassle your father too much, okay? His back is hurting him and he hasn't been sleeping well."

"Do you have to go right now?" Ruby took her mother's hand. "I can't tell which interview outfit makes me look wholesomely sane. Or sanely wholesome."

"*Astute.*" Her mother kissed her on the cheek. "The look you're going for is *astute.* But I can't help today. You should have asked me last night. I'm already late."

Then her mother folded up her dress. No garment bag at all, it turned out. She placed the dress directly into a rolling suitcase, right over a few balled-up pairs of socks. Somehow this made Ruby's heart hurt. "I just wish you weren't going," Ruby said, and then focused on the rug's blobby amoeba shapes, embarrassed by the childishness of her words. Ruby's mother really had helped keep the peace between Ruby and her father this last week. Ruby acted out less when her mother was around. Even as a teenager, she hadn't fought with her much. "Probably that's because she got home late so often when you were a kid," Caroline had said to Ruby a few days ago under the blue whale when they'd gone to the Museum of Natural History together to help Ruby prep for her interview. "My mother and I fought about everything and she was always around. Always." Caroline shrugged.

"But probably you felt like you had to be really well-behaved when your mother was around so she didn't leave you again."

"She didn't *leave* me," Ruby said. "It's not like she abandoned us. She took night classes for her college degree for a few years. And then night classes for her library science degree for another few years. She only took one or two classes a semester so it wasn't like she was gone that often. She was always back in time to read to me before bed."

"You don't have to sound so defensive," Caroline said.

"I'm not defensive," Ruby said, gazing up at the blue whale's fiberglass belly. Years back, museum staff had renovated the whale to make it more accurate—the old 1960s model had been based on photographs of a dead female blue whale found in South America. The new twenty-first-century museum whale had more accurate blowholes, less bulgy eyes, and, Ruby had read, a belly button. But she'd never been able to spot the belly button in the hall's dim light. Ruby was looking hard at the whale's navel when Caroline said, "It doesn't make you a bad anti-feminist person if you wish your mom had been around more. Aren't you a little resentful?"

Caroline and Ruby no longer played Holocaust-orphans-sisters-survivors, of course, but they had new games, and one of them Ruby had titled in her head the resentment game, which they wound up playing almost anytime they walked around together in the neighborhood where they'd grown up. The best way to really feel like legal adults seemed to be cataloging their childhood resentments toward their parents. Ruby spoke about how her father always seemed disappointed in her, and Caroline spoke about her parents' divorce (Caroline had better parental resentments, just like she'd had better dolls). But when Caroline asked Ruby if she resented her mother's absences, it was hard for Ruby to say. As a child, during those evenings when her mother didn't get back until after dinner, she would usually feel more irritated at her father, the way he hovered over her, making sure she did her homework, his eyes shadowed under his baseball cap. Once when he had knelt down beside her and told her to put the drawing stuff away and do her math assignment, she had grabbed his baseball cap right off his head, covering her face with it like it was a mask, and screamed into the hat that she hated him. During her mother's night classes, such outbursts at home were common.

But they were followed, always, by her mother holding her when she got back, the big softness of her arms, the relief, the love, her mother's voice urging her to apologize to her father, okay, none of them had it easy, and if Ruby apologized then she'd read to her more of the *All-of-a-Kind Family* books; those girls *really* had it rough, immigrant sisters who didn't even have a bed to themselves, and they had no books of their own, and they had no TV, so Ruby shouldn't complain, she should go tell her dad she was sorry, okay, because she was, wasn't she?

Later, Ruby would write essays in her high school English classes about how her mother was her hero, how she'd graduated from college while working a full-time job, had always been home to read to Ruby at night, and now *she helped people in prison gain access to books and information!* Her teachers wrote in the margins, *Your mom sounds like such a superstar!* If Ruby had held resentment toward her, it was hard to excavate today, buried under those more vivid moments when Ruby had raged against her father.

"I'll be nice to Dad today," she told her mother as they stood together now. "I promise."

"Good girl." Her mother smoothed down Ruby's hair. "And don't worry about the interview or what you'll wear. If anyone should be worried, it's me. This lady isn't the best at public speaking."

"You'll do great," Ruby said.

"Text me after the interview, okay? When is it? Eleven? Do you have time to get ready?"

"I washed my hair last night," Ruby said. "I just have to put on some nicer clothes and walk over. Easy."

"Okay. Just try to get there early. First impressions and all that. And have fun at Caroline's party thing tonight, too."

"Good luck with the conference people."

"Where's your dad? I want to say bye."

"He's taking care of a pigeon nest in the courtyard. The one across from 2D's terrace."

"What do you mean 'taking care of a pigeon nest'?"

"Destroying it," Ruby said.

5 FIVE POTENTIAL HAPPY ENDINGS

A *nd so the super stands in the courtyard, eyes the pigeons, raises the broomstick to knock free the nest, it's the invisible hand of capitalism making him do it, economic ghost forces that will lead to benefits for all, they say, Martin's own hand visible to them now as he lifts the broom even higher to reach the ledge, can't get rid of my voice, can you, Martin; he lowers his hand again, he lowers the broom, he can't do it! He can kick out a human being, but he can't get rid of these birds.*

The pigeons cooed. 2D had said he must destroy this nest. That was the voice Martin needed to listen to, not the Lily voice, which had returned full force ever since he'd stepped out into the courtyard with the broom. He needed to make 2D happy to make the management company happy to keep his job to keep his home. Part of being in charge of the building was demarcating what spaces were and were not potential homes. The foyer could not be a home. This ledge could not be a home. Rats could not make their homes inside the garbage room. Lily's home could not stay Lily's home, could not become a museum to Lily, but *could* be destroyed and remade into a home for someone else with enough money.

He lowered the broom. He had forgotten to mop this morning! The floor in the garbage room must be sticky. More people would complain about that than about this nest, and he should take care of the problems that would attract the majority of tenant whining—democracy and all that. He threw the broom onto the ground, went back inside. The nest could be dealt with as soon as the floor was clean.

He grabbed the custodial bucket out of the utility closet and filled it with hot water from the sink in the laundry room. Then he poured in a decent amount of generic lemon soap from the hardware store's gallon-size bottle. A few board meetings back, there'd been a big controversy because several tenants pronounced the smell of the generic pine-scented soap Martin used "deeply nauseating." Martin had then tried out the cherry-scented soap, which had caused even more reports of nausea, and many comparisons to children's Tylenol. Lemon so far seemed to be going over fine. "It's a little too hospital-esque, isn't it?" 9B had said at the last meeting, but not loudly enough to cause any sort of re-vote. Martin mixed the soap in the hot water and got to work.

Whenever Martin mopped long enough, he began to see the world in wet and dry. First, of course, he just saw the wet and dry patches on the floor. But his perception soon expanded to the body as patches of wet and dry. The wet of an eye white. The dry of a cheek. The moisture of mouth pocket. The stickiness of the ear shell. The giant swatch of torso with its prickles of wet in the chest hair, dewed armpit hair, the slight wet of genitals and the skewers of dry pubic hair, the desert stretch of legs, and the feet, the fungal fury that might be unleashed between the toes because of just a drop of moisture.

And next he would think about the city, first the dry parts of the sidewalks and the parts wet with dog urine or spilled coffee. Next the wet slosh of the Hudson and the dry stretch of the highway above it. Wet, dry, wet, dry. It was sometimes beautiful and rhythmic, this work. It could, in its better, quieter moments, put you into a meditative state without a single mantra, with movement alone.

Sometimes, yes, this work could do that.

But other times.

The birds looking down at him.

His chest was glass again. And someone was pounding against this glass, striking out, trapped inside. The glass bottles he'd have to clean up after Caroline's party. The key was to get up there tomorrow as soon as the sun rose. In the morning, cleaning up would not be so bad—the green glass could, on sunnier dawns, catch and hold the early light. Was this a heart attack? The feeling ripping through his chest? He wished he could have asked his dad, *What was it like?* He closed his eyes. He concentrated. He counted out his breaths like they were coins and thought, *Not the end not the end* because how could it stop here? He and Debra would have a happier ending, after how hard they both worked. His daughter, too, would have a happier ending. But he shouldn't think about Ruby, or the way she had looked at him after he kicked Lily's cousin out of the building. That hard, hurt stare. That was not a happy-ending look. He knew what her happy-ending look should be because Martin had begun to develop, in waking life, a series of detailed dreams, each concerning possible happy endings for his daughter.

Dream #1: Ruby would become an award-winning diorama artist. Did diorama artists and curators have something like the Oscars? Well, this would be something like the Oscars. She would show off her gold statue and beam and say, *This is for my parents.* No, no, she would say, *This is for my father.* (Sorry, Deb.) *This is for my father for always supporting me, for inspiring me to follow my dreams, for giving me paper on which to draw, and art supplies, and even though he did not make enough money for me not to take out all those loans, things still actually wound up great. Maybe better than great because I needed to work for what I had and so thusly acquired the lifelong power of perseverance. Anyway. I'm so, so grateful. Dad, you made me who I am. Thanks!*

Dream #2: She would want to be a super. She'd say to Martin, *Teach me your ways.* She'd say, *There is something noble in your work, with the exception of the occasional killing of birds, which is unfortunately unavoidable.* She'd say, *Also, I want a rent-free apartment.* She'd say—actually he didn't care what she'd say, what reasons she gave for wanting to be a super, the point was she would see in him a life shape to aspire toward.

Dream #3: High-strung, distant Ruby would suddenly become a meditation guru. She'd have a revelation and would stop always looking back at the past or ahead at the future. She'd sit with a straight spine. She'd lead retreats on mountaintops and heal the jerks of the world with her message of mindfulness. She'd even deign to meditate with Martin, and Neilson in 3C. At the start of the session Neilson would say, in his nasal voice, *The key is zooming outward to see the inward.*

And she would say to Neilson, *No, Neilson in 3C, oh, Neilson, I'm sorry but?* And she would say, *The key is not just zooming out. You don't know what the key is, despite your real efforts. You've never actually known what the key is.*

Neilson would start to weep.

Ruby would say, *It's okay. Enlightenment doesn't come easy. Except, of course, when it does.*

If diorama artists had something like the Oscars in his imagination, wouldn't that imply meditation practitioners had something like the Oscars? Well, Ruby would win something like Best Picture at the Oscars of meditation. She would get up onstage and say, *First, I would like to thank the universe, and its cosmic forces, obviously. But specifically I want to take this moment to send loving-kindness to my father for helping me better understand who I am, which is tricky, because identity is a constantly shifting and unstable force of mutability. Thanks, Dad!* And she would wave. Or bow. Or something.

Dream #4: Ruby would get some regular nothing-job. But she would be happy. She would leave the city. She would go on long walks in the woods and send pictures of owls she found to Martin. She would become a photographer, maybe. Not as her main job. Just as a hobby. Pictures of snowy owls, and barn owls, and great horned owls. Pictures of huddled feathered breathing things blinking wisely on icy branches. She would call Martin and Debra twice a week. She would say,

I'm doing great. And how are you old people doing? Each photo from her would feel like Martin had won an award.

Dream #5: Simultaneously the most and the least ambitious dream: Ruby would agree to go bird-watching with Martin, after months of eye-rolls at the suggestion. They'd find the great horned owl he'd been looking for in the park, and the owl would be even more otherworldly than he'd imagined, its beak gunmetal gray, the white patch at its throat like an elongated moon. When Ruby lifted the binoculars to her face, all of a sudden he'd be looking out of her eyes. He'd see the owl as she saw it and he'd have access to her thoughts in that moment, he'd hear her thinking in his mind like he heard Lily's voice sometimes. And she'd be thinking, *This bird is even more otherworldly and majestic than I'd imagined. I am so glad I'm here. I am so glad my father brought me here, I am so content.*

His heart felt better now.

A lot of renovation today. Three crews Martin had to let in, one crew Jamaican, one Mexican, one Romanian. The Jamaicans were continuing the demo job on Lily's apartment to combine it with the apartment above, the Romanians were fixing the ceiling in 3A, the Mexicans were replacing some of the steel lintels above the windows overlooking the north courtyard. Martin would let them all into the building. Would consult with various guys in charge. Would arrange approximate times of arrival/departure. Would account for everyone. Plus the bedbug dog coming by, along with Pumpworks Tony. And Neilson in 3C with the clogged shower drain, which he had just started wailing about to Martin in a series of text messages.

Martin had a policy of never giving out his cell number to tenants. The landline and answering machine were pain enough—his
job followed him into his sleep, the last thing he needed was for it
to follow him on his brief escapes from the constraints of the building. But he'd recently made an exception with Neilson because
Martin wanted to know when his impromptu meditation sessions
happened so he could sometimes join in. Of course, Neilson's texts
right now were all very drain-based. His messages popped up along
with messages from the birding e-group about the owl. *Is owl still
near turtle pond. Drainage is REAL issue need to not be standing in
puddle of water while showering? No great horned just spotted near
sheeps meadow. WHAT time again did you say ud check out drain
again working from home let me know hope I didnt wake u up 2 early
with my call. saw the owl last night in the locust grove, majestic. Martin? U there? What time? Saw owl around dusk. What time 4 drain?*

The birding e-group's messages and Neilson's muddled together
in Martin's mind. He pictured an owl slowly turning its massive
head to reveal shower drains for eyes, two unblinking stainless-steel
strainers.

Deep breaths.

He was done mopping the garbage room. He moved to the hallway in front of the passenger elevator. Some faint footprints. A
powdery spattering of detergent had been spilled by somebody on
the way to the laundry room. If he looked hard enough at the detergent, maybe he'd see the face of a celebrity, or even a saint to whom
he might pray that Ruby get this job at the museum. A contact of
Caroline's had gotten her the interview, which meant she had a
good shot, probably. And museums had to pay decently, right? All
those priceless artifacts that people in movies were always trying to
steal. Probably the gig had really good benefits, maybe even dental.

When she got the job, she'd move out again. Things would be back to normal and he would stop constructing dreams of his daughter's future to calm himself.

Was he expecting too much of her? Martin had moved out of his mother's place as soon as he turned eighteen. He had supported himself ever since. Martin at that age had been sad and skinny, his dad newly dead, his mother's new boyfriend a guy who didn't hit him, but did hurl insults at him whenever he could, no-good-freeloader-cut-your-hair-you-bum kind of thing. A few days on the street when he moved to the city from New Jersey after trying to follow a girl to college, and then he'd done the whole bootstrap thing. He found a job as a "facilities staff member" for a historical society, mopped their wooden floors with Murphy Oil Soap that made at least three curators seize his arm and say, misty-eyed, that the smell brought back memories of their old beloved housekeeper from childhood. He made do, saved what he could, met Debra at the library and now, look at him. Living walking distance from both the Metropolitan Museum of Art and the Museum of Natural History.

Living below street level. Mopping beneath the electric-meter boxes.

Well, trade-offs. Trade-offs were a natural part of life. Trade-offs weren't the same as being scammed. Martin was very sensitive to that difference. He hated being scammed. But he didn't mind playing the fool so long as he was aware that was the part he was playing. When you were self-aware, you weren't being scammed. You were just moving inside whatever role the universe had cast you in this time around, an actor winking behind the mask. It could be artful, fooling could. Like when he'd kicked the woman out this morning, he was playing a part. He wasn't really, deep down, the kind of person who would do such a thing. But he had to act like it to stay alive. Still, he wished he could have helped her. What memories of Lily did she have? Did she hear Lily's voice in her head, too? Or did her memories of Lily manifest in other ways, did she see Lily sometimes, or just feel her presence?

A hand on Martin's shoulder. He jumped. "Whoa," Debra said. "Relax." She clutched a rolling suitcase in her free hand.

"Sorry," Martin said. "A little lost in my head. You off on your big adventure?"

"You look upset." She moved closer. "You caved in to 2D and destroyed the nest finally, huh? Ruby told me."

He kissed her on the lips, then along the centered part of her hair.

"There'll be more birds on that ledge," Debra said. "Don't worry. There will be endless nest-building birds for 2D to complain about."

Right next to them, machines measured the electrical illumination in bedrooms, bathrooms, the powering on of large TVs, the sleep mode stealing over new computers.

"Martin." Debra squeezed his hand. "You okay?"

"I'm fine." Martin smiled as big as he could. "It's good you're getting out of here. Miss Conference USA. You deserve a little vacation."

"It's not a vacation." How fast Debra's face seemed to fold up into something smaller. "Do you really think that's what my day will feel like? It's work."

"Isn't there a banquet?"

"I'm trying to build a network of donors. The banquet is also work."

"I wish my work looked like your work today."

"Are you *trying* to piss me off right before I leave for the weekend? Don't you know how nervous I am? This is my first real panel conference thing."

"You have nothing to be nervous about."

Debra gripped the edges of her shawl. She said, "I'm going to make them laugh."

"Who?"

"My panel audience. One of them will raise their hand and ask 'What's the craziest question a prisoner ever sent you for the reference-by-mail program?' and I'll babble about the Dungeons & Dragons group in Delaware. They keep writing in, asking for more and more complex D&D rules."

Martin snorted.

"See," Debra said, "that's exactly the problem. I'll bring it up because I'll be too nervous to tell that person in the audience that it's kind of messed up to ask what's the craziest question I ever got. And then everyone will laugh at the idea of prisoners playing Dungeons & Dragons, and I'll laugh, too, because I have no spine and I'll want the audience to like me, and after, I'll just feel like a jerk. Just this fat white lady on a panel for mindful outreach, going ha ha ha at the incarcerated populations she's supposed to be helping. I know that's what's going to happen."

"Maybe just don't bring up the Dungeons & Dragons group?"

"You don't get it. I won't be able to think clearly. You don't know what it's like to be speaking in front of a group of strangers."

"You're right. I don't know what it's like to be listened to like that, Deb." He pressed the call button by the elevator. "You'll be late."

"Martin."

The meters swerved. A maid was running a vacuum cleaner. A

babysitter was microwaving her coffee, which had gotten cold on her commute. Martin said, "I didn't destroy the nest."

"What?"

"I couldn't. I came out here to mop instead."

"Babe? They're just birds. They'll rebuild."

"I know. I know. It's only that this nest—"

"You'd rather preserve their home and compromise ours. Makes sense to me."

"You're being overdramatic."

"It's only that 2D's pretty vocal on the board," Debra said. "But I guess you know how far to push things."

"Have fun," Martin said. "Enjoy the banquet." He added, as neutrally as possible, "Try not to work *too* hard."

"Yeah," Debra said, with the same look Ruby had given him when he'd returned downstairs from kicking out the intruder. "I'll give you a call later on." And she gazed out in the direction of the courtyard.

"Fine," Martin said. "I'll take care of the nest. I'll do it right now. I promise."

"You do what you can today," she said. "Try to get out of the building a little, okay? Breathe some fresh city air." The elevator doors opened and she stepped inside, the wheels on her suitcase wobbling, squeaking, and the doors closed, and she rose up.

6 ALL OF THE ANTELOPE

R uby sat on the toilet.

The apartment was empty and her stomach ached. She bent forward so that her nose nearly touched her knees. She pushed. If she could just shit, she'd feel okay. Her phone buzzed. A text from Caroline. *Good morns and good luck today with interview rubyyyyyy.*

She pushed.

The Clogged Toilet. That could be the title of a diorama, too.

Near the end of their relationship, John had told her she was being self-centered with her diorama ideas. "You won't actually ever have a museum dedicated to your life," he said, looking through her sketchbook of plans. "It doesn't make sense, like, holistically."

"But it wouldn't be a *literal* museum," Ruby said. "It would be an imagined space that viewers could interact with somehow. There would be an element of participation."

"An element of participation," John said. "For someone who didn't go to art school, you sure have picked up a lot of bad habits."

She pushed. John had gotten surprisingly good with the zingers after Ruby had said some critical things about his own work. "You spend more time hosting these crazy galas for the rich volunteers than helping the kids," she told him. "Is what you do really about the students who need help, or about making the volunteers feel like virtuous people?"

He would sigh, seem to agree with her, say something about the complex systemic issues perpetuated by complex systemic evils and how yes, despite his best intentions, he was probably a cog in that machine, but at least he was a self-aware cog, right, trying to do good, ha ha? Then a few hours later, he would drop some equally critical bomb on her diorama visions. She knew deep down he wanted to understand her whole obsession, and it was her fault that she had never really been able to explain to him that imagining dioramas was, for her, like meditation was for her father. Her father liked to say that everything was constant change, but when she'd seen him meditate a kind of immobilization stole over his face, a tranquil stillness.

Caroline texted again. *lemme know how it goes and if you see Nate (my connect there) say hi for me.*

Caroline's *connect*. Why was that word so annoying? Ruby pushed harder.

The Clogged Toilet. The diorama would show two girls (Caroline, Ruby) who were lost. No, who were just pretending to be lost, pretending that they'd run so far from the imaginary Nazi guards, they now couldn't find their way out of the imaginary woods. Of course the viewer would not be able to see the imaginary woods. They would only see a roomful of dolls. When she constructed this diorama, it would be important for Ruby to make the girls look animated—to differentiate them from the dolls—despite their artificiality, their stillness. Their sweat must look like real sweat, and not the sheen of plaster. Their eyelashes must not look like loose thread and fringe. Their bodies must not look soft and posable, but should seem full of tough muscle, full of breakable bones.

Caroline's childhood room would take up two-thirds of the diorama. Then there would be a divider, meant to represent the wall between Caroline's room and the guest bathroom. The remaining third of *The Clogged Toilet* diorama would show Ruby's father fixing the toilet in this bathroom. (In real life, the toilet had broken, and Caroline's father had called Ruby's father upstairs in the middle of the girls' playdate.) The bathroom would be full of little colorful soaps, rendered in the background of the diorama, in two dimensions. Rendered in three dimensions: The toilet. The tool kit. The plunger.

Both of the girls would be pretending not only that they were Holocaust-orphans-sisters-survivors running from Nazis, but also that they weren't aware Ruby's father was making repairs so close by. And this second game of pretend would be deeper, more frightening, not really a game at all. How to convey, in a single diorama, multiple levels of pretend?

Ruby stood up, sweating. Nothing in the toilet bowl. Just an ache inside her gut. She flushed anyway. In her room, she buttoned up a light blue blouse and pulled on her old rayon/nylon/spandex knit skirt, what she thought of as her professional skirt. It looked not great. She texted Caroline back and told her she was worried about her interview outfit. Caroline responded immediately. *I'll just come right down, Rubes. I can help with outfit.*

Ruby was in middle school when Caroline and her parents moved out of 6A and into the new penthouse apartment on the roof. "My mom's more excited about not sharing a bathroom sink with my dad than she is about the view," Caroline told Ruby. During the housewarming party in the penthouse, Caroline's grandmother Dora had called out Ruby's name when she walked in. Dora was a skinny old woman with dark eyes that looked lacquered with protective solemnity, just like Caroline's. Dora took Ruby's wrist in her right hand and Caroline's wrist in her left hand and said, "Yes, yes, Ruby, I remember you. From when you were tiny. So tiny, Ruby. Listen. You only get so many friends from youth. Okay, girls?" Dora had turned to Caroline. "Hold on to each other and you hold on to your childhood!"

Caroline was obedient to her grandmother's wishes. She kept tabs on Ruby not only through high school, but also in college, calling her once a month. Usually Caroline would call on the first day of her period when she said she needed a distraction from her painful cramps. Ruby's period almost always started a day or two after Caroline's menstruation-centric call. "That means you're syncing your period to hers," Ruby's freshman-year roommate said once, "which means Caroline's the alpha female in the friendship." Ruby's roommate was always stoned, and Ruby decided not to share her observation with Caroline. Anyway, during their phone calls Caroline never acted alpha, but would dissect the disparaging things her professors said about her work or talk about a boy she liked who didn't like her. Near the end of their call, she would often speak sweetly about how much Ruby meant to her. Sometimes after Caroline complained about cramps, she would say, "We knew each other before we knew what menstruation was, even conceptually. Do you think about that ever? We knew each other for our whole childhood."

Here was one real obstacle presented by habitat dioramas: They were actually very specific but needed to represent the universal.

You saw an antelope behind the glass and even though you were looking at one antelope that had had its one particular antelope life, now, in the educational space of the museum, that individual life came to represent All of the Antelope. And sometimes Ruby felt as if Ruby didn't represent Ruby to Caroline, but All of Childhood. And vice versa, probably, right? Because what did Ruby actually know about grown-up Caroline today?

She knew: That Caroline had painful cramps for approximately two and a half days every month. That Caroline threw parties at her dad's apartment anytime he was out of town. That these parties were actually pretty mild, just people talking and drinking and wandering around on the roof. That Caroline always wore great dresses to these parties. That Caroline now had short hair and a sideways smile. That when people asked Caroline what she did for a living she flashed a bright smile and said, "I make sporks," which always made people laugh, but almost never in a mean way. That after saying "I make sporks" and disarming her audience with what sounded like pure satire, Caroline would then speak very eloquently about the way people dismissed "disposables" in society and about the decadence of most art in the epoch of the Anthropocene and about whales killed by plastic garbage in their stomachs and, really, how disposable were the disposables, how expendable was any of it, and she felt lucky, just very lucky, to be part of the conversation, to be able to devote herself full-time to her art.

What else did Ruby know? That Caroline did not actually make very much money from those sporks but that Caroline, being Caroline, did not have to work another job, and so could claim art-making as her principal employment. That Caroline's grandfather did things with stocks. That Caroline's uncle did things with stocks, too. That Caroline's mother had let Caroline's father have the penthouse because she had wanted to get out of what she took to calling "that toxic city" and now lived in a huge house in the Hudson Valley. That Caroline believed her mother was a drama queen. That Caroline was friends with several semi-famous actresses who would one day be truly famous, Caroline believed. That her friends were all great wits, Caroline said, and she said it to be witty, since who called anybody a wit these days?

Nobody but Caroline.

Ruby knew this.

Ruby also knew, from conversations participated in or overheard at Caroline's parties, that Caroline believed in the power of positive thinking, that Caroline had once said her dream was to become a social-justice-artist-warrior-princess, that maybe Caroline had said that in an ironic way, that Caroline could be ironic and earnest at the same time, somehow, that Caroline had a sometimes-boyfriend, who sometimes lived in London and sometimes in Italy, that Caroline liked trees and occasionally did volunteer work planting baby trees near ancient parking lots, that Caroline believed in the power of education, that Caroline thought Ruby, also, should cut her hair very, very short and just see what happened next, that Caroline had a trust fund but that John (after a bad day at work when his organization's funding got slashed) told Ruby not to act like the trust fund was somehow Caroline's fault, not to go all "Occupy batshit, please, because Caroline's dad has donated in big ways to Hover Up," that John told Ruby that Caroline was a resource Ruby should make use of, that before trees Caroline once volunteered her time at animal shelters helping them find their "forever homes," but gave up because the animals made her just a little bit too sad. "It's their eyes," Caroline said. "You can tell they've seen more than any Labradoodle should."

What else did Ruby know? She knew that last year Caroline had gotten the beauty mark on her cheek removed—she said her mother worried it might be cancerous—but Ruby could make out a tiny ruffle of the skin where the mark had once been. She knew that most people would not even notice that ruffle. She knew that it was important, during the resentment game, for her to never breathe a hint of resentment toward Caroline because such a hint would cause not only a full-on weeping session on Caroline's part, but also, probably, hours of conversation in which they would have to unpack and describe and compare their own various privileges, which would seem like a healing process, but which would actually leave Ruby feeling worse, she was pretty sure, though she wasn't entirely sure why.

Of course, at times she'd found Caroline insufferable or dense. But she could never picture just walking away from a friendship that had been such a constant part of her childhood. Half the old stores in the neighborhood where she'd grown up were gone. Losing Caroline's friendship would be like gutting something in her own internal landscape. Maybe that was why, since moving back into her parents' apartment and into a neighborhood that already seemed a little unfamiliar, she had felt an almost frenzied need to spend time with Caroline. Or maybe she felt that need because, right now, Caroline was the only person she didn't feel embarrassed around, perhaps because they'd known each other so long, perhaps because Caroline didn't seem to have a sense of how much debt Ruby was in. Ruby had other friends, of course, but since her return home, those friends seemed less distinct, had become simply the non-Carolines—and Ruby would not speak to them when they called. She left the non-Carolines' texts unanswered, ignored the strings of *you okay??* The baristas she'd worked with for years at Mellow

Macchiato, Tamar, who sang opera under her breath when a customer was rude, and Jane, who always wore a Sailor Moon T-shirt beneath her apron. Olivia with whom she'd survived the terrors of high school math. She even ignored Nadia, whose dad was also a super, in a building a few streets away, and with whom Ruby had hung out a lot in middle school, despite the way Nadia liked to brag about how *her* dad once had been an engineer. In high school, Nadia began spending all her time with a small insular group of other Romanian immigrants. It had been hard for Ruby to break into that group, not being or speaking Romanian, and the two had fallen out of touch until a few years ago when Nadia and Ruby had reconnected online, just before Nadia moved to Alaska to count vanishing caribou for a nature conservancy.

How is it being back with The Folks, Nadia had asked yesterday, but Ruby had ignored her text, both because she couldn't think up a response, and because Nadia right now was like the background painting in a diorama, a flattened-out figure far away, from some other part of Ruby's life. Ruby could not speak to her caribou-saving friend. There were no sound waves in the second dimension and Nadia, right now, was two-dimensional to Ruby.

So why was Caroline still so vivid to her?

Well, Caroline was right upstairs for starters.

No, no, Caroline was downstairs—the doorbell rang. Caroline had arrived to help Ruby with her outfit.

When Ruby saw Caroline in her father's building now that they were adults, it sometimes felt a little like attending a séance, like they were raising up the long gone, witnessing a somber congregation of the spirits of their former selves. The spirits shook hands, did their little ceremonial spirit bows, while the living human receptacles acted casual, pretending not to see the ghost girls at all. Caroline was wearing leggings and a belted saffron-colored dress with on-seam pockets. "That's a beautiful outfit," Ruby said as she led Caroline to her room. Caroline laughed and told Ruby it wasn't an outfit, just a dress, and Ruby looked down at her own skirt, which Caroline had not yet commented on. "Did you get some sleep last night?" she asked Caroline. "After we talked?"

"Some," Caroline said. "I was definitely way less panicked by the time we hung up."

Yesterday Caroline had been to see her grandmother Dora, who had not recognized her, had thought Caroline was Dora's own long-dead sister. This had happened before, but it was the first time her grandmother had not realized, eventually, who Caroline was. Caroline had called Ruby in tears. "It's like I've lost someone who's technically still here, and feeling like I've lost her when she's still breathing makes me feel guilty *and* bereft."

So Ruby had talked for a while, trying to distract her from feeling sad. She had spoken in dry tones first about her breakup with John and then about the way her father clearly was disappointed in her. She had done impersonations of both men, mimicking their attempts to exude male authority and still seem like sensitive, reasonable guys. She kept her own panic about her return home out of the conversation. She had simply tried to make Caroline laugh.

Now, as Caroline stood in Ruby's room and surveyed Ruby's interview outfit (or maybe just her interview clothes), Ruby wondered if she'd make Caroline laugh unintentionally. Caroline simply squatted down and touched the fraying hem of Ruby's skirt, inspected the bunchy elastic waistband. At last she said, "Do you have anything else to wear?"

"Not really."

"I might have something that would fit?"

"Your clothes don't fit me. You know that. They never have."

"You're superskinny. Don't get into a body-shaming zone."

"I'm not in any zone. I'm saying, in a no-shame way, that your clothes won't fit me. I just have to go with the fact that I look frumpy."

"It can be good to look frumpy. Not that you *do* look frumpy."

Ruby touched the hem of her fraying skirt.

"If you're *aware* that you're refusing to occupy a traditional feminine space, Rubes, you actually create a powerful statement. If anyone says anything bad about your clothes, just tell them you're being deliberately frump. What about your hair?"

"It's deliberately tangled."

Caroline smiled. "I could at least brush your hair."

Ruby found a brush and handed it to Caroline. "Are you excited for the party?" Ruby asked, as Caroline moved behind Ruby and smoothed down her hair.

"Oh, I guess. I've honestly been feeling distant from a lot of people lately. I think the marble-spork-feature thing has made my friend Annabel and my friend Kirsten kind of weird and jealous."

Ruby had met both Annabel (impressive botanical arm tattoo) and Kirsten (made short films without dialogue) a few times before, but Caroline still always talked about them as "my friend Annabel" and "my friend Kirsten," as if Ruby had forgotten who they were. It gave Ruby the impression that Caroline was an ambassador from a faraway land.

"Speaking of the party," Caroline said, "the terrace door is kind of jammed? Do you think you can ask your dad if he'd come upstairs?"

"You should call him," Ruby said. "Call him and leave a message on his machine."

"You can't just tell him?"

"Leave a message. That's one of his rules. No intermediaries."

Caroline began to brush. Nobody had been this close to Ruby for such a sustained amount of time since John. She felt so grateful she became discombobulated. Their childhood selves and their adult selves seemed not so separate.

"Keep still," Caroline said. "I'm trying to comb out this rat nest." It felt like she was brushing out the neural tangles of Ruby's brain. Was *this* what meditating was like for her father? Ruby felt an uprising of love for Caroline so intense, she had to take a deep breath. Her nose filled with the scent of tangerines. The smell came from Caroline's shampoo, but it made Ruby think of the orange peels Lily would leave on her windowsill. When she exhaled, instead of staying silent, she whispered, "I let a homeless woman into the building today, Caroline."

She had not meant to say a thing. Something about that swell of love, that tingling along her scalp—the confession had simply happened. Caroline stopped brushing her hair. She moved in front of Ruby, her eyes wide. "What?" she said.

"You can't tell my dad, is the thing." Ruby clutched Caroline's hand. She tried to squeeze enough to express urgency but not enough to produce pain. "I buzzed this woman in. She said she was related to Lily."

"Lily? Lily in 5A? Like, Lily who is dead?"

"Yes. She *looked* like Lily, and so I did it, I just buzzed her in. I just reacted. My first instinct was to help her. To get her warm."

"Oh, jeez, Ruby." Caroline scooted closer, her long face distending with something like wonder. "Is she still in the building?"

"I don't know. I went to the lobby after with my dad and didn't see her."

"She needs help. We need to get her to some services if you think she's really homeless. She needs external resources. Oh, oh, or we could reach out to my friend Andy. He lives right around here. Remember that guy from my last party? He sort of had a crush on you, I think." Caroline put the brush down on the bed. "He takes photographs of homeless people, and he has them tell their stories, and one homeless guy went viral and a TV network gave him a *house*. I've been wanting to collaborate with Andy for ages."

Ruby closed her eyes. She remembered Andy and she hadn't liked him very much. Why had she told Caroline anything? It was like she'd restarted the kind of game that she and Caroline used to play together.

"Where's the woman now?" asked Caroline.

"I think she left." She must have, right? Ruby would have heard something if she was hanging around. Her father would definitely have said something.

"You *think* she left?" Caroline said. "Or you know? Are you sure she isn't in the building still?"

Ruby touched her professional skirt. How stupid she'd been. She'd romanticized this woman just to make herself feel better. She'd let her into the building without thinking about helping her once she was inside.

"Don't do that thing where you get all dazed, kiddo. Are you sure she's not still here? Are you *sure*? If you let her in, it's a little bit your responsibility to make sure she's okay."

She felt like her interview had already begun. A new panic cut into her.

Caroline said, "Have you checked out Lily's old apartment? She could just be alone up there, surrounded by dust."

"I don't know," Ruby said.

"Do you want me to check 5A?" Caroline asked. "I could go to 5A and see if she's there, while you get ready for the interview."

"I told you. She's gone."

"Where did she go?"

"I don't know." Sweat spread down Ruby's back. "I didn't follow her. I just know she left the building a little after I let her in. I saw her leave on the intercom."

"That's not what you said a minute ago."

"Caroline, forget it."

Caroline sighed. "You're upset."

"No, no," Ruby said. "I think I just need to be alone, to compose myself before the interview."

Caroline got up to leave. She turned at the door. "We're okay, right?"

"Yes. Of course."

"Are you still coming to my party tonight?"

"Yes."

"Even though John might be there?"

"Yes."

"Well, Andy will for sure be there. We can tell him about the woman you let into the building? If we can find her, maybe he can take her picture. Maybe we can help her."

If *we* can find her, if *we* can help her. Ruby shook her head. "The woman left, Caroline. I'm positive. Let's forget I mentioned it. My dad would freak out if he knew."

"I know things have been tense with your dad," Caroline said. "I just feel bad for the woman."

"Me, too, obviously. That's why I let her in."

"But then you forgot about her?"

"I don't want to talk about it, Caroline. I just need to be alone right now, before the interview."

"Okay, okay. I get that." She stepped into the hall, but then she ducked her head back into Ruby's room. "I really feel like you're mad at me, Ruby."

"I'm not mad." And to get her to leave, Ruby knew what she must do. She rose to her feet. She gave Caroline a hug. She said, "I'll see you tonight, okay? Thank you so much for checking in on me, Caroline. And for getting me this interview. Seriously. I'm so grateful."

After Caroline left, Ruby looked at herself in the mirror for a long time and tried not to think about Lily's cousin, possibly in the building somewhere right this moment, lost, alone. She hadn't seen the woman leave, but how, really, could she still be here? The building was full of people coming and going. If she had stuck around, someone would have reported her by now. Once more, Ruby appraised her interview outfit: her blouse with the buttons, her skirt, her tights, her flats. If she could *own* her frumpiness, like Caroline suggested, it might even seem expensive. She would try her best.

She said to the mirror, "I have always loved dioramas."

She said to her own reflection, "There's something really artful about them. Right? I think so, too. That balance between preservation and mystery, education and the creative force. My favorite?

The antelopes. Or the rhino. Or the hunting dogs. Or the blue whale. Which, yes, not technically a diorama. But I love the belly button addition. Oh, I just can't choose one favorite. Every diorama presents its own specific delights."

She said to the dark spit-smoothed arches of her eyebrows, "Oh, yes, I know I'm early. I always get to appointments half an hour early because, right, punctuality is so important."

She said, "My grandmother gave me a book about dioramas, mmhmm. When I was very young. She died recently, yes. I miss her every single day. But I memorized the book. Mhm. Exactly. It would mean so much to me to work here. Because the legacy. Oh, wow. Yes. Health insurance? With dental, even? Oh my god. I mean, oh my goodness. Wow. Yes. Thank you so much. Would you believe I actually *brought* the book with me? For luck? Looks like it worked! Yes, yes, thank you, wow."

Then she grabbed Lily's copy—the library's copy—*Ruby's* copy—of *Behind the Glass: A Chronicle of Habitat Dioramas* and slipped it into her tote bag, in case it was a necessary prop for the scene she envisioned creating during her interview, which now was in about an hour. She glanced into the mirror one more time, and there was child-Caroline's voice again. *They have no place to go.* The words repeating like one of her father's mantras. Caroline, keenly aware of the treatment of what was deemed "disposable," was right to admonish Ruby. The woman was not disposable, not expendable. She was Ruby's responsibility now that Ruby had buzzed her in. Plus, if the woman *was* still here, if she made trouble in the building, or trouble for Ruby's father, it would be Ruby's own fault. If she wanted to feel less like a child, if she wanted to speak with authority during this interview even, she needed to follow through on her own decisions, the good ones and the dumb ones. She should figure out if the woman was still in the building before she headed to the museum. If she was here, Ruby would find a safe, warm place for her to go before her parents found out what Ruby had done.

The basement floor outside the apartment was slick, newly mopped, though her father was nowhere to be seen. Probably he was in the middle of some job upstairs. She ducked her head into the laundry room in case the woman had huddled there. Dryers spun, shirt-sleeves flailed, skirts were upturned, but no human beings. The garbage room was also empty. Ruby was wasting her time down here. If the woman was still in the building, she would probably be in Lily's old apartment, at least until the demo crew showed up and reported her.

Ruby pushed the elevator call button. But it was morning rush hour now, tenants leaving for work, childcare providers taking their young charges to school, and the elevator was slow in making its way down. If Ruby exited the fire doors by the garbage room, she could use a maintenance stairway from the basement's courtyard to get to the street. But there was no stairway to the lobby from the inside of the basement itself. When the building was first built, the basement was seen as entirely separate from the upper floors, a site designated only for the boiler and coal delivery and the delivery of foodstuffs sent up the dumbwaiters. Some kind of architectural symbolism lingering from the late nineteenth century. The only way to reach the upper floors from the inside of the basement, even today, was the elevator. Because of an old idea about what this building should be, Ruby would never be able to power herself upward and out of the basement into the rest of the building on her own two feet.

At last, the elevator made it to the basement again. If the woman was in 5A, Ruby would declare: "Your cousin Lily said I was like a granddaughter to her. That means in a way, you and I are family. And I want to help." Just rehearsing the words in the elevator made Ruby feel close to crying, but in a noble single-tear-down-the-face kind of way, the kind of way that would make Lily's cousin trust her. Maybe she could keep the woman in her room somehow until her interview was over? Her father would be busy with building stuff all morning. After her interview, she would rush back and do just as Caroline had said. She would find this woman some external resources.

Ruby hadn't been to the fifth floor since Lily's death. When she stepped off the elevator, the ripe-onion aroma left from Lily's many stir-fries was all gone. The demo crew had taped a plastic door with a central zipper over the entranceway to 5A, to keep out the plaster and dust. Ruby pushed the plastic aside. The real door was not only unlocked, but ajar. "Hello?" Ruby called. No answer from cat or human. She stepped inside. Well. What had she been expecting? Lily's blue-and-brown-plaid couch, still covered in Mel Blanc's cat hair? The orange peels everywhere? The scratchy rug? The lamps with the shades askew? The piles of videos and books and news-papers?

No books, no cat, no hair, no newspapers, no couch, no fridge, no rug. The demo crew had already gotten rid of most walls that weren't load bearing. Instead of orange peels, orange extension cords snaked across the floor. Bare light bulbs hung from wires where the lighting fixtures used to be. Wooden molding and pieces of door trim were piled where the easy chair had sat. In every re-maining corner, there were plastic bags filled with debris. "Lily," she said into the empty space. "Lily?" Ruby would have promised some deific neighborhood creditor five dozen sessions of people-watching at Bethesda Fountain, a summer's worth of sunny days with bagels in Riverside Park, all personal memory of light in her favorite Hopper paintings at the Whitney, and one-third of the Museum of Natural History's dioramas, just to hear Lily's voice fill that wrecked apartment for a single instant.

But nothing.

Her face had become wet. Ruby walked to the bathroom, looking for paper towels or toilet paper, but of course Lily's bathroom didn't exist anymore. The tub had been broken out, and half of the original subfloor exposed. Thin wood slats where there once had been tile. Yet at the edge of the tile still intact, there, there—a pink tissue.

So it had been just as Ruby told Caroline: The woman had come to Lily's old apartment after all, but once she had witnessed its changes, she had realized she had nowhere to stay here. She had left the building.

A creak, a slam, the front door opening and shutting again. Ruby raced out of the gutted bathroom. Somebody screamed. A man. Four Jamaican guys, part of the demo crew, stood in the doorway. "I told you this place was haunted," one of the guys joked to another, but he was glancing nervously at Ruby as he said it, like he thought maybe she truly was a ghost or at the very least a tenant who might find a way to get him in trouble. "Excuse me," she said, ducking her head, and walked around the men and out of the apartment.

Back in the basement, she washed her face. Then she grabbed the tote bag with Lily's diorama book and took a great steadying breath. It wasn't healthy for her, being back here. Thank god for Caroline and Caroline's connections. Today Ruby would get a real job, the kind of job with benefits, the kind of job that aligned perfectly with her own artistic interests and her educational background, the kind of job that kept her out of basements and out of destroyed apartments. She would get the respect she wanted from John, from Caroline, from her mother, from her father. She would pay off her debts and find a new place to live and at last have the space and stillness to make her own art. She would talk about her future projects without feeling presumptuous. She'd perfect a little sardonic smile that she'd wear any time she said something seemingly sophomoric—like "autobiographical dioramas"—and the smile's self-awareness would undermine whatever sounded stupid in her words. She would begin constructing dioramas of moments from her life, her own human history. The dioramas would be beautiful and wonderful and strange.

But on her way down the hall to the elevator, she saw that the fire door to the courtyard was propped open with a brick. She hadn't thought to look for Lily's cousin in the courtyard—she hadn't thought the woman would want to go back outside. Elbowing the fire door open a little more, Ruby stepped out. The air was still cold, but not so bad as it had been earlier that morning.

The woman wasn't out there. Ruby's father was. He stood next to the alleyway where he dragged the garbage out in the evenings. On a ledge that belonged to the church next door was, still, the nest. Inside the nest, still, the two pigeons he had fawned over. The birds' heads were tilted to the side. They watched Ruby's father hard. He must have been standing out there for a while, watching them back, unable to move, to complete the task he had told 2D he'd finish.

Her father turned to see Ruby watching him, too. He said, "Your mom told me I had to do this. So."

"Do you need help?"

He turned back to the birds. He raised the broom. He held his shoulders stiffly, close to his neck. He paused. He lifted the broom still higher. "I'll tell you what Caroline's dad in the penthouse made me do once," her father said then. "When he had a pigeon problem. I'll tell you what he made me do, Ruby."

"Okay."

"He put a sticky gel around the cracks where the birds were nesting."

Ruby lifted her leg and scratched the back of her calf with her toe.

"Then a bunch of the pigeons got gel on their wings. They couldn't fly. They were stuck. Caroline's dad called me to hit the flopping pigeons with a two-by-four, put them out of their misery. I thought maybe a hawk or owl would get them, which happens sometimes up there, but no hawk got them. No owl. And the pigeons were starving. So I had to do it."

Ruby could not look at him.

She looked up instead, to the roof of the building. She imagined the penthouse apartment, and Caroline back up there now, looking down on her.

"You still mad at me for before, Ruby?" her father said. "About the woman? You seemed really, really mad."

"You had to kill those birds," Ruby said to the sky. "I understand that." She looked down again. "But you didn't have to kick Lily's cousin out today. It's not the same."

"You're very well-educated." Her father reached into his pocket and pulled out a key. He took Ruby's hand and pressed the key into her palm. "This is for 2D's apartment. So you can take care of her fish after your interview. We each have our tasks, right?"

Then he took a step forward toward the nest, lifted the broom a little higher. The birds looked back at him. He winced. And everything angry and hardened in her turned, for a second, soft.

She was dressed for a job interview and she could do a job. "Let me get the nest."

"It's not that I can't," her father said.

"I know," Ruby said. "It's your back, your back hurts."

"Yeah," said her father.

"But my back is fine."

"Yeah," said her father.

"So," Ruby said, and took the broom and took account of the small brightness of one pigeon's left eye and then swept the broom over her head, and knocked the nest off the ledge. The pigeons flew up. The whole nest flew up with them into the air, hovered there for a microsecond, as if the fluttering of the birds' wings were enough to lift it—then fell.

Ruby half expected several eggs to roll out of the nest and crack open and, in fact, that was just what happened.

7 THE STRIKER

The expression on Ruby's face when she destroyed the nest was an expression Martin had seen his daughter wear just once before. It was a few months before she turned eighteen, and she had come downstairs from the penthouse apartment with a folder. Debra was at work, but Martin was on the couch, soaking his left foot in a bucket and watching TV. A British man was describing the way certain seabirds in Japan climbed tall trees to have "keen jumping off points for their spectacular flight." Ruby sat down on the couch next to Martin and made what he'd later remember as a bit of a show opening the folder. There were two typed pages inside. Martin said, "What's that?"

She smiled a strange smile. "Caroline gave me an early draft of her college application essay to read."

"What, to edit? I thought they hired some fancy private counselor person for that."

"It's not to edit. She wanted to clear it with me."

"To clear it with you?"

"Just don't tell her I let you see. Her dad would probably find some way to sue." She held out the pages and, after he rubbed his hands on the rolled-up leg of his pants, he took the essay from her.

"You don't have to wipe your hands," Ruby said. "It's not some sacred document."

"It's just a habit."

"It reminds me of a story Ms. Ramseur told us in drama class once," Ruby said. "All these people were rehearsing a play and Bertolt Brecht was the director and this actor couldn't get this scene right. Do you know Brecht, Dad?"

"Not well but kind of," Martin said. He'd definitely heard Lily call things "Brechtian" more than a few times.

"So the actor is playing a worker in a factory I think, and the employer hands the factory guy something and the scene wasn't right. There was something off. And Brecht calls in the woman who is cleaning the theater—"

"The cleaning woman," Martin said.

"Yeah. And he says, 'Excuse me, miss, but would you hold this?' and he holds out a blank piece of paper. And the woman wipes her hand before she takes the paper. Which is when the actor playing the factory guy realizes what he was doing wrong when he was acting out the scene. He hadn't wiped his hands when he was given the document."

How hard did the cleaning woman's heart go, when that Brechtian motherfucker called her forward?

"I only bring this up," Ruby said, "because I don't think you need to wipe your hands to hold Caroline's essay. She's not your superior, Dad. She's your daughter's friend."

"What happened to the cleaning woman?"

"I don't know. That wasn't in the story."

"It wasn't in the story."

"I guess she went back to cleaning."

"Did they give her a raise after that?"

"I don't know." Ruby sighed. "The lesson was about the power of detail, not about the cleaning woman."

It wasn't about the cleaning woman. Ms. Ramseur didn't think to have them wonder about how the woman herself was probably wondering, when they called her over, if she was in trouble. Had she been accused of something? Had she lost her job? Nope. That woman lived on as a nameless example in how to accurately capture the working class for the rich people showing up to see a play.

Martin handed back Caroline's college essay to Ruby. Then he dipped his hands into the bucket of water where he was soaking his left foot. He got his hands nice and wet with toe water and then he reached out for Caroline's essay and took it from Ruby without wiping his palms. "Is that better?" he asked.

"Jesus, Dad."

He said, "I sure hope the cleaning woman found a new job."

"Could you just read the essay?"

Some drops of toe water had blurred the ink, but it was all legible. *My grandmother survived the Holocaust,* Caroline's essay began. *Many of her immediate and extended family members died. Because of her experiences, she and my parents instilled in me from a young age the idea that the lines we place between us with regards to religion, race, class, gender, and sexual orientation are boundaries that obstruct what really matters. We are all human. We all suffer. Life is not easy for anybody. It is up to us each to try to make it a little easier for those less fortunate around us. Even as a child, I looked for small ways to make the world more equal to prevent such a large-scale tragedy from happening again, through seeing the potential and full human in everyone.*

For example, I played with the super's daughter all the time as a child and my parents allowed her to sit in on some of my tutoring sessions and even paid for her to attend my art classes. (She is, by the way, extremely talented!) I also volunteered with Head for Hope and played a major role in organizing donations and designing posters for the See Me As You As Me Foundation.

He scanned through the rest of the essay. No mention of Ruby again. Really, just a passing glance. So why did he feel like freeing his cramped foot from the bucket and kicking something?

"It's only a sentence, I guess," Ruby said. "Caroline made a big deal about how she'd get rid of it if it made me feel used in any way."

"How nice of her." Martin splashed his foot a little in the bucket.

"Honestly, telling her it makes me uncomfortable makes me more uncomfortable than the actual sentence does."

"So you'll just say nothing?"

"I never realized those art classes weren't free. Her mom always made it seem like this spontaneous trip."

"Well, I guess now you know they weren't free," Martin said. "Now you get to know that for the rest of your life." Ruby stayed quiet. Martin read the essay again and said, "The grammar in this is awful."

"I think the grammar's mostly fine," Ruby said. "I didn't notice anything, anyway."

"It's awful," he said. "It's shit."

And the expression, the bird-nest-destruction expression, happened then. She had looked down as if she had ruined something. No—as if Martin had made her ruin something. His hands were still wet. He turned back to the TV and Ruby left the room. How those seabirds could leap, how they could climb.

————

After Ruby left for her interview at the museum, Martin swept up the nest in the courtyard, head bowed low.

The nest inside the dustpan looked like any other clot of building crap. The shells resembled plaster from a remodeling job. Martin took the dustpan, went inside to the garbage room, and dumped the pan's contents into the trash. He had had a fight with Debra, he had seen his beloved pigeons' home destroyed, he had made his daughter do his job for him, he had kicked out a woman related to someone he loved. *Mired in the grime of self-pity, the super stands in the garbage room feeling sorry for himself,* said Lily. *The culture of grievances in this country is an unseemly stain, spreading fast! Wherever you come from, rich or poor, there is suffering. The problem is the way we quantify that suffering, revel in suffering—tired of those pesky self-pity streaks? Try growing a pair. Martin tries not to listen to his own tiredness. Martin tries, Martin tries, Martin tries, Martin tries.*

A broken record of a ghost now. It wasn't fair. His own dead parents and vaguely traumatized Eastern European ancestors had not haunted him in this way. But the Lily voice screamed in his thoughts: *Martin tries, Martin tries, Martin tries.* The words in tune with his own heartbeat. As his heartbeat sped up, so did Lily's chants. He left the garbage room, went through the courtyard, unlocked the service door, and ran up to street level. The Lily voice never followed him out of the building, as far as he could tell. As soon as he stepped onto the sidewalk, he could hear his own thoughts again. He was breathing hard. He felt dizzy.

He began to walk fast in the direction of the JCC, where a late-morning meditation class was about to start. Although he hadn't been back since the time he'd farted during class, he had memo-

rized the schedule in case he had an emergency need for mindfulness. Right now, running from a ghost voice, his heart walloping
against his rib cage, the emergency seemed real. He moved as fast as
he could without breaking into a run, passing banks, Starbucks, cell
phone stores. A lot of the stores that had been here when he first
moved to the neighborhood were gone, but Martin tried not to veer
into sentimentality about it all. Utopia diner was still around, and
the hardware store he liked, and one or two of the old Irish pubs.
Anyway, even those places had been something else at some point,
right? The small stores had once been the manors of rich nineteenth-
century New Yorkers fleeing the dirt of downtown, and before those
proto-yuppies showed up, there had been trees and trees and trees,
plus some tribes who were about to get their land stolen fast, and
before them, primordial muck, the greatest gentrifier of all time.
He passed the Duane Reade where around Halloween many years
ago, he had seen Caroline—then in her early teens—slip a pair of
plastic cat ears and a tube of red lipstick into her bag. He'd barked
out, "Hi," down the aisle, and she'd looked up and smiled at him,
guiltlessly, cheerfully. She had not put the cat ears or the lipstick
back. He had not confronted her. But he had mentioned the incident that night to Debra and Ruby.

"Why didn't you stop her?" Debra said. "Jesus, Martin. Be the
grown-up in the room."

"I'm not *her* grown-up," Martin said. "She has parents."

"She only steals stuff from big companies," Ruby piped up. "It's
this whole Robin Hood phase she's got going. No day but today,
steal from the corporate overlords, all of that. Sometimes she almost sounds like Lily."

"Never, ever tell Lily that," Martin said.

"It hurts the salespeople," Debra said. "Not the corporation."

"I'm just saying, with Caroline, it comes from a good place."

"You don't shoplift, Ruby," Debra said, "right?"

"I don't shoplift," Ruby said. "I know if I got caught, you'd disown me and throw me out on the streets or whatever."

"We wouldn't disown you," Debra said, and Martin said, "Speak for yourself, Deb." He was almost positive he had been kidding and Debra, to affirm this, had laughed. But Ruby had not smiled back.

The Duane Reade a whole block behind him now. Where had he been? Lost in his mind. Hearing not the Lily voice, but the voice of Rubys and Debras past. This was the problem. His thoughts could not stay zipped up in the now.

He headed through the glass doors of the JCC, which had most recently been not a small store, but a gas station the center had bought straight from Exxon. A large security guard nodded at Martin and gestured to the metal detector. Martin put his ring of keys into the gray plastic bin, along with his wallet. The guard waved Martin through the full-body detector. Did the guard look at Martin and see a white-guy yuppie? Or could he tell by the streaks of plaster on his hat that he was some other species of neighborhood white guy? The guard handed Martin back his keys and wallet, and Martin said, "Thanks."

Then he took the elevator up to the community spirituality/ reflection room, which was several floors above the pool but still smelled, very faintly, of chlorine. Eight other people were already meditating, their eyes closed, some of them perched on folding chairs, others sitting on pillows. He'd worried there'd be a tenant there, maybe even Neilson, but no, strangers all. This time, there were even a few people in cargo pants like Martin. While his heart still raced, Lily's voice wasn't in his head, so that was progress. Also, he hadn't eaten any gluten. No farts to worry about, no stomach growls. He would be fine. He took off his shoes. His right sock had a hole in it, he saw now, and his calloused big toe stuck out. But nobody was watching. He got onto a cushion and closed his eyes. The chlorine smell made him feel like he'd just dived into a deep dark pool. If he got through this session, if he could just calm his heartbeat and slow his thoughts, he could swim through this day. And then it would be tomorrow: Ruby would have a job, Lily's cousin would be forgotten, Debra would call him after her panel, full of relief and love and ready to come home.

On his pillow, he counted his breath in cycles of five. A couple more people trickled into the room, but Martin registered them less as people than warm columns of air, changing the currents around his face. He opened his eyes again. The teacher, a thin man with scruff on his long jaw and no hair on his egg-shaped head, said, "We will begin with fifteen minutes of silent mindfulness meditation, followed by a group activity with a singing bowl."

A group activity?

Martin tried to breathe himself back into the moment. But the group activity loomed. He had never had this teacher before. Who knew what ideas about enlightenment he had? Would they have to do an interpretive dance of their inner soul? Do trust falls while putting their childhood traumas into song? But he was not supposed to leap ahead like this in meditation. He must breathe. He must become the sole inhabitant of his breath. All morning, his thoughts had looped him forward and backward in time. His mind had become possessed by a voice from the actual past. What he needed was to be present. What he needed was to see the instructor's head not as egg-shaped but merely pleasantly ovoid. He inhaled so deeply, air seemed to sluice through his body like liquid. He relaxed.

But then a low, ringing sound filled the room, like an owl's hoot combined with the dirgelike moan of old plumbing filling with newly heated steam. Martin opened his eyes. The teacher said, "We will now begin part two of our session." He held out a gigantic shining singing bowl, intricately carved, and a rosewood striker with a leather wrap. He placed the bowl on a blue silk pillow filigreed with gold thread and said, "Please, repeat the following mantra after me: 'I transcend anxiety. I transcend despair. Together we are present here.'"

Everyone in the room repeated the mantra.

The teacher explained that they would pass around the singing bowl atop its pillow. The person in front of the bowl would say today's mantra, and when they were finished, they would strike the bowl with the rosewood striker. "No, no, I misspoke, we don't *strike* the singing bowl," the teacher said quickly. "The language we want to use now is 'make contact.' Each of us will have the opportunity to make contact with the singing bowl, and then pass it to the person on your left. Please keep up your breathing meditation while the singing bowl makes its way around the circle."

Martin was not sure he'd understood all the instructions, but everyone else in the room was nodding. A short forty-something man next to the teacher recited the mantra, loud and clear: "I transcend anxiety. I transcend despair. Together we are present here." Then he struck the singing bowl, or made contact, or something. The sound rang through the room again. Everyone but Martin kept their eyes closed. At last the man opened his eyes and, balancing the singing bowl perfectly on the pillow, passed it along to an old woman with a delicate rash creeping up her neck. The neck-rash woman began to speak: "I transcend anxiety. I transcend despair." Martin should close his eyes. But he wanted to see how the woman struck the singing bowl. What if when Martin's turn came, he struck it wrong, so it didn't ring out, but only burbled? Everyone would think, There is a man who doesn't know what he is doing. They would think, There is a pathetic man with one toe out of his sock, and he's not even enlightened enough to make a singing bowl sing. Then they would think, This is a judgmental thought. I send love to this man. And brain waves of condescending love would start cresting in Martin's direction.

Martin sat five spots away from the teacher. In a few minutes, the singing bowl would be in front of him. How did people pass the singing bowl along without it falling off the pillow? That would be even worse than a faulty song—if he somehow toppled the singing bowl from the pillow, denting it in some crucial manner that robbed it of its acoustic gifts forever. Everyone's eyes would open. The teacher would look at him. The others would look at him. Already his palms had gone sweaty. When he held the striker, it would slip from his grip. Butterfingers, everyone would think, reverting to their middle-school gym-class selves. He would turn this room of enlightenment-seeking adults into juveniles. He would ruin their quests.

The neck-rash woman struck the singing bowl. The sound was less powerful than the teacher's strike, but still there was a good resonance. How had she angled the striker? No! He wasn't supposed to be watching how people angled the striker. He was supposed to be paying attention to his breath. The singing-bowl thing was a communal experience, not a competition. What if he forgot the mantra? "I transcend anxiety. I transcend despair. Together we are present here." The words melded in his mind. He remembered his daughter destroying the pigeon nest and Lily's voice screaming at him about a culture of grievance. His hands were shaking. When it was his turn to move the pillow with the bowl, the bowl would fall. The sound it would make upon falling would be the worst sort of song, the song of an old man who did not know his own damn self. His ignorance and shame would manifest as fatty deposits blocking his arteries—there was something lipid-like about shame—and he would have a heart attack right here, among strangers. Or he would cough and his heart would just slip out of his mouth and fall right into the singing bowl. What kind of sound would that make? Plop, probably. Just plop. Now it was his turn to recite the mantra. The man next to him held out the striker. Martin took the striker and then reached for the pillow with the singing bowl on top of it. He scooted it carefully along the floor until it was directly in front of him. It did not topple over. A silence had fallen. Everyone was waiting. Somebody cleared their throat. Was it him? No, the teacher. Martin could not remember the mantra. Something about anxiety, despair? *Martin tried, Martin tried, Martin tried.* Not the Lily voice, only the memory of the Lily voice, but that was enough. The teacher's fingernails were clean and Martin's were black. His armpits and his banged-up back had slickened with sweat. He stood. His knees cracked and his right foot hit the edge of the pillow. The singing bowl wobbled but did not fall. Nobody opened their eyes. They were all so swaddled in their breaths.

He pushed open the door and stepped out into the hallway where the pool smell grew even sharper. He took the elevator downstairs, did not nod at the security guard. When he'd exited the building, he realized he was still holding the striker. Could he stomach returning inside, to that meditation room? No. Just the idea caused an acidic filminess to rise to his throat. Instead he headed home, past the Duane Reade, past the cell phone stores, gripping the striker as he went. He paused at the Starbucks. He had to pee. But when he ducked inside he saw a group of men as old as him, all with giant backpacks and greasy hair. They looked like they had nowhere to go. Two of them were waiting by the bathroom door.

He could pee at home.

He left the Starbucks and went back to the building. Down to the basement. Silence in his head. He put the singing bowl striker next to the meditation bench. Lily's voice, thank god, offered up not a single word of praise or of rebuke. He went to the bathroom and peed. He washed his hands and his face.

He was so hungry. There were a few rolls he'd saved for the birds on top of the fridge. He swallowed three rolls down. He should never have stopped eating gluten. What a yuppie-tenant thing to do. Here, in the present moment, the bread did not hurt his stomach. It was simply delicious. The sound of his own chewing filled his ears.

By the time the doorbell rang, Martin was full and calm again. Pumpworks Tony, maybe, was outside, with a question about the demo work. He took a minute to shake off any residues of panic, and then he opened the door. Caroline. "Good morning, Martin," she said, in a wobbly singsong tone. "I was—"

"Yeah?" Martin said.

She bit her lower lip.

"Something wrong?"

"I wanted to talk to you," she said, her eyes so wide that for a second Martin was convinced she was there to accuse him of stealing the JCC's singing bowl striker.

"What is it?" he asked.

She tugged at the collar of her dress like some invisible starchy ruff was constricting her breath.

He tried to make his voice less gruff but not too soothing—not blue-tile-pulling gentle, maybe closer to sorry-UPS-didn't-drop-off-your-package mild: "What did you want to talk about?"

"Ruby told me about the woman in the foyer this morning."

"Uh-huh," Martin said. "And?"

He waited for her to declare that he had been too harsh. He had ignored his privileged position. He had failed to act with empathy, compassion. Under his stare she quickly looked away. "Forget it," she said.

Still she stood there.

"Did you need something else?" Martin asked.

"The terrace door." She spoke with so much hesitation she almost seemed to be improvising her demand. "The door's jamming. I have the party tonight. I want my guests to be able to go outside, if they want. Though I guess it'll be cold. It might rain. But the view is so nice. People always want to go outside."

"You're supposed to call and leave a message," Martin said. "You know that. Leave a message about the door jamming and I'll fit it into my schedule."

"Okay," Caroline said. "You're right. I should have left a message. My grandmother's been sick. I'm all over the place. I'm sorry, Martin."

The apology softened him. "Well. I guess I can take a quick look now." Martin grabbed his toolbox, which he'd left by the door, and stepped out.

"Now?"

"Is now not good?"

"You'll just look at the door, right? Because my room is a really big mess. Just piles of old childhood stuff. You know, I'm usually in my apartment in Brooklyn, so I don't really clean my room in my dad's place. It's embarrassing."

And a further softening in him. She was *embarrassed* that her room was a mess. Few people in the building ever had enough respect for him that they might express self-consciousness over a messy room. Perhaps all those afternoons he'd watched over Ruby and Caroline continued to exist in some messy room inside Caroline's mind. And unexpectedly he and Caroline were smiling, like old friends who had recognized each other on a street in a different city.

"I'll just look at the door," Martin said. "I should be able to get a small job like that done fast. I'll go upstairs with you."

She seemed about to say more, but then he pressed the call button for the elevator and she fell silent again. "How have you been?" Martin asked as they waited.

"Oh," Caroline said. "I'm okay. How about you, Martin?"

"Mostly, when people ask how I am, I answer that I'm old." Martin shrugged. "How are your folks?"

"Also old. I mean, I don't think of them that way, but my dad's always telling me he's getting ancient. He's talking about retiring, actually, and moving to Portugal."

"Wow," said Martin.

The elevator at last arrived. When they stepped inside, Caroline turned a key under the button that said *PH*. The doors closed. "Where will you go?" Caroline asked.

"What?"

"When you do finally retire. Will you stay in the basement?"

"The new super will live there. The apartment comes with the job."

"Right. I forgot. So where will you move?"

"We'll figure it out, I guess." Inhale. "We're saving up still."

"You know what would be legitimately hilarious? If you got an apartment *in this building*! And just stayed here!"

Exhale. "That would be very funny."

"I know nobody here would want to lose you. Everyone would miss you so much, Martin."

The doors opened on the fifth floor. Pumpworks Tony stood before them, reeking of men's body spray that smelled like aerosolized metallic bathroom cleaner and the cheapest cologne squeegeed out of the armpit of a T-shirt. He waved wildly and shouted to Martin about needing to talk.

"There's this weird pipe in 5A," Tony said. "You wanna check it out before we move forward with it?"

Martin said okay, in a second, he had a quick job to do first in the penthouse. The doors closed just as Pumpworks Tony tried to say something more about the pipe.

"Wow," Caroline said as the elevator began to rise again. "That was the worst-smelling body spray ever."

Martin didn't really like Pumpworks Tony's smell either, but now that Caroline had called him stinky, he felt a new fierce loyalty. He wanted to tell Caroline that her penthouse apartment wouldn't even exist without Pumpworks Tony. Before the penthouse was built, all the water that flowed through the building was first pumped up to a large water tank on the roof. The tank was used both for water pressure and fire safety. But when the penthouse was constructed, the tank that had been fine before, now wasn't high enough above the penthouse plumbing fixtures to meet the New York City plumbing code for water pressure. They brought in an engineer to make the forces of gravity and city code align. The only options were to raise the five-thousand-gallon roof tank or to install pressure pumps, which was the choice the engineer made.

Pumpworks Tony was the guy who had installed those new pumps. In some way Pumpworks Tony was responsible for the water Caroline drank and washed with and defecated into for years, *years*, which meant Pumpworks Tony had contributed directly to her being alive in the world, and Caroline didn't know and Martin didn't tell her because dramatizing the story of two water pumps seemed impossible and if he opened his mouth to narrate such a tale, later Caroline might go to Ruby and say, "So, your dad went on and on to me about water pumps and water pressure in this weird, like, quasi-*parable* way?"

The elevator opened up directly into the penthouse apartment, with its vaulted ceiling, its hardwood floors, its leather couches and swivel chairs. They stepped out together and Martin immediately pulled the turquoise shoe covers out of his toolbox and over his sneakers. He tried to say, in a jaunty tone, "And what are you up to these days, Caroline?"

She twisted her hands. "Well, this will sound like complete fiction, but my marble sporks are kind of taking off."

"Sporks?"

"A friend of my dad's . . . It's a long story. But they were featured in this pretty big design magazine. So, these days I'm in the studio making sporks." She looked a little sheepish. "It started as this kind of comment about disposability and eco-devastation? But then people actually wanted the sporks as, I guess, ironic decorative objects. Which is . . ." Her eyes darted nervously down the hall, to the closed door of her messy room. "Ironic, I guess." She blushed. "It's always a little awkward to say the spork thing. I actually really believe in the project. I wish I knew a way to make it sound more professional and less twee."

"Or quirky," Martin said.

"Yeah." She smiled at him. He tried to focus on the smile and not his own vexation. Sporks. She made them in a studio she paid for with her trust fund. Her father's rich friends bought them, displayed them. He counted his breaths again.

"I showed a few to my grandmother and she thought they looked like human bones. At least that's less quirky, right?" And Caroline laughed, a small sound. Her gaze kept flitting to the messy room, as if she was afraid he would march down the hall in a class-warfare rage, rip open the door, and reveal the true extent of her disarray.

The thing was, Caroline had all the right to make and sell eco-devastation-fighting sporks. If she didn't need to work in some more traditional way, why should he expect her to do so? Anyway, it wasn't his job to cogitate on this crap. He said, "I'll look at the door now." *That* was his job.

He went past Caroline, to the glass terrace door, which was, indeed, jammed. Martin examined it closely although he longed to just gape at the view from up here, an expanse of water towers and spires and roof decks and sky. The sun behind a thin streak of clouds. Something was wedged in the door's upper track, or maybe in the roller. He worked the door back and forth carefully, not wanting to damage any part of the terrace. Whatever crud was jammed in was still not revealing itself.

The wind rose. A flock of birds on the breeze. Once he had seen a hawk land on that water tower over there and his heart had stopped—not in a translucent-chest heart-attack way, but in a way that had to do with wonder. A couple dozen buildings away was Central Park. The owl was there somewhere, probably thanks to eco-devastation. Those birds of prey had learned to make the city and its rats work for them. You could sit out here and see all sorts of birds riding thermals of warm air, rising on their own invisible elevators.

Back to work, Martin! You can fix this terrace door in three easy steps.

The Lily voice again.

If you can fix a jammed door the door is yours, that is how it would be in a real utopia, in a real utopia the super wouldn't exploit the voice of the dead to think the thoughts that he can't let himself think on his own because his own voice is too quiet, too soft, too accommodating, he's so good-natured they all think, not knowing that he's only that way because if he acted out, if he shouted at Caroline over her little sporks, it would only confirm what they hoped was most true in him, he was a beast, he deserved his position in this world, he deserved to be exploited, I mean, that temper they would say, no wonder he's living down there, he deserves it, troll under the towering bridge, so best behavior, Martin, best behavior.

He turned back to the door and very carefully lifted it. A stone, round and flat and smooth, the culprit of the jammed door. He kicked it out of the lower track, bent down, and picked it up. Caroline was on the couch in the living room, crouched over her laptop, a cup of coffee in her hand. She was typing furiously. When he showed her the stone she said, "Oh, wow. Thank you, Martin. I really appreciate it." The words rushed.

"No problem," he said.

"That's all I need here. You can go." Her blush had vanished. This was more familiar: The supercilious command. The sense that he was in the way.

"Cool," Martin said. "I'll get out of your hair now."

He must have sounded surlier than he'd intended, because Caroline said, "I hope I didn't mess up your schedule with this. I'm sorry I didn't leave a message like I was supposed to."

"It's okay." Martin should say a nice thing now, so she'd stop wincing like he was mad at her. "I appreciate the strings you pulled for Ruby. It sounds like a cool opportunity. The museum."

"It's better than cool." Caroline put her laptop aside, her eyes widening again. "From what I've heard, it's just this incredible behind-the-scenes experience. My friend Annabel did it and she got to retouch this habitat diorama with, like, a flamingo on the horizon. She helped build crates for dinosaur fossils. She loved it. It's an amazing internship."

"An internship?" The stone in his hand felt warm. "You mean a job."

"Internships *are* jobs, Martin." Her hands fluttered up like doves. A gesture of exasperation, of impatience, but if he focused on the dove image, not so bad, so yeah, he must do that, he must focus on the dove image and not on Lily's voice, which said, *Martin lifts the stone and throws it right at—*

"Does this internship pay?" Martin asked, holding the stone, but not not *not* throwing the stone.

"I don't think so. But the point is, it'll help her get a better-paying job down the line." She lifted her cup of coffee and took a long sip and here was Lily: *Delicious organic coffee beans, harvested from sustainably robbed workers.*

"An internship," Martin said.

"Well, but you know the value of an internship like this one, Martin. Of course, there are problematic aspects. But that's true of everything. You know an internship is a great opportunity."

"I'm not stupid, Caroline. I know those internships, even the ones that pay, pay . . ." He almost said *pay shit*, but he paused. Breathed in. Breathed out. "They pay almost nothing."

"Yeah, but some internships turn into paying jobs in hardly any time at all."

"She thinks it's a job, you told her it was a job."

"It *is* a job."

He thought of Ruby, and the intruder this morning, and once again the stone felt so warm in his hand. He held the stone out to Caroline. He said, "Here. This belongs to you."

Caroline squinted like he had spoken in a language she didn't know.

"It was in your apartment," he said. "It belongs to you." *Martin realizes he needs to get rid of the stone in three easy steps, one, two, three!* And Martin stepped forward. He envisioned himself dropping the stone into Caroline's cup of coffee. No, no, he could never do such a thing. But then his fingers were uncurling and before he could grab it back, the stone was rolling, pulled by that demon gravity, and then the stone had dropped. It dropped into Caroline's cup of coffee.

The coffee sloshed out over the sides of the mug, droplets sliding onto Caroline's lap, down the skirt of her dress. She jumped to her feet, like the liquid had scorched her. The mug fell to the floor and broke into many shards. Caroline looked like she might cry. But a second later she said, "My fault. Don't worry about it. I'll clean this up. You can leave, Martin."

He had vowed never to hit his child the way his own father had hit him. He had not struck Caroline. And Caroline was not his child. Yet still he felt like he had broken a vow. Everything had been controlled and full of mindfulness and full of *thought* and now, thoughtlessly, this. A stone dropped in a cup of coffee.

"I'm sorry," Martin said. "I'm so sorry. That was an accident. My fingers slipped."

Caroline was many things, but she was not a total idiot. She drew her shoulders inward. They both knew it was not an accident.

Still, it was important to act like it was, important to pretend, so that nothing else shattered in this moment. "They called me butter-fingers when I was a kid," Martin said. "I always was dropping the ball."

The super grovels. The super lies.

"I made this mug a long while ago," Caroline said, looking at the shards. "With a celadon glaze."

"Can I at least help you clean up?"

"I told you, don't worry about it." Now Caroline looked at him. Her voice reverberating like the singing bowl, she said, "You've done enough. Thanks for all your help."

AFTERNOON

8 THE TOP OF THEODORE ROOSEVELT'S HEAD

An internship.

A free-MetroCard-college-credit-what-you're-not-in-college-well-you-can-take-home-the-leftovers-after-certain-functions-and-fund-raising-events-you-will-share-your-desk-with-Francie-who-comes-in-M-W-F-and-leaves-specks-of-cottage-cheese-all-across-your-limited-supply-of-Post-its-on-good-days-the-specks-will-look-kiiinda-like-stars-on-bad-days-feminine-discharge-and-Francie-is-a-sophomore-in-school-college-university-yes-will-ask-you-what's-your-major-every-week-and-even-if-this-doesn't-turn-into-a-job-it's-*such*-an-opportunity-looks-fan*tas*tic-on-a-résumé-even-while-your-sweaters-pill-and-molt-and-turn-to-dust-an-opportunity-did-we-mention-it's-an *internship*.

Ruby did not get the job at the Museum of Natural History because there was no job at the Museum of Natural History. Assisting in diorama maintenance and research, Caroline had told her. When, in the middle of her interview, Ruby found out what she was actually dealing with, she admitted she didn't have the financial means to take a nonpaying position right now. The man interviewing her, very young and sweetly round faced, looked distressed. Ruby had to reassure him for almost half an hour that it was nothing that the museum had done wrong. She loved dioramas, she said, yes, more than almost anything, for reasons slightly beyond her own comprehension, to be perfectly honest, and she wanted dearly to step inside one, but she just couldn't take a nine-to-five without pay, and no, of course, the MetroCard was a great benefit, just not enough for where she was at this time in her life. No, she wasn't interested in the paid summer internship for college students. No, she didn't need college credit. She had her degree. Nobody to blame, nope. Just a miscommunication. Understandable. These things happen.

She exited the museum's administrative offices.

In front of the entrance to the Museum of Natural History stood an equestrian statue of Theodore Roosevelt. Roosevelt's chin jutted out and he gazed forward, surveying the perimeter of Central Park as if scrutinizing a vast unknown. His horse, on the other hand, seemed to be panting in a way that was less than dignified, bronze nostrils flaring, oxidizing horsey eyeball bulging out, equine stare directed not just downward, but straight at Ruby. Ruby tried to admire the horse—the physics of equestrian statues were tricky (she remembered from a class at school), requiring feats of balance and weight support. Roosevelt and his horse were flanked by a statue of a Native American man and a statue of an African man; both of these men were on foot, mere accompaniments to the rugged melodies suggested by the horse-mounted Roosevelt who loomed above them, seemingly leading them onward.

The top of Roosevelt's head was covered in thin spikes to keep pigeons from landing on it. Some buildings in the neighborhood had done the same thing: placed spikes near entranceways to keep people from sleeping there. Would her father ever be asked to install spikes like those? Would he do it?

Of course he would do it.

Her mother called. "Babe," she said, "how did it go? Look, I can't talk long, because I'm on the bus, and there's traffic, and did you know there's a rule now on Greyhound against talking for a long time on your cell phone? How did it go?"

"Mom, you can text me if you can't talk."

"I hate text. I need an actual voice. How did it go?"

"What?"

"The interview, Ruby."

"Oh, it was okay."

"Something went wrong. I can *hear* it. See, this is why I need to call. Even though the woman across from me is narrowing her eyes—yeah, I *see* you, lady, it's my daughter on the other line. My only kid. Okay? Can you—"

"Mom. I'm fine. Let's talk later."

"Well, sure, if you really don't want to talk."

Her tote bag was slipping off her shoulder, heavy with the weight of Lily's book on dioramas. She shrugged it back up her arm. She said, "It was an internship."

"An internship?"

"Not even an hourly wage. They said maybe after a few months it might turn into a job, but I can't wait that long."

"Oh, sweetie. I'm sorry."

"It's fine. It was just a misunderstanding." A few steps below her, a child hurled an entire pretzel to the ground. Ruby's stomach grumbled. A fleet of pigeons descended on the food. "I haven't told Dad yet."

"Well, he'll understand."

"I don't know. He already seemed kind of miserable today."

"It's those birds. Do you know if he finally got that nest out?"

Ruby glanced at the spikes on Roosevelt's head. "Yeah," she said. She sat down on the steps heavily. "He got it."

"Oh, thank god. He was really dragging his feet. I love your father, but he has a habit of projecting emotions on creatures who can't speak."

"You mean animals," Ruby said.

"Well, I don't want to make him sound like a child."

"Just say animals."

"Fine. Animals. So, if Dad's sulking, too, that means you'll need to cheer each other up. You guys should do something nice tonight. Go out to eat. Can you get him out of the neighborhood after work? Sometimes when he gets miserable like that, the only thing to do is show him the world is bigger than the building."

"It's a big world," Ruby said, scrunching her knees up to her chest to make herself smaller as a group of schoolchildren trotted up the steps.

"And listen, you've got a whole afternoon ahead of you. You can use the time to apply to jobs, right? Or even to go to a résumé workshop at one of the libraries. There's kids your age that go to those now all the time, Em's told me. And you know, there's a couple new coffee shops in the neighborhood that are probably hiring. Not coffee shops I'd go to, of course. If it costs more than two dollars, I say—"

"I should have known it was an internship. I never look into things hard enough. I always romanticize. Like with the woman this morning. I wanted to let her in. I wanted to take care of her, so bad. I got into a whole thing with Dad about it."

"Let's not confuse the issues, sweetie. Right now we're just talking about you getting a job."

"I just feel really stupid, Mom."

"Ruby, no. You're a smart girl. Woman. You know that. I'm so, so proud of you. Listen, shut up, give me one second."

"What?"

"Not you, honey."

"Mom, if you need to get off the phone—"

"I should, I guess. Your dad should meditate on Greyhound. The buses are silent places now, apparently. Don't want an uprising. But if you need to call, then call, okay? Listen, lady, yes, I'm about to hang up. Right. On my flesh and blood."

Ruby ended the call. She wished her mother hadn't said she was so, *so* proud. The extra *so* felt like a spike in her side, too vehement to be believable. She put her face in her hands. A woman descending the stairs said, "I thought the whale would just be, I guess, bigger?"

"Bluer," said the man by her side. "At least bluer."

"It was more, what's the word, mottled?"

"Well, that's not the whale's fault, I guess."

"I guess."

Ruby needed to get off these steps. She should go home, apply for more jobs. But she couldn't move. She sat on the steps and watched the crowd for a while, her tote bag on her lap, the contours of Lily's diorama book visible through the cloth. Then she looked at her phone. Nadia had sent her a picture of a caribou. Something about this image inspired her to scroll through a whole series of the photos she had of herself and John, smiling in front of city park trees so gnarled the trunks seemed to be frowning. She took her time examining each photo for signs of discord. Then she took her time deleting the photos, one by one.

"Basically the museum started because a bunch of one-percenters had too many hunting rifles." Ruby's head shot up. Lily? No, just a woman around Ruby's age, sheathed in ripped black fabric. Lily wouldn't say *one-percenter* anyway. *Bourgeois swine* is what Lily would say right now. No, that wasn't right either. Lily, if Lily were here, would grab Ruby's head and pull it close to hers and say something like, *Ruby, get it together. My parents were not sweeties like yours, you lucky duck, my parents were emotionally abusive and yet even still, I learned to keep my head held high. Life will shit on you. The asshole of life is designed to shit on you, Ruby. This is called nature. This is called biomechanics. What you must do when you face biomechanics? Is you must not keep your head down, because you cannot dodge the shit. You must keep your head high, see the shit coming, accept the shit, and help others get past the shit. Do you understand?*

Ruby stood up and headed in the direction of home, down Central Park West.

Her father always told her he was glad they didn't live on Central Park West, because the supers there had to deal not only with extra-entitled celebrities, but also huge rodent problems. "There are ancient rodent tunnels leading from the park into those buildings," he liked to say, his eyebrows high.

Ruby did not notice any rats now. But she did notice that many of the buildings were in the throes of reconstruction. Rusticated limestone bases, terra-cotta trim, stone-hewn cherubs, rams' heads, and rosettes were covered in a protective mesh, through which scaffolding appeared in glimpses. The mesh turned the buildings into hulking phantoms. She went west, so that she was walking across a street between Central Park West and Columbus instead. No mesh here. This block was lined with prewar brownstones.

Halfway down the block, a guy sitting on the steps of one of the brownstones called out to her.

It was Caroline's friend Andy. She walked closer. The same Andy that Caroline had wanted to call about Lily's cousin, the Andy with whom Caroline wanted so badly to collaborate. He wore a camera around his neck. The collar of the shirt under his gray cardigan was half down, half up, which gave him the sartorial look of a friendly dog unable to coordinate the orientation of its ears.

Ruby had met Andy once before, at one of Caroline's parties, while lingering by a table crowded with cheese and wine. She was waiting for John, who was downstairs on a call with one of the boys he mentored who was anxious about an application deadline. She was drunk, and frank with herself about her own observations: Andy was much skinnier than John, she noticed, his chin rounder, his voice reedier. He told Ruby he was a full-time photographer, which she thought might mean he had a trust fund. But she must keep an open mind. How did Ruby know Caroline, he asked, and Ruby told him they'd grown up together. Tentatively, thinking about Caroline's grandmother and her tight grip on Ruby's wrist, she'd added, "Caroline is my oldest friend."

"So you're a native of the city, too. Like me." Andy's mouth was waxy wet with cheese. "Almost everyone else here tonight is a transplant." He gave a mock-theatrical sigh, and Ruby laughed, though she felt a tinge of guilt—John was a transplant. She hoped Andy wouldn't ask her to go into detail about her background. She had just talked for a long time to a woman who described her job to Ruby as writing features on restaurants that sourced from local farms. When the woman found out Ruby's dad was a super, she had begun railing at her about how her building's super sucked. "He never fixes things," the feature-writing woman had said. "He's the worst. And he barely speaks English, I mean that not in a racist way, just if something is wrong he doesn't even understand what I'm asking. It's so frustrating."

Thankfully, Andy didn't ask about Ruby's parents. Instead he asked, "Are you an artist like Caroline?"

She wasn't sure how to answer, so she told him she'd taken a lot of art history classes when she was still in school, written papers on narrative stillness in the visual sphere. "I've always been really interested in the diorama form," she said.

"Interested?" In Andy's half question, half echo, she heard how clinical her own statement must have sounded. Trying to overcompensate for that detachment, she'd actually seized both of Andy's own thin arms and, in a moment of wine-fueled earnestness that might (she thought later) have been read as a come-on, said to him, "I don't want to just make things for people to see. I want to change the *way* people see things."

At the time, Andy had hardly seemed to notice the arm grab. He kept his face very blank, so blank she could tell he wanted her to see the effort it was taking him to be neutral, to not roll his eyes. "You want to change the way people see things," he said. "That's awfully ambitious. Are you sure you're not a transplant?"

She dropped his arms and poured herself another glass of wine. "What do you photograph?" she asked.

"I take photographs of people on the fringes. Homeless people and old people and drug addicts."

Ruby reached for more cheese.

"Not exactly trendy subjects, fringe people," he continued, while Ruby chewed. "Not exactly the kind of stuff you can buy for a trillion dollars and hang up in a bank. But I feel called to the work and I'm grateful there's been some response. Can I get your number?"

"My number?"

"I'll text you the address of a gallery where a few of my works are being shown."

She swallowed the cheese and gave him her number. Andy said, "It's getting hot in here. Shall we step outside?"

"*Shall* we!" Ruby said.

"I definitely don't speak with an English accent," Andy said, "or whatever accent you're trying to do." But he was smiling at her. They walked out together onto the terrace. The city spread out before them there, like a carpet woven with a wild design of soft window glow and bright streetlights and moving headlights.

Andy said, "Have you noticed when the wind picks up like that, and howls like that, it sounds like all the female opera singers in this city have climbed to the rooftops and are belting out arias?"

This kind of lyrically charged statement was how certain people at Caroline's party made small talk. Usually, Ruby ignored these people. But Andy was looking at Ruby eagerly, so she said, "That's extremely poetic." She thought the wind sound was more internal, like a head-howl, the harmonics of an interior monologue. She looked down, shuffled a small rock around with her feet. They started a little game, blessedly free of lyricism. She kicked the rock toward Andy, he kicked it back. Then she kicked the rock at a funny angle and it hit the terrace door, which was opening. John was opening the terrace door.

He nodded at Andy when he stepped out, then put his hand on

the small of Ruby's back, so that when she turned, she was eye level with his jawline. He looked especially superhero-ish next to Andy, who said, in a too-loud voice, "Howdy, John."

"Hi, Andy, hi. Great to see you again. There are some friends inside I want you to meet, Ruby. They're good people."

"That's code for they're important, serious people John thinks I should network with so I can stop working at a coffee shop," Ruby told Andy, who laughed and said, "Enjoy that rat race."

"It's not like I'm part of some corporate tech giant," John said. "I work for a nonprofit."

"Ah," said Andy. "Enjoy that *noble* rat race."

"Why did you try to make me look like an asshole out there with that networking stuff?" John asked when they were back inside. "Why am I a jerk for wanting to help you?"

"I'm sorry. I'm just a little tipsy. Let's go meet your friends."

"Your teeth," John said. "They're purple."

"I don't care." And she really didn't. Ruby met the serious people, smiling.

The next day, after work, she had gone to the gallery, only a few blocks away from Mellow Macchiato, to see Andy's photographs. The street had been mostly swept clean of actual three-dimensional homeless people, and now there was a bank, a shoe store, and a shop selling vegan cupcakes that tasted like cured meats. A sign outside the shop said, *Try our new "bacon" flavor!*

Quotation marks in a food name made Ruby nervous. Still, she peered in and saw what looked like Billy the Exterminator pointing to a number of cupcakes in the display window. An exterminator in a vegan cupcake shop. She must have the wrong guy. She walked on.

The gallery, to her surprise, was one Ruby had actually heard of, a place known for its roster of emerging artists. She had passed by before, though she had never gone inside. Museums felt easy to wander around in, but galleries had always made her a little nervous. There was a woman about Ruby's age inside the gallery, too pretty to look at directly, and a man wearing a purple blazer so gloriously silken Ruby guessed it would be called not purple but lavender, and another man whose round face seemed to burst over his turtleneck like an overripe peach. Nobody spoke. Ruby was a little disappointed—and disappointed in her own disappointment— to find that Andy's photographs were, in their way, beautiful. The shopping carts full of garbage bags were always moving in or out of the frame in his photographs, the backgrounds were out of focus in a good way, and the lumpy faces and bodies of his "fringe people" were nicely composed. Some of the photographs were very grainy, as though taken with a camera phone and blown up, which lent a no-fucks-given artfulness to the portraits.

Later, she looked Andy up online. He occasionally posted pictures with paragraph-long stories of the people he met, stories about their desperation, the things they'd lost, the past sky-high dreams they'd had for their present falling-down selves. Hopping from one link to the next, she discovered that one man, with a big beard and darkened eyes and a sad story about his regrets, his guilt, his abusive father, and his lost son—this man had hit a nerve with people. Donations had poured in. The man Andy had photographed was invited to a daytime talk show during which he'd cried and become exponentially more famous. He was given a house. In an interview about this man and his own work, Andy said, "I believe my images tell stories that make viewers see the humanity all around us, even in the places where that humanity seems most absent."

After Ruby and John broke up, Andy sent her a message while she was packing her clothes into old grocery bags. Caroline must have told him the news. *How are you?? This is Andy from Caroline's party in case you forgot. It has been a while huh Ruby.*

She had thought of the man with the beard, the look in his eyes. Andy had captured how unwanted he felt. And if Andy looked right at her now, as she was leaving John's apartment, what would he see? She hadn't replied to his message.

But now here Andy was again, sitting on this brownstone stoop, calling out to her. Best not to read too much into his sudden reappearance. The city just operated this way sometimes; you could have a day fueled by coincidences that lined up wearing the mask of fate, trying to fool you into thinking there was some secret order to your life. People from your past might present themselves at any moment, even at your most despairing needful times, but it didn't mean anything special. She would refuse to find anything special in this now—Andy, calling her name after a depressing nonjob interview. She kept her voice casual. She said hi back. She pointed to the brownstone behind him. "You live here?"

He looked over his shoulder as if he were surprised to see the structure still standing. "This is my mother's place, technically," he said. "Though probably not for much longer. She's hoping to sell it."

Ruby had passed his block many times, since it was near the park, the museum, and the subway. But until this moment, the brownstones that lined this particular street had never been more than a two-dimensional façade off which her thoughts bounced in the same way light bounced off closed windows, illuminating nothing inside. Growing up in the city meant that huge swaths of streets appeared mostly unreal to her, sets designed to enclose her childhood.

"What are you wearing?" Andy was staring at Ruby's rayon/ nylon/spandex knit professional skirt.

She tried to smile brightly. "It's deliberately frump."

Andy nodded as if this were the right answer. "Do you want to come in for a minute? It's a little chilly out."

"Then why are you sitting out here?"

"I'm scouting for subjects, but so far, no dice. Too bad. This cloudy weather's perfect."

"I should probably head home."

"Where are you living now?"

"I moved back in with my parents. In the basement."

"Don't look so embarrassed." Andy's voice had turned soft, soothing. "I know quite a few talented people who have spent some time living in their parents' basement."

"My parents live in the basement, too."

"Your parents live in your parents' basement?"

"Yes," Ruby said. "We all live in the basement together."

Andy tilted his head.

"My dad's the super," she said.

"Oh, yes." He nodded again, a little too quickly. "I think Caroline mentioned that to me once."

Maybe he'd known what she meant all along and had just been teasing her. Flirting, even. She imagined sitting down and reading to him from Lily's diorama book. She shrugged her tote bag up her shoulder again. "I really should go."

"Wait," Andy said. "Would you want to come inside for a drink?"

"It's kind of early, isn't it? Barely afternoon."

"If it's after anything, it can't be that early."

"I need to get home soon. To feed these fish."

"Of course you do."

"It's really true."

"I can't give you a very brief tour of my place? It's a unique real estate experience. That's what my mother says. Maybe you might even know some potential buyer? It's prewar. Also, the basement is amazing."

"Now you're definitely making fun of me."

"No, I swear. There's something really amazing in the basement. I want you to see it. You, specifically, would appreciate it, I think."

"That sounds kind of like a serial killer line."

"I guess it does." And Andy laughed in a way that seemed more self-conscious than serial killer–esque, which was encouraging. The door behind him was open partway and the piece of brownstone insides that Ruby could see pulsed with biotic darkness. Maybe the brownstone contained life forms she couldn't imagine, stalactites hanging from prewar ceilings, stalagmites puncturing prewar floors. The inside of the building looked, from out here, like a new ecosystem. And once she was inside, maybe she could tell Andy about Lily's cousin, just as Caroline had wanted. Maybe they could track her down, comb the neighborhood for her. Andy could take the woman's picture and Ruby could interview her, get her story. They'd write it up in a compelling little paragraph or two, like the wall text accompanying a diorama. If the woman made her eyes sad enough, or interestingly defiant, maybe she would go viral and find a home. Ruby and Andy would be do-gooders, equalizing the city's injustices, humble heroes who were also, obviously, artists. Andy, grateful to her, would encourage Ruby in her future artistic pursuits, but not in the patronizing way John did. He would put her in touch with the gallery by the scare-quote bacon shop and Ruby's own creations would be gazed at by everyone, people like Lily's cousin wandering in off the street, people in silken lavender blazers, her father, her mother, Caroline. The whole of the city, maybe.

"Okay," Ruby said. "Give me the tour."

Andy smiled, stood up, and put his hand on the small of her back, guiding her inside. They walked into an entry hall that had nothing in it besides a coat hanging on a hook. The amount of open space startled her. In the apartment Ruby now shared with her parents, they were always fighting for an inch of room: on their couch, in their closets, in the kitchen. The space around their front door was filled with shoes and a bucket of umbrellas and coats piled up on a few straining hooks. The emptiness of Andy's entrance hall felt, by contrast, like some cool quiet chapel.

Her phone buzzed in her bag. She didn't touch it. "You live here alone?" she asked.

"Now I do. That's why there's not much by way of furniture. Especially on the first floor."

The next room in the brownstone was large and contained only two objects. The first was a lamp with a white electric cord stretched taut over the hardwood floor, toward an outlet. The second was a shopping cart.

"That cart's from Irene." Andy stepped up to the cart, grabbed its handle, and rolled it back and forth until one of the wheels squeaked. "She kept all her belongings in here. After I sold the photograph I made of her, I gave her some of my proceeds. So she gave me her cart. She said with the money I'd provided, she wouldn't need her cart anymore."

"That's amazing."

"It was a little optimistic of her. It was only a few hundred bucks. But, you know, I guess she had the right attitude." He shrugged. "Her story never quite blew up the way Mr. Jay's did. Not sure where she's at these days."

Ruby walked over to the cart. Her phone buzzed again. "You can put your tote down," said Andy, "if you want. And maybe check your phone? It's distracting. Sounds like an animal trapped in the walls."

She looked at her phone. Missed calls from her father, probably telling her he'd heard about the interview. A text from her mother, reminding her that she was so, so proud. The knot in Ruby's stomach tightened until it felt less like a knot and more like a barb, something hooked. She turned off the phone, placed it in her bag, and then put both her coat and bag inside Irene's cart. "Nowhere else to leave them," she said, trying to cant her head playfully. "Do you not even have a coffee table?"

"There's a little bit of furniture in my old room but only the bare essentials. Everything else is with my mother and her new husband. Upstate."

"So why aren't you upstate with your belongings? Or in some apartment here with your belongings? Why are you living in an empty house?"

"I don't need all that stuff. It's distracting. Clutters the visual part of my mind. And I might as well use this space if no one else is, right? Rent-free until it's sold."

"How much would this rent for?"

"A lot of cups of coffee." Andy smiled.

Ruby felt relieved by that smile. There was a kind of candor in it, this admission by Andy: he was rich. Maybe this honesty came from being a native of the city, from growing up knowing his role in the place. John, as a transplant receiving financial help from his family, was extra self-conscious about his function as a relative newcomer to New York, and about New York's meaning to him. The city, for John, was still partway a symbol. It had sometimes been exhausting for Ruby to find herself a native of a place that was a symbol to her boyfriend. She wouldn't have that problem with Andy should she decide to start something with him. She would have other problems with Andy, and maybe those problems would be more interesting ones. Imagine if they walked into Caroline's party together tonight, laughing in near-unison, with their heads close, and imagine if John saw them? She didn't want to hurt John, but after they broke up, he kept asking—in this irritating overly concerned way, in the way he probably talked to the first-generation college applicants at Hover Up—if she would be okay. Will you be okay, Ruby, no, really, I need to know, will you be okay?

Walking into the party with Andy would be an extravagant display of okayness.

Andy guided her toward another door, opened it. An empty room much like the one she'd just stood inside. The only difference was there was no shopping cart. Instead there was a rainbow tangle of wires sticking out of the white wall.

"My parents slept here," he said.

What had happened to the wall? She tried to envision a bunch of wires crawling out of the wall of her own childhood home, like veins ripped free from skin. No wonder Andy wanted to sit outside on the brownstone's steps. She felt a sharp pang in her stomach, and realized a moment later that the pang was not one of hunger but of sympathy. Although Andy wasn't paying rent, it could not be easy dwelling inside the vacancy of the house where he grew up. Maybe that was why a flask sat squat and serene on this room's windowsill.

When Andy saw what Ruby was looking at, he walked toward the window, and handed the flask to her like he was presenting her with a trophy. It contained some kind of whiskey that smelled more like iodine. "Mr. Calvin gave me that flask," Andy said.

"Another one of your subjects?"

"Used to hang out on the church steps at Seventy-First. He decided he'd stop drinking one day. Don't worry. It's clean."

She drank, despite her earlier protest about the time of day. Andy stood close.

"I heard about you and John," he said. "You know, I've talked to his new girlfriend some. We were actually in some of the same classes at school. She's not as smart as you. She's in public health."

"New girlfriend? Already?" She took another gulp from the flask.

"I thought Caroline would have mentioned it."

"No. She probably thought she was protecting me."

"That sounds like Caroline."

"A new girlfriend in public health." Ruby said the words slowly, experimentally. "I don't even understand what public health is, really."

"Well," Andy said, "don't worry about her."

"It's okay."

"My whole grand point was just that John's an idiot."

She turned her face so Andy would not see how grateful she was for those words. "At least he's trying to do good in the world," she said, hoping that by defending John a little, she herself might seem less wounded.

"He's doing good in the world for now, sure," Andy said. "But do you know how many guys I know who work in nonprofits for a few years, then realize they won't inherit their family's money for a long while, and hop right into tech? Or finance? Or fintech?"

"How many guys?"

"So many guys," Andy said. "But not me. Never me. For better or worse, I'm committed to my own stuff."

Ruby sipped from the flask again. "I believe you," she said, and found she meant it. She handed the flask back to Andy.

"Did you ever get a chance to see some of my photos?" Andy asked. "At the gallery? I gave you the address at Caroline's party that time, right?"

"I saw them."

Andy drank. "And?"

"And I think you have a good sense of composition."

"Thanks, Ruby."

"Sure."

"That actually means a lot. Because I'm actually very concerned with meaningful arrangements of space." He turned the flask around in his hand. "You think they're exploitative, don't you?"

"What?"

"I can tell that you think they're exploitative. Caroline doesn't, you know. It's a question I've batted around with her because it's a big concern of mine. She finds them, ultimately, honest."

"I guess they could be honestly exploitative."

"Is that a joke?"

She wasn't sure. But she hadn't meant to say anything cruel. She drifted toward the window facing away from the sidewalk. Here she could better see the backsides of a row of brownstones the next street over. Each had its own little quadrangle of garden space, some with wooden benches and wire chairs and clogged birdbaths black with city rainwater. "Are there any birds that you see out here?" she asked Andy.

"I only see pigeons out there."

"Some really rare birds come through around Central Park. Like, birds that make people's life lists. My father's always telling me about some blue-eyed warbler-thrush thing that's been spotted in the Ramble." She took the flask back from him and swigged. "So what's incredibly amazing about your basement?"

"I'll show you now. Okay?"

Andy's eyes had become the same wet dark color as the water in the clogged birdbaths.

A feeling like excitement flowered in Ruby's solar plexus, petaled her ribs and thighs. Nobody had watched her in that unclog-me way in a long while. Andy really wasn't bad-looking. And he wasn't so much shorter than John.

"Okay," Ruby said. "Let's see this basement."

They walked together down a black steel spiral staircase, a palimpsest of white shoe scuffs, marks of the movers coming and going, shifting big boxes on their shoulders. At a certain point Andy must have picked up a camera, because he was wearing it now around his neck, like a tourist in his own home.

When they reached the bottom of the stairs to the basement, he pushed open a large door and pulled a string. A bulb turned on, swinging back and forth, a bell ringing weak peals of light across the room. Old pipes ran above their heads, crisscrossing in places. Parts of the wall were peeling, and right beside the stairs sat a box of black garbage bags. Cool air and a metallic tang from the pipes filled her nose. Ruby smoothed down the professional skirt yet again. Her tights had bunched up a little around the ankles. Something about the tiny ripples in the fabric caused a small starburst of panic inside her chest, a feeling that made the excitement from moments earlier start to recede. What was she doing down here, in this strange basement, with someone she didn't really know? Her phone and bag were upstairs. If she called out, nobody would hear her.

But she was being ridiculous. Andy was Caroline's friend, was fine, wouldn't hurt her. They had plenty of shared acquaintances. She was just having a kind of capital-*E* Experience, the kind she could tell an elaborately zany story about at the party later on. She was in a weird brownstone! With a weird boy! Who was probably richer and definitely more artistic than John—things John would pretend didn't bother him, but which definitely would bother him. John would be jealous.

Plus—it was interesting in here. The basement in the brownstone wasn't empty like the rest of the place. Stacks of cardboard boxes were everywhere. Some of them were duct-taped shut, but the majority were open and overflowing with old papers and yellowing photo albums and even skinny doll arms and doll legs sticking up at funny angles, as if a whole shipload of Barbies were drowning in a scrap-paper sea. Some of the boxes were labeled in scrawls of Sharpie. *Helen's*, said one, *5-7 gr.* said another. *Photos (Dakota)*, *Photos (Andy)*, *Photos (H.)*. Most of the boxes said nothing.

"The movers haven't taken care of the basement yet." Andy gestured to the boxes. "My mother isn't sure if she wants to keep all these scraps. She's still determining her true feelings about nostalgia."

"Does it make you feel nervous?" Ruby asked. "Having all these mementos sort of fermenting beneath your feet?"

"Not really."

"I feel kind of off just being in my childhood room again."

"It's just stuff." Andy was now looking at a great hulking mass, enshrouded in bubble wrap, sitting on top of a pile of cardboard. "Can you guess what that thing wrapped in plastic is, Ruby?"

"Nope."

"That is the bubble-wrapped head of a black rhinoceros." Andy beamed. "That's the surprise."

A rhinoceros.

"My great-grandfather shot it a long time ago and left it to my grandfather. Who left it to me. Do you know there's only about thirty of this particular type of rhino left in the world now? Maybe fewer. They're going to be extinct one day soon. They might be extinct already."

The bubble wrap seemed like it might start to move with the rhino's breath. Ruby's own breath changed the drift of dust motes down here. This basement wasn't a set piece, wasn't a diorama. It was a wrecked museum.

Andy tugged at the strap of the camera around his neck and asked, "Will you put the head on?"

"What?"

"I want to take your picture. Will you wear the rhino head?"

"Um."

Andy must have taken that as a yes. He began to slowly unwrap the bubble wrap. The rhino's glaucous, glassy eyes reflected the slightly swaying light bulb. Its nostrils were bigger than its eyes, and somehow more real.

The basic physics and logistics of wearing the head were unclear to Ruby.

What was it like to own something your great-grandfather had killed, to be able to hold the skin of a beast and point to it as physical evidence of an ancestor's human life? She didn't even know in what sorts of ways her own ancestors had fled their own deaths. "They got out of Dodge!" was all her mother would say, Dodge presumably being the most official name she had for whatever vaguely Eastern European place they had left behind.

Andy finished unwrapping the head. "Okay! You ready?"

"How exactly am I supposed to wear that?"

"So, technically, you won't *wear* the head. You'll lie down and I'll place the head on your chest in such a way that your actual head will be concealed."

"Oh."

"It's like a magic trick. The camera creates the illusion."

"You've done this before."

"With my sister, once or twice. Just goofing around."

"Why didn't you take *her* picture?"

"I did, but I want to take yours."

"I don't know."

"I'll pay you."

"Oh, yeah?" She must not sound desperate. "How much?"

The number he told her made her gasp audibly. It would cover her credit card bill for this month, and even some of her student loan payment. Andy smiled again, the same a-lot-of-cups-of-coffee smile. "You're worth it," he said. "Your body's expressive, you're fairly tall, you've got a long torso, proportionally speaking, and your features are symmetrical enough."

"That's all I've ever aimed for in life." She tried to smile back. "Symmetrical enough."

"My point is you could definitely model, like, in this cool *unexpected* way."

Which was definitely another line. Or an insult. Or both. How often it wound up feeling like both.

"Actually," Andy went on, "thinking about it as modeling is

probably the wrong approach. It's not like you have to be my subject. This could sort of be like an artist collaboration. I mean, if you're interested. I won't demand you put your name on anything."

A collaboration with Andy. The very thing Caroline had spoken of so longingly this morning.

"Well?" Andy said.

Ruby pointed to the rhino head. "Don't you feel bad?"

"About what?"

"About your grandfather shooting one of the last black rhinos."

"My great-grandfather. Anyway, it wasn't one of the last black rhinos when that my great-grandfather shot it. That was a long time ago. We can't retroactively assign guilt, you know?"

She stayed silent.

"But if you want," he said, "we could frame the piece as a kind of *statement*. Like an awareness piece. Like we treat these rhinos as aesthetic objects in the same way we treat women as aesthetic objects?" Andy scratched the tip of his nose. "I think that could actually be extremely powerful." He removed the lens cap on the camera around his neck. "The head isn't too weighty. I promise."

Maybe being that close to the rhino head would kind of be like existing inside a diorama for a few minutes. It would be weird. And she remembered that she liked weird. "Okay."

His cheeks rosy now, boyish. "Okay?"

"Yes. Fine. I'll pose for you with the rhino head."

And Ruby lay down, carefully as she could so that her skirt didn't ride up. The floor was even colder than she'd guessed. Andy lifted the head and she closed her eyes as he lowered it on top of her. The rhino head was heavy on her chest, and dusty. She fought back a sneeze.

"You look really great," Andy said, and Ruby wished she could see his face, but the rhino head was blocking her view of him. "Amazing, really." A sloshing sound. He was drinking again from the flask. "Ruby? This series will be a stunner."

"Okay."

"What I need you to do now is let your arms go limp. Pretend like you're very weak. It's just that it'll be a better photo if you let your arms go limp."

She let her arms go limp.

"Great," he said. "Great, great, great."

It took him a long time to adjust the lens and to figure out a way to, as he put it, "make peace with the light." After a while Ruby could hardly stand the silence or the shifting. "What do you know about rhinos?" she asked.

"What?"

Probably the bulk of the rhino head had muffled her voice. She said again, louder, "What do you know about rhinos?"

"I know my great-grandfather shot one."

"What else?"

"I don't really know anything else."

"Not even from the Museum of Natural History? There's a black rhinoceros diorama there."

"I never went to that museum much, except on school trips. And then we just looked at dinosaurs." The camera started clicking. "My mother has a fear of germs, and my father has a fear of crowds. I hate him."

"Your father?"

"Not to be, like, a Freudian cliché. My grandfather I loved, though." Click. Click. Click. "That's why the head is still here. He gave it to me."

"You seriously never saw it?"

"Saw what?"

"The rhino diorama. There's three rhinos in it. A baby one and parents. It's beautiful."

"I never really saw the draw of the museum, honestly. It's a little phony? This whole concept of sanctimonious scientist-hunters. Conservation via killing. You're still looking great, by the way, Ruby. Yeah. Keep your legs like that. Maybe turn the right ankle out a little? Yes."

She heard him swallow wetly and screw the flask shut again. The two sounds in concert created a new streak of fear inside her, sharper than the one she'd felt when she first stepped into his basement. Had her skirt inched up when she moved her ankle out the way he asked? She felt a little paralyzed, beneath the head. When she took a deep breath, the rhino head seemed to grow heavier.

Unlike Andy, she had visited the black rhinoceros diorama many times. At first she had mostly paid attention to the rhinos themselves, the hulk of them, the way the baby rhino in the display stood slightly off to the side. But as she got older, she became more interested in the tiny birds perched on the rhinos' backs. *The red-billed tick bird*, the sign next to the rhinos said. The birds liked to eat the little bugs that burrowed in a rhino's skin. The birds *had* seemed kind of phony at the time, an afterthought of realism. But now, under the rhino head, Ruby found herself anticipating the whir of wings. Birds must have balanced on this very rhino head many years before, talons digging in to maintain their equilibrium. Perhaps whole flocks of red-billed tick birds lived on this rhino and fed on this rhino and shat on this rhino and mated on this rhino and scattered into the blaze of sky when they heard the shot, one day, from Andy's great-grandfather's gun.

"You're twitching a little," Andy said. "Stay still. The light is dim here, so the exposure has to be long."

If she moved, she would come out a shadow, a ghost, a blur in every shot.

"Think about something calming, Ruby, okay?"

She thought about this rhino growing up in what the museum called, in the informational wall text, *dry bush and thorn country*. In this imaginary thorn country, she heard the shot of a gun.

"Ruby. You just *twitched* again. Stay still. Or is that asking too much of you?"

What informational text would she write about Lily's cousin, if she and Andy found her? Would she write about Lily? Waves of warmth began to spread to her splayed legs and arms. Her right foot was asleep and she knew soon it would become tingly. The anticipation of the limb waking up was almost too much to bear.

"Look," said Andy, "these are all going to be unusable if you keep moving around like that."

"I'm trying to stay still."

"I'm *paying* you to stay still," he said, and something about that sentence seemed to wake a new life in him. His breathing shifted to a different, more jagged rhythm. He had another drink from the flask. She listened for him to say something else, but he didn't. Instead he walked forward and knelt down next to her so that she could see his face again. The part of his collar that was sticking up no longer looked endearingly cockeyed but like some growth that had broken out of his neck, a tumor with the texture of a cardigan. His eyebrows were very straight and his mouth, too, held itself in a firm straight line. He took hold of her wrist.

"What are you doing?"

"I'm just going to try to rearrange you a little, so you're more comfortable, so you don't twitch. Okay? Just don't move. It's good for the photo." He held her other wrist down against the floor, reaching awkwardly around the rhino head on her chest, so that his arm pushed against her chin. The sun cleared a cloud for a minute and light shone through the small basement window, waving back and forth on the wall, like *hello hello hellooo*. Andy's whiskey breath wafted over the rhino head. Ruby stayed very still.

"Good," he said. "Like this. Don't move. Okay? This is what's needed for the photograph. Okay-okay?" He released her wrists. But he was still kneeling beside her. "I didn't appreciate what you said before, Ruby. That accusatory tone you took against my great-grandfather."

"What?"

"The way you talked about him killing the rhino."

The trick was to remember all the money he would give her. She should stay silent. Silent. Silent.

She said, "But he *did* kill the rhino."

"Except it wasn't one of the last rhinos when he killed it. I don't think."

Neither of them budged.

"You have to consider historical context, Ruby."

She tried to laugh at him in a large, guffawing you-are-an-idiot way, but it came out as something else. A small giggle. Childlike, coy even.

One of Andy's hands moved to her right hip bone. He pressed down on the place where the hip bone jutted out.

"What are you doing?" she said. "Stop."

"I'm getting a sense of these textures, how they'll photograph," he said. "Polyester fabric doesn't have pores, so it can't breathe like other fabrics." A hitch in his own voice. "But it feels like it's breathing beautifully on you."

"Um," Ruby said.

"I mean," he said, "it feels good. You feel good."

"Andy," she said. "Stop."

It was as if he couldn't hear her at all, he was so focused on recomposing this scene, and in his focus she felt his former friendliness decompose. His hand was still on her hip bone. She thought about the way his eyes had resembled birdless birdbaths upstairs. Maybe remaining motionless really was her best bet. But then his hand crept up under her professional skirt and her sleeping limbs awoke. "Stop," she said again, and lifted the rhino head off her chest.

Its weight pressed hard on her hands and her arms quavered. Andy's hand kept creeping.

But she found some reserve of upper-body strength, some power that had been fomenting unbeknownst to her. With a great grunt, she hurled the rhino head forward, at Andy's own head. He cried out.

The rhino head rolled over onto its side with a thud.

Ruby's chest now felt very light. The rhino head seemed undamaged. Andy moaned. He lifted his hand to his nose and it came away sticky red with blood. He gaped at Ruby. They were both breathing hard.

"Stay here," he panted. "We are going to have a real *conversation* when I get back."

"A conversation. Is that what you call trying to grope me?"

"You can forget about getting paid."

He was already running upstairs to the first floor. A door opened and shut. She trembled all over. The rhino head had rolled on its side. Its glass eyes were still shrouded in dust. Its real eyes probably *were* dust. Despite the adrenaline flowing through her, she found herself stalled by the rhino's gaze. The animal's head was trapped in Andy's basement, among all these old school papers and toys, as if it were not a rare thing at all, but as common as an old exam or childhood doll, and as easily forgotten.

She should not leave it here any longer in its bubble-wrap shroud. They were both getting the hell out of here. She walked to the box of trash bags beside the basement's boxes, removing a black garbage bag as if she was pulling out a soft tissue covered in aloe lotion. Next she rolled the rhino head into the black garbage bag. This would not be borrowing. But it would not exactly be stealing, either. This would be something else, what she was about to do. A sort of reclaiming. Art-making, maybe?

Hauling the rhino head up the basement steps was difficult. She could hear running water—Andy was in the bathroom, wiping up nose blood Ruby guessed, snuffling quietly to himself, probably unable to hear her footsteps due to the outrage pounding in his own body.

When she got upstairs, she placed the garbage-bag-swaddled rhino head inside Irene's cart. She put on her coat and grabbed her bag and then pushed the cart through the entrance hall and to the doorway. It squeaked as it trundled forward, galumphed down each stone step, but Irene's cart held true. She was on the sidewalk and pushing the cart past Andy's brownstone and past other brownstones and she was at an intersection. The streets had changed. They seemed brighter, seemed like they might soon grow brighter still, even though it was now sometime in the early afternoon, and mounting illumination was against the usual order of things. Well, forget the usual order of things.

She looked back once, sure she would see Andy running after

her, but there was nobody behind her at all. A jogger with a stroller all the way down the street. That was it.

What if she left the rhino head on the steps of the Museum of Natural History?

Yes. Yes, yes, *that*. She would leave the rhino head on the steps of the museum, the way mothers in old novels left babies in baskets on the steps of a church, hoping someone would arrive who could connect to the infant, make up for the child a sweeter history, a clearer future. The rhino head and Ruby were almost there, almost at the museum.

One of the cart's wheels had become damaged during the descent down the brownstone's steps. It twitched to the right when the rest of the wheels knew to move ahead. But Ruby kept pushing and eventually the broken wheel grudgingly aligned itself in a forward-moving direction. As she approached the museum, no one even gave her a second glance. And she was not surprised. She was only a woman with a shopping cart. The city was full of people just like her.

At the museum steps, though, she paused. She gripped the cart. If she left it here, would someone think the rhino head was a suspicious package? Would they accuse her of something? The key was to act casual. She let go of the shopping cart—"Goodbye and good luck, rhino head," she whispered under her breath—and drifted in what she hoped was an inconspicuous way over to a food cart.

Lily, when she took Ruby to museums, would never buy her food from the nearby vendors. Tourist traps, she said. But today Ruby bought an overpriced hot dog. Even though she had no job. After what she'd been through with Andy and her bold rescue of the rhino head, hadn't she earned it?

Then she walked away from the museum, trying not to look back over her shoulder at the cart. When she was out of sight of the museum, she found a bench along the park and sat down. Gray clouds gathered overhead. She began to feast. Midbite, the hot dog's mustard dripped onto her professional skirt, a big, ugly yellow streak surrounded by a spattering of smaller viscous drips. She imagined one of her old professors coming up to her, praising the way she had produced a tongue-in-cheek Pollockian imitation using nothing but condiments. "Are you perhaps crafting a pointed commentary on the artistic-industrial complex?" they might ask, and she would reply, "Yep, that is exactly it."

Despite her stained skirt and her joblessness, she felt good about taking the rhino head, about taking any sort of action against Andy at all. But then, after a while longer staring at the skirt, she imagined Andy's hand bubbling up from under the fabric, and she felt very cold. Her phone was still off. She didn't want to look at it. If Andy texted her, she knew she would be tempted to respond, and she liked the idea that their dialogue was over, that she would come out of the day with, if not lasting employment, at least the last word in something. She opened her tote bag and took out Lily's book on dioramas. She read through it all, cover to cover.

At last she stood from the bench just as the sky began to drizzle down rain. Students passed her, wearing big backpacks. School was out and she still had to feed 2D's fish. It started to pour. She raced back to her father's building. She had not run in weeks, although for a time John had tried to get her to lose weight by jogging around Prospect Park. Now that that was over, she had vowed never to go faster than a speed-walk. But here she was, sweating, heart pounding, hair again a mess. She ran through the lobby, up the stairs, up to 2D, jamming the key hard.

The apartment smelled like fake pine trees and lemon soap. It was full of carefully placed furniture. A large taupe couch by the window. A brass bar cart. A gleaming glass table that had been showcased in a magazine's feature piece on modern coffee table styling. (2D had left a dozen copies of the magazine in the laundry room, in a way that reminded Ruby of how her mother hung Ruby's old drawings on the fridge. Which maybe made the coffee table 2D's child?)

And, of course, there was the fish tank. Ruby had imagined a whole school of darting fish, but in fact there were only two clown fish. A few instructions on how to feed the fish had been left near the tank and a note had been propped on top of the containers of fish food. *Ruby thank you SO much, a lifesaver stunning heroine!!!* Next to the note was an envelope labeled *FOR RUBY!*

When she opened the envelope, there was no money inside. Instead there was a MetroCard with a Post-it note on it that said, *To take you wherever you dream!* There were also two Starbucks gift cards and another Post-it note that said, *To give you the caffeine you need to get there ha ha!* Tenants did this to her father sometimes, too: gave him gift cards for jobs he did, mostly for fancy restaurants in the neighborhood, a couple of times for pedicures. "They don't understand that I would pay *not* to go to those places," he told Ruby once. Oh, her father. She had disappointed him so much.

But it was important she not disappoint the fish, too. She tossed a few pinches of fish food into the tank and the fish immediately began to feast. She sank into the couch, not even removing the rain-damp mustard-streaked skirt. She was exhausted. On top of the Lucite coffee table, 2D had placed three gigantic vintage pool balls, a red vase, and a candelabrum. It *was* a beautifully styled coffee table. And the fish were both so alive, full of frantic to-ing and fro-ing. They didn't seem to notice anything other than their own movements. They really were spectacularly relaxing. She watched them until her adrenaline slowed. Was this a form of meditation? She stopped watching the fish and began to watch her breath, as if her own inhalations were some strange shy animal. Finally, she fell asleep.

I t was almost four, and Martin still hadn't heard from Ruby. He had spent his day playing many roles besides a worried father. A rat killer (one caught behind the wet garbage). A garbage hauler (wet trash dragged into the alley). A courtyard sweeper (bird nest, yes, and also used condoms tossed from a window).

But mainly—in the hours after he'd done the stupid thing, dropping the stone in Caroline's coffee—he had been a translator, a go-between for the mostly immigrant crews and the building's inhabitants. Here is when the men will enter your doorway, 3D, and at this time, 2C, the Romanians may cross your threshold, and yes, 7C, trust me to schedule the strangers who will be here to redo the ceiling of what will be your child's nursery, and uh-huh, 4B, the bedbug dog has been here but not for as long as we expected, Bed-bug Scott said the dog was fatigued, was exhausted and trauma-tized by an especially bad infestation uptown, no, far *far* uptown, no worries, everything will be fine, sorry, 2A, the exterminator is coming not today but next Friday, right, that's right, you've got it!

Booming his voice, loud and boisterous when the crews came in, so they'd know to trust him as one of the guys. Lowering his voice with the tenants so they'd feel respected.

In between saying the things he had to say in the ways he had to say them, Martin checked his phone again and again. He'd sent Ruby messages all afternoon. *How was interview you okay look your mom told me what happened hey just message me when you get this let me know.*

He had not heard back.

He had heard many times from the birding e-group, though, about the owl in the park. And he had heard many, *many* times from Neilson in 3C about the drain. But zero messages from his daughter. Well, she was an adult. Probably she was fine, and when his heartbeat sped up, he needed to stay in the glistering present moment.

Still, despite all his attempts at staying present, by the midafternoon Martin found himself huddled in the garbage room, next to the motor room, checking his phone repeatedly.

A text from text-averse Debra, a real rarity. *conference going ok not much free food also forgot to say before told R you would take her out for dinner she seemed BLEAK.*

A blurry photo of the owl in a tree, being dive-bombed by blue jays. E-birders he had never met responding in utter reverence: *wowowow, what a majestic, beautiful shot, I hate jays, beautiful.*

Neilson: *hey M, r u on yr way drain is still clumped full would really like to shower sometime today if that's not 2 much 2 ask haha?*

Neilson wrote texts the way he probably thought kids Ruby's age wrote texts. A guise of youth. But Ruby's texts were almost always grammatically correct. He'd one hundred percent hear from her soon. Maybe she'd gotten back and he hadn't noticed? He went into the apartment and checked her room. Nobody. But her sketch pad was there.

He picked it up. There was the drawing from the early morning, a plan for a diorama of Lily's old apartment. A rectangle on the page and inside, a sketch of Lily surrounded by her stuff. The sofa with pulls on the fabric from Lily's series of cats. The three-speed box fan. The piles of books. On top of the drawing, Ruby had written, *TOOOOO SENTIMENTAL O WELL.* She had begun to draw Lily, it looked like, sitting on the couch, but only had a thin outline of hulk.

Martin took out his phone.

Where are you? he texted Ruby. *Am very worried.*

He needed to do something about the way his shoulders felt, like the entire weight of the building above him was pressing down. The weight of all those tables, all those couches, all those other people and their own worries. But he still had work to do. He texted Neilson back: *Be right up.*

thanx martin Gr8!1

When Neilson opened the door for Martin, he said his shower drain was still clogged and he'd had to wash with dirty water pooling around his feet after his run, and while he appreciated the difficulty of Martin's job, he just couldn't help but notice that there did seem to be a certain lack of efficiency to the way Martin ran things, he'd been holding back saying these words because they were by this point old friends, but honesty was necessary for friendship, too, right, and Neilson knew efficiency experts and perhaps he could put them in touch with Martin, or the building's board, or Frank at

Sycamore Property Management, because these efficiency experts were really very very good.

Neilson flipped his hair back over his shoulder. Something was going on with him. He was pissier than usual. Martin said, "Efficiency experts. Neat. Okay."

In the bathroom, Martin placed a paper towel at the side of the tub. Then he looked down at Neilson's ornamental chrome plate that served as the tub's pop-up stopper handle. He needed to remove the slender cotter pin that connected the chrome plate to the stopper. With the ache in his back, it would be less painful to lie down in the tub to remove the pin than it would be to twist his head and hunch over the chrome plate. The tub had looked dry, but after lying down Martin realized there was a thin layer of dampness on it. The moisture plastered his shirt to his back. Best not to think of Neilson's gross hairy feet in here, right where he was lying.

Once he had removed the chrome plate, he pulled the cotter pin so he could get to the handle to activate the pop-up drain stopper. Then he hauled himself up so he was kneeling in the tub. He removed the handle and now he had the overflow pipe right there. He put the augur in the drain and got the drill motor spinning, down through the overflow, down through the trap. He began fishing out clumps of Neilson's hair, placing the clumps on the paper towel.

What do you do when those hair clumps are so stuck in there? An e-z solution! You—you—Martin—you did not let her in, you did not deliver the news of my death kindly, I've tried to hold this back all day long but listen, you did not make an effort, you let her walk down the street, a basic courtesy to tell the family with compassion, and in this you failed, in this as in so many things, as bad as the worst of the tenants in that moment though it breaks my heart to say so, as if she were not human, don't get me wrong, I had issues with her, I called her sometimes that sad moron of a cousin because of her general problems with the ole drugboozesex trifecta, you heard me time and time again say how my family was scheming always scheming yet without imagination, still, they are my family, and you acted like the worst of the tenants the worst, you're mad at Neilson for seeing her as a bundle of blankets but you saw her as a human without history, how we would play together as kids, me and my cousin, creating tents out of blankets and chairs, like your daughter did as a kid, too, sometimes, and the way you dropped that stone, I saw, into the coffee, oh, it will be bad, Martin, bad the way sweet Ruby is going, how she looked at you, not like you were a human she didn't know, but like you were a human who should know better, I've been thinking about the arc of systems and the arc of the nest falling, those eggs, how you do what they say, you just do what they say, how she looked at you, and where is she now, anyway, where is your daughter now?

He was on his back again, reconnecting the ornamental chrome drain operator, trembling a little, when Neilson walked in. Martin sat up in the tub, his elbows jammed against the sides.

"Yuck," Neilson said, looking at the drain hair. Then: "Martin. Are you okay?"

Martin was coated in sweat that kept dripping itchily down his spine. It made him feel like his actual nerves needed a deep private scratch, the kind people usually reserved for their butts. He was exhausted and he stank, and there was Neilson.

"I'm done here," Martin said. "We're all good."

"Do you want to meditate? Before you go? You look like you could use it."

Neilson did not own a singing bowl. So Martin, feeling his own nervous heat, nodded.

In the living room, Neilson had set two cushions on the floor, their shams embroidered with spiraling golden thread. When Martin sat down on his cushion, his knees cracked. Neilson sat down, too, his legs folding nimbly and silently, in a way that reminded Martin of the blue heron he'd seen in the park by the boathouse.

"Are you ready to start?" Neilson asked. "If so, put your phone away and breathe through your nose."

Martin closed his eyes. Phosphenes behind his eyelids, moving here and there, like birds, like fish. When you closed your eyes too tightly, you stimulated retina cells and made your brain believe that you were seeing light. Who had told him this? Ruby? Lily? Neilson? Their voices blending in his mind with the force of their confident fact-giving. How much they all knew. How much they all wanted him to know they knew.

He closed his eyes even more tightly.

Behind his eyelids now, the shapes of falling pink tissues.

He shouldn't say anything. He shouldn't say a word.

Whoops. But here was Martin, clearing his throat. "Why did you tell me there was nobody in the foyer, Neilson?"

Neilson's eyes opened.

"This morning," Martin said. "You called. And you said there was just a bundle of blankets in the foyer."

"There was."

"There was also a person."

"Well," Neilson said, "I just looked out of the corner of my eye and then I hurried inside. I had to keep my heart rate up for my exercise regimen. The whole thing's a waste if you aren't operating at a consistently aerobic pace."

"So you didn't look at the blankets long enough to know."

"To know what?"

"If there was a person under them."

"It's not my job to know that."

Martin looked down at his shoes. He had forgotten to put on his shoe covers when he walked in here. A big mistake. Not hearing from Ruby—and the thing with the birds and the brooms—and the stone in Caroline's coffee—and the intruder this morning—all of it was getting to him. Throwing him off his deferential-'n'-distant game.

"Didn't mean to criticize you," he said to Neilson. "Let's meditate."

"I told some friends about you, you know." Neilson shifted forward on the cushion. "I said I meditate with my super. They said you were maybe the only meditating super in all of New York!"

Just a dancing bear of a bearded dude, that was Martin! And yet he knew Neilson was sharing this anecdote as a way to make amends. So Martin smiled and said, "I bet I'm not so rare. It's a big city. Probably there are other supers who meditate."

"You think so?"

"Some of them are probably in child's pose under a busted pipe right as we speak."

Neilson did his polite laugh before closing his eyes again. Martin waited a second. Then he took out his phone. No messages.

"Isn't it hard to meditate with the phone out?" Neilson asked, eyes open again. "I sure as hell couldn't do it. Karla was always checking her phone. Drove me nuts. Not why we ended things, of course. Well, not the only reason why. But a distraction. Right? I used to say to her, why do you have to mediate the world like that?"

Martin put the phone back in his pocket.

He envisioned Neilson's big white feet with dirty shower water pooling around the toes.

Then they both began to meditate in earnest. Martin and Neilson breathed in through the nose. They breathed out through the mouth. They breathed in, and out, and in, and then Neilson intoned, "Let us take a moment now to awaken fully and *efficiently* in our inward vision, to sit with ourselves as we are and without judgment and with our hearts also full of mindful loving-kindness."

A big-hearted inefficient dancing bear of a bearded dude that Neilson spoke of to his friends.

A sideshow freak.

A character in the stories Neilson told at dinner parties.

Wide-eyed, mindfully alert, Martin farted into the golden-threaded cushion.

It was a very quiet and definitely accidental fart—too much gluten today, all those damn rolls—but once it had sallied forth into the container of 3C, once it was far too late to call it back, Martin didn't regret it. He hoped Neilson smelled a slight stink in his nostrils as they flared out with his mindful inhalation. And then? Maybe Neilson would laugh. When the smell reached his nose. And Martin would laugh. And whatever had caused Martin to drop the stone in Caroline's coffee, whatever was curdling up the good and respectful impulses in Martin—that would vanish, leave his mind and heart. If Neilson would only acknowledge the smell Martin had made. If Neilson would only laugh.

But Neilson did not react. Maybe he remembered that this had happened before at the JCC group class. Maybe he was just trying to spare Martin any embarrassment. Except Martin was not embarrassed. He wished Neilson wouldn't assume he was ashamed that he had farted on the gold-threaded pillow. Had his phone buzzed just now? But okay, he must focus.

Martin allowed himself to sink a little farther into his breath. His heartbeat slowed. Whatever grease might be clogging his arteries was now melting away into lotus-shaped grease droplets, whooooosh, there was his healed heart, a baby-new blood-pumper. Breathe in, breathe out.

He had made a definite smell.

The way Ruby had turned to him, scrunched her nose just a little, holding that stupid broom. An unpaid internship. And Caroline hadn't thought to tell her. Hadn't seen why it would matter. And breathe. Breathe in, breathe out, just breathe, everyone suffered! Compassion for all! Even Caroline and Caroline's family, they suffered. Hell, Caroline's grandmother had given a lecture or two at the JCC on her experience of suffering. Martin's parents had said their parents and grandparents never wanted to talk about their time during the pogroms in—where? Somewhere near Kiev, Martin's dad would say vaguely. He said his parents liked to pretend like they'd fitted in seamlessly in America, and Martin figured out that meant no stories of the past. Stories *always* had seams, they always had stitches and pieces that didn't quite connect. Besides, Martin's dad had said, nobody really cared about their stories. Martin had figured out what that meant, too: His grandparents were poor and everyone around them had some trauma, wherever they had come from. Having some trauma was called being alive. They wouldn't think to write an article about it and insofar as they gathered, nobody would ask them to give a talk. *Without social capital*, Lily screamed in his head, *it's not a narrative, it's only a thing that happened to you!* So: No tales from Martin's family. Only hurtling forward into the future until your body turned into dust motes.

There were so many different types of dust in the building,

especially in the apartments under construction. Plaster dust, cement dust, limestone dust, paint dust, cobweb dust, fiberglass dust, the dust of the dead, too. Lily's dandruff floating around somewhere, probably, still. Dandruff was dead skin cells, right? Ghost cells people shed all the time. Maybe Lily was talking to him through her dandruff, which remained in the building, zipping around. Little phantom scalp flakes delivering telepathic messages through Martin's skull. Or possibly he was just going insane.

His phone had not buzzed. He was pretty sure.

How Caroline had drawn her shoulders in.

Here was the thing. He could feel compassion for Caroline, who was really just a kid. But feeling compassion for Caroline did not erase these facts: Caroline was having a party tonight. Caroline could tell her father that Martin had been horrible to her, that he had dropped a small rock into her cup of coffee causing her to drop the entire mug, hot coffee scalding her legs. Kenneth had power over Martin and even if he decided he would not complain to anyone about Martin's rudeness toward his daughter, even if everything went Martin's way, even if he spotted the owl in the park, even if he found out Ruby had got a decently paying job, even if Debra's conference panel led to tons of donations and a promotion and erased her feelings of burnout, even if Lily had not died on the toilet, and even if someone else had been the one to let in the construction people who were right now tearing up the bathroom in which Martin had seen the specific pale blueness of her corpse— even if all those things had or had not happened? The party upstairs tonight would be Caroline's party. The party upstairs tonight would never be Martin's party, or Ruby's party, or Debra's party, or Rafael's party, or Pumpworks Tony's party. It always would be

Caroline's party and it would be Caroline's guests vomiting in the lobby and it would be Martin cleaning that vomit up and those were the present-moment facts, no changing them.

But what made today the day those facts felt like shards of glass in Martin's feet?

If he'd only been wearing the shoe covers when he walked into 3C.

Neilson nickered like a horse. This happened sometimes when Neilson was immersed in his breathing. He seemed to channel some inner equine state and his exhalations went near whinnying. Dude was in the I'm-a-pony-man-galloping-through-the-green-fields-of-my-deeper-consciousness zone while Martin cheated himself out of calmness by thinking about his beleaguered ancestors and working himself into a frothy anger. Neilson's eyes were still closed, the crepe-thin skin of his eyelids unwrinkled, and Martin closed his eyes again, too, tried to settle back into the now, but now, oh, now he could only envision the smug smile on Neilson's face and his mostly wrinkle-free eyelids, and so the next time Neilson did the nearing-nirvana nickering thing, Martin answered by farting again into the gold-threaded pillow, less experimentally this time, this fart warm and noisy, practically explosive, definitely ranker than the earlier one.

Hm! Yikes!

What had gotten into him? Some off-kilter vibrations in the building today? Maybe Lily's ghost was haunting Martin's gastrointestinal tract? Not good. But it was kind of fun to watch Neilson struggling to keep up his deep breathing, pretending to be so in the moment, like the smell was nothing more than the texture of a present of which he, Neilson, was infinitely accepting. Still, the nose . . . Yep, there it was. A crinkle. A little unconscious crinkling.

In the nose and in the eyelids, too. Martin snorted back laughter. Neilson's eyes opened.

"What is it, Martin?"

"Nothing." A surprise to hear himself actually giggling. He tried again: "You know when you're just so profoundly *present* that you start to laugh?"

Neilson nodded. "Yes," he said quickly. "Yes, absolutely. I'm glad you got there, to that open, childlike place, my brother." He stood up and, without another word, opened a window.

A cool draft and the voices of the crew at work in the courtyard today, just starting to wrap up. They called to each other in Spanish. Martin and Neilson listened and did not understand much. The men out there seemed even to be laughing in another language.

"Jesus," Neilson said. "They're so loud. Do they not know people here work from home?"

"We're not working right now."

"But I *will* be, Martin. Once you leave, I'll have to get back to work and instead of listening to the changes in the currency marketplace, I'll have to listen to all that hollering out there."

"They're just goofing a little. The workday's almost done."

"Not *my* workday. I telecommute. My job has no boundaries."

"Okay," Martin said. "I understand."

"Could you talk to them later on? Tell them to keep it down when you're back in the basement?"

Martin said nothing. His silence caused Neilson to turn from the window and raise an eyebrow. His face resembled a white garbage bag barely cinched closed, near to bursting. He wanted so badly to say something, Neilson did.

"What?" Martin said.

"I'm not sure how to put this." Neilson folded his arms over his chest. "But were you purposefully farting into the meditation cushion?"

"Yeah, my man." Martin stood up. "I purposefully farted into your meditation cushion. I was feeling very Zen."

Dream #1: Neilson would say, *That makes sense to me.*

Dream #2: Neilson would say, *Fuck, I was being an asshole, and I should just let the guys outside laugh if they want to laugh.*

Dream #3: Neilson himself would start to laugh. And Martin would join in. They would laugh so hard, they'd fart in sync. Which would mean they'd laugh more and then Neilson would give Martin a big early Christmas tip, even though it was March and he hadn't given him much last time around anyway.

None of that happened. What happened was: The cinched look on Neilson's face got tighter. If Martin stayed here much longer, the garbage in Neilson—whatever trash in him had the sharpest edge— would rupture the bag of his face and everything would erupt at Martin. The worst words. A few threats. Guaranteed.

"I'm just joking with you," Martin said quickly. "It was an accident. Too much gluten."

"Uh-huh," Neilson said.

"I really like bread. That's my problem."

"Right," Neilson said.

"Yeah. So. I should get back to work myself before it gets too late." He hoisted up his toolbox and, under Neilson's stare, left 3C. Behind a door, he could hear 3D's Yorkies howling.

The dozens of garbage bags in the courtyard had made their slow migration to the curb in front of the building as the afternoon wound down. Martin saw them when he went to hose the sidewalk. A crew had come, had pulled the bags through the courtyard, through the trash alley, up the stairs, to the street, where the bags would stay until a truck arrived to haul them off. When Martin squinted, they resembled dozens of slouching people, puffy-coated, who seemed to be waiting for something. The insides of 5A, scrunched within black polyethylene, had reshaped into something skeletal. The slabs of Lily's drywall had turned into deformed spines, the bulge of Lily's insulation into hunched shoulders.

He turned the hose on and let the water unfurl into the air. If he arched the hose right, it was like he was hanging a beaded rodless curtain over the sidewalk. The water droplets caught the sun and cast a shimmering rainbow. A shimmering rainbow! Way better than the garbage visions.

Sodden trash and storm-softened coils of dog shit and wet leaves were all over the sidewalk. Feeling more coolheaded now, Martin used the hose to force a candy bar wrapper over the curb and into the street. He was in the middle of hosing away some of the dog shit when a skinny guy around Ruby's age approached.

"Excuse me," said the guy. He wore an unbuttoned wool coat and a cardigan that looked deliberately threadbare. But the collar under his cardigan was messed up in a way that didn't seem deliberate, one side up, one side down, cockeyed, and for a second Martin crossed his own eyes in a surprising twinge of sympathy. For the guy or for the shirt? He couldn't tell.

"Excuse me," the guy repeated, his voice high.

"Yeah?" Martin was suddenly aware of the dust in his beard and on his hat. Grease smudges on his chin. His late-middle-aged-urchin look, Debra called it.

"Are you the super at this building?"

"Yeah. How can I help you?"

The guy seemed unsure. He looked at the gum wrapper being forced by the water to skip along the sidewalk. "Are there any apartments available in your building?"

"I'm not the one you talk to about that." Martin turned off the hose. "You need the property management guys."

"Oh."

"You want the number?"

"That's okay. Do you mind if I take a picture of the façade?"

"Sure," Martin said. "Free country." He returned to hosing down the sidewalk while the guy photographed the building. Soon 8C walked by, saw Martin, seized his arm. "Do you know if a package arrived for me? It is supposed to have arrived, Martin." 4B walked by with her child in tow, saw Martin, asked, "Do you think you could give the babysitter spare keys when I'm gone this weekend, I just can't find my spare—Martin?"

Martin answered all their questions and nodded politely at their requests. When they were gone, he looked down the street. The guy who had asked about apartments was standing there, holding his phone high above his head, where it glowed like a torch.

He returned to the basement. No Ruby still. The striker he'd stolen was a shadow under his meditation bench. The red light of the answering machine blinked at him. Frank at Sycamore Property Management. "Martin, you there? Look, we have to talk." A long pause in the message. Martin waited for Frank to say the name *Caroline*, but that didn't happen. Instead Frank said "Neilson." Neilson had called and ranted about how he had reported a clogged drain and waited days for a response. Was this true, Frank wanted to know, and didn't Martin appreciate Neilson was on the board? Was Martin actively *trying* to put his job in jeopardy? This was not a one-strike situation, Frank said, but it wasn't exactly a three-strike situation either. A two-strike situation, maybe. Two strikes and you're out, Martin. Okay?

Frank had a joking tone in the message, but he wasn't really joking. Frank could get a newer, younger Martin, pay him less. As far as reasons for firing went, a delayed response to a drain clog was a pretty ridiculous one, but Frank could find some way to spin things if he wanted, in just the way Neilson had spun things. Neilson hadn't been upset about the drain. He'd been upset that Martin had intentionally farted on his golden-threaded pillows. But "farting with intent" would be a weird thing to complain to the Sycamore people about, so he had gone with the drain delay.

Which meant Martin needed to work extra hard to avoid pissing anyone else off for a while. He needed to hope that Caroline kept the moment with the dropped stone to herself.

10 EDWARD HOPPER MEETS GODZILLA

It was dimmer out when Ruby awoke. She sat straight up. She was on an unfamiliar couch warmed by her own body, in an apartment that smelled like a fake forest of pines. Across from her, a fish tank glowed cyan. She was in 2D. The fish were still alive, drifting back and forth. Beyond the fish tank's glug, the apartment was soothingly silent, the way a museum might be at night.

But the silence in 2D did not really belong to her. Her skirt was still damp, still mustard-streaked. And she could still feel Andy's hand, inching beneath it. It would be impossible to hide out much longer, pretending the earlier events of the day had never occurred. She rubbed sleep from her eyes. She turned on a lamp. She must stop avoiding her phone.

She reached for it now, digging around in her bag, and turned it back on. Some texts from Andy. She would not look at those now. Other messages, too, from her father, her mother, Jaida from high school, Ellen from Mellow Macchiato, and Caroline from this building, Caroline from childhood, Caroline, patron of unpaid in-

ternships. She read through the messages from Caroline before anyone else's.

ruby where are you are you in the building?

*Andy called me said you STOLE family heirloom from him under
his nose???? Also gave him a nosebleed? He sent a picture . . .*

Please call back.

We can fix this . . .

Did interview go ok at least?

Look Ruby, Andy is blowing up my phone . . .

RuUuuuBeee. Rube Rube Rube. Rupeeeee.

Andy wants to know where heirloom is

Ruby I know you are there and ignoring me

Where is heirloom he is freaking out

look are you okay

She felt a little faint. Her grip loosened, and her phone fell from
her hand. It skidded under the Lucite coffee table. She flopped
down on the floor to retrieve it, but once she reached her arm under
the table, something compelled her to crawl under the Lucite surface entirely, to lay her whole body beneath it as if it were a shield
protecting her from invisible fiery arrows. The rain-damp of her
professional skirt pressed against her butt and thighs. The ceiling,
seen through the underside of the table's clear surface, turned
shimmery.

For a second, she felt like a knocked-out helpless Snow White in
a Lucite coffin, but after a few moments, it was the apartment that
looked defenseless and comatose, and Ruby who felt more awake
and witchlike, potent with secret poisoned apples. Apartment 2D
turned into an artifact behind a display glass. She propped herself
up on her elbows and pressed her nose against this new lens.

At last she scooted out from under the table and stretched her arms above her head, bouncing on the balls of her feet. She was most definitely *not* Snow White in a coma. She had taken the rhino head. She had effected change. It was important not to avoid Caroline like some scared little kid. Ruby felt oddly empowered, until she glanced back down at the table. She squinted. The table was now streaked with long foggy marks, like cirrus clouds. Her breath had smudged its spotless shine.

She went into the kitchen and opened up the small cabinet under the sink, retrieving Windex and a roll of paper towels. She would take care of this. She maneuvered her arm beneath the table and sprayed the underside with Windex. For good measure, she sprayed Windex on the tabletop, too, rubbing it in with the paper towel—maybe 2D would be so impressed when she noticed Ruby had been cleaning that she would decide to give her actual cash instead of gift cards.

The smudges remained.

She sprayed some more Windex. Possibly the magic of the solvent could only work without a human being watching? She sat on the couch again, trained her eyes on the fish. It no longer seemed like they were aimlessly drifting back and forth. They looked like they were running from something.

She glanced, finally, at the table again. And dug her fingernails into the taupe cushions. Not only did the smudges remain, but the table had also become pitted where the little shots of Windex had hit, as if some special ants had decided to build their anthill inside the Lucite.

Ruby could already hear the throaty sadness in 2D's voice as she read aloud the shipping costs and the manufacturer's bill. Ruby would say, I am so, so, so sorry, Ms. Brody, and 2D would say, Please, call me Christine. A payment plan would be decided on. Ruby would owe 2D so much money. On top of her debts. On top of her joblessness.

And what would Ruby tell her father?

Another text from Caroline. *WHERE ARE YOU.*

Am fish-sitting in 2D, she texted Caroline. *you in PH? you can come downstairs, visit if you want?*

Caroline responded almost immediately. *be right there.*

Ruby ran her hands over the pits in the table as if the pits were some kind of braille her fingertips might read. It was fine, it was fine, it would all be fine. The fish would calm her. She would speak quietly and politely with Caroline. A knock on the door. "It's open," she called out. Her own voice sounded strange to her. Another knock. She tried to stand, but her legs felt weak. "It's open," she screamed.

Caroline burst into 2D, her dark eyes comically wide, a circus act of concern. She had a different dress on, this one featuring a geometric print. "Ruby," she said, "what's going on?"

"I'm fish-sitting," Ruby said.

"Andy called me essentially in tears."

"He's a sensitive boy."

"Ruby. Be up front with me. I can't take any more drama, especially not today, which has already been weird and hectic."

"What's so weird and so hectic about *your* day?"

"The party. Getting ready for the party has been a lot." But Caroline said these words in a way that suggested whatever was really going on was entirely outside Ruby's comprehension of the weird and the hectic. She looked at Ruby's rumpled and stained professional skirt. "How was the interview?" she asked. "I've been waiting for you to text me about it. Did you rock it?"

Did Ruby *rock it*. Like Caroline was an aerobics instructor. Did! You! Rock! It!

Ruby said, "You told me it was a job."

"It *is* a job."

"It's an unpaid internship."

"An internship is still a job."

"It's not the kind of job I can take."

"I don't get what the big deal is." Caroline flopped down on the couch next to Ruby. "What's wrong with an internship? You're not even paying rent right now. You take a pay cut for a few weeks, you go to Starbucks less—"

"I don't go to Starbucks." She glanced toward 2D's gift cards. "Why do people think that I go to Starbucks?"

"My point is, you'll be setting yourself up for something sweet down the line."

"I don't have *down-the-line* time." Ruby found the strength in her legs. She stood up and closed the door to 2D, which Caroline had left gaping open. She turned on the overhead light and walked to the couch but did not sit down. She needed Caroline looking up at her in order to say what she needed to say. "I have a lot of debt, Caroline."

"You never really told me that, Ruby." Caroline looked at 2D's two fish. "I mean, I guess I knew you had *some*."

"I should have been more clear."

"But that's all the more reason to take the internship. I had a professor at school who said the ultimate problem with student loans is that they discourage people from taking on risky but valuable opportunities." The full force of her positive thinking twisted Caroline's mouth into a smile. "The kinds of opportunities that could change your life."

Ruby took a deep breath.

"And you have friends. You have to remember that. You have

family. You have people who love you. You have a place to stay. It's not that bad."

"I can't live with my parents much longer. My dad looks at me like I'm some sort of skin disease."

"Yeah, well, your dad has been having his own issues." Caroline laced her fingers together, like holding them that way was the only thing preventing her from going into full-on flail mode. "He came upstairs to fix the terrace door and freaked out at me."

Ruby went very still.

It felt like an elevator chute had formed from her brain through her rib cage. It felt like some thought at the top of her skull was waiting to descend toward the center of her heart.

"He just sort of lost it." Caroline cocked her head. "Is there a crisis or something going on? A death in the family? Because who does that, who drops a stone in someone's cup of coffee out of nowhere?"

Ruby still could not speak.

"Thank god it just spilled on my dress and not my laptop," Caroline said. "He tried to play it off like it was an accident."

Ruby began to cry. Something hot and alive had cracked open inside her. She remembered the way she'd held the broom this morning, and swung it, and how hard she'd hit that nest, and how her father had tried not to look her way after the eggs cracked open with an amniotic slosh.

A stone plopped into coffee. Somehow, now, she felt responsible—the way she should have felt, probably, when she had buzzed Lily's cousin in.

"Rubes, Rubes." Caroline reached for Ruby's arm and pulled her onto the couch. They both sank into the cushions. "I'm so sorry, babe. I didn't think you'd react like this."

"Are you going to tell your dad about my dad?" Ruby whispered. "About the stone?"

"Of course not."

"You promise?"

"I won't say anything." Caroline reached out and dabbed at Ruby's cheeks with a tissue, the same pink color as Lily's cousin's tissues, and oh, oh, she'd forgotten about Lily's cousin. Ruby cried even harder. Caroline sighed. "It's been a long day, huh? Shh. Breathe, kiddo."

"People are always telling me to do that," Ruby said. "They want me to breathe and go to Starbucks."

"What are you talking about?"

Ruby just took a long, unsteady breath.

"Listen, in your own words, what happened with Andy?" Caroline stroked Ruby's hair. "That's what I came to talk about. Not the semantics of job versus internship."

"Your friend Andy's a creep." She was shaking a little, the way she had after she'd thrown the rhino head. "What did he tell you?"

"He said you came over. He said he showed you the rhino, and you did a photo shoot, and then you hit him across the face and stole the rhino head. That rhino head means a lot to him, Ruby. He hates his whole family, except for his grandfather, and that head belonged to—"

"I know. His grandfather."

"I told him you just didn't understand what you were stealing. Right? And that you'll give it back? Look, it's an incredible honor that he asked you to collaborate with him in the first place."

Important that her voice remain quaver-free. "You don't understand, Caroline." There was that elevator feeling again, the sense of bored-out chutes inside her very bones. "He put the rhino head on my chest for the photo shoot. But when I was under the rhino head, he was kind of putting his hand up my skirt." It was like someone else was telling the story. She had stopped crying. Now her voice sounded too placid, too distant.

"*Kind of* putting his hand up your skirt?"

"I mean, it didn't go all the way up."

"He told me he made a move on you." Caroline waved her own hand as if to demonstrate the body part's harmlessness. "He told me all of this, Ruby, *and* he said he backed off once he wasn't sure where you were at."

"He didn't back off." The words came out loudly. "He was pinning me down."

"He's not that strong, Ruby. Have you seen his arms? He has chicken arms."

"The rhino head was pinning me down, too." She could feel its weight again.

"So what happened when Andy and the rhino head were pinning you down?"

"I threw the rhino head at his head before he could really do anything. That's how he got a bloody nose."

"But he wasn't trying to hurt you in the first place." Caroline rubbed Ruby's arm. "Andy and I have talked a lot about his issues with traditional courtship rituals. He's got an interest in radically undermining false sentiment, is all. Not only in relationships. You see that concern in his art, too, right?"

Ruby stiffened.

"Listen, Ruby." Caroline scooted closer. "Probably some progressive-education-teacher type got Andy to read *Story of the Eye* at too young an age and it's corrupted his conception of what flirtation should look like. But if I thought for a second he would really hurt you, or try to play some misogynistic mind games with you, I'd kill him. I'm really sensitive to this stuff. Remember when I kicked Scooter out of my party last June? But I *know* Andy. We've been friends since high school. It's a misunderstanding." Caroline squeezed Ruby's hand. "He's a superhuge feminist."

A superhuge feminist. Ruby looked down at the fat of her own arms. The waggle-bag of her biceps. Caroline was smaller and thinner than Ruby. She sat there, smaller and thinner than Ruby, yet holding her face so heavy, heavy, heavy with concern.

"You *know* I'd be outraged if I thought Andy would really try anything," Caroline went on. "I wouldn't defend him for a second."

"You're defending him now."

"No. I'm telling you the truth, which is a good truth. He wasn't going to do anything. Now you don't have to go around with the weight of feeling like a victim. I'm giving you the gift of knowing. When it comes to Andy, nothing would have happened. I wouldn't lie about that or be delusional. You're my oldest friend."

Her oldest friend. In that moment, it was as if Ruby's entire universe was made up of the shadows of all the things Caroline had that Ruby did not: financial security, an apartment, a studio, so many dresses, a clear sense of moral certitude, several boyfriends from foreign countries, a sunny, optimistic outlook that turned solemn and grief-stricken at the appropriate times. Their friendship had once seemed to stretch a great distance, but Ruby suddenly feared that if she looked too hard, if she really investigated, she would find that she and Caroline were simply trapped together in a diorama and that great distance was the work of some scientist-artist, a flat, two-dimensional rendering. Lovingly crafted, deeply illusory, a lifelike depiction of something already extinct.

She pushed Caroline away and looked at the place where

Caroline's beauty mark had been, as if the ruffle of scar was some kind of eye to gaze into. "If you don't believe me about Andy, if you're taking his side on all this, then I can't talk to you right now."

"I'm not taking sides," Caroline said. "Don't make this about me not believing you, like I'm some asshole male football coach and you're the sorority girl or whatever. I'm the one with context into Andy's life and worldview. If you just throw out accusations like that, it hurts women who really need to say something."

Ruby stood up from the couch.

"I want to help you," Caroline said. "I've been trying to help you, and it's like you won't let me in."

"Because it's not *me* you want to help. It's some idea you have of me."

"What idea do I have of you?"

This, Ruby did not know.

Caroline, too, stood up. "I'm noticing a pattern."

"What pattern?"

"Your whole problem is follow-through, Ruby. You make grand gestures and you don't think about them."

"What do you mean?"

Caroline headed for the door. "I'm getting out of here."

"Tell me what you mean."

"I'm not trying to lecture you, is the thing."

"Just say what you want to say."

In the doorway, Caroline turned and looked at Ruby. She crossed her arms over her chest. "You go to an expensive college to study some bizarre mix of studio art and art history and writing and you don't think about what you'll do afterward, you don't take internships or anything, you just work summers at that coffee shop. You move in with John—too quickly, Rube, obviously—and you don't think about if you two are really compatible until it's too late. You let a lost, scared woman into this building, you don't think for a second about really helping her, about where she'll go next. And now this, with the rhino head. You're barely touched, there's a misunderstanding, and you react by stealing a meaningful object from someone who's been through a lot in his life, accusing him along the way of what could be some serious reputation-destroying stuff, and you don't think about the follow-through, you don't even *think*."

Caroline exhaled mightily.

The oldest friends. The fish going back and forth and back. How nice it would feel to dip Caroline's head into that glowing tank, to wash her face with the fish water. That would be a grand gesture.

"Well," Caroline said, "are you just planning on glaring at me? Do you have, like, some sort of thing to say? I'll listen, Ruby, because I actually care."

Ruby pretended to think. Then she pointed to the Lucite table. "Do you have any idea how to fix that?" she asked. "I sprayed some Windex on it and fucked it up."

"Wow."

"What? You have much more expensive tables in your dad's apartment than we do."

"I have more expensive tables."

"Yes."

"That's what you want to say to me. You want to make me feel guilty because of how I grew up."

"I'm just stating the facts." Ruby smiled with enough sweetness to hit, hopefully, the nervy center of each of Caroline's teeth. "Your dad's rich. You have more expensive tables."

"And you have mustard all over your wet skirt, kiddo. Did you know that?"

"I know about the mustard," Ruby said. "I know *all about the mustard*." Still, she looked down at her skirt. The mustard stain had streaked almost the exact area where Andy's hand had crept. Or maybe it hadn't. Maybe she was remembering his touch wrong. Under the force of Caroline's doubt, her own memories began to feel like fabrications.

"You shouldn't worry about my dad being rich," Caroline said. "Worry about *your* dad being violent."

"Leave." Ruby looked up. "Get out. Okay?"

"I was already going."

The fish went back and forth, back and forth. Their bulgy little eyes like buttons now, something to be undone.

It would have been nicer, more satisfying, if Caroline slammed the door. But she didn't. She closed it like a normal guest, politely leaving a space that was not her own home. Everything in Ruby felt very hot. Her blouse was too tight. The professional skirt was wrecked with condiments. She was having trouble breathing. The table, the rhino head, Andy's hand. And then the way Caroline's own hand had fluttered dismissively in the air—that had felt like stealing, like something had been taken from Ruby. Caroline had had a short but efficient shoplifting streak in their adolescence, one that Ruby had halfway admired. But she wanted to take something from Caroline now. She wanted to run upstairs, head for Caroline's closet, take her nicest clothes and squirt mustard across all of them. She wanted to take 2D's payment of Starbucks gift cards and throw them at Caroline's feet.

How would 2D look at Ruby when she learned about the table? How much would Ruby owe her?

Her feet began to move before she was aware of telling them to go. Suddenly she was in 2D's bedroom. Its speckled beige walls gave her the sense of being inside one of the organic eggs John scrambled for breakfast. The carpet, soft underfoot, swallowed Ruby's ankles. The big bed was so plush, it looked like it could consume entire people. When 2D had sex, when someone was on top of her, did she sink into some alternative uterine mattress dimension? How could Ruby get there? She flopped onto the bed. She sank but did not disappear. No new dimension. Just this world.

She rolled off the bed. To the right of the bed was the walk-in closet. Ruby opened the closet door, which unfolded in pieces, its joints oiled into silence. No rainbow workout clothes kept in here. This space was for the articles of clothing in danger of wrinkling. The small column of dust that wafted up with the opening of the closet doors looked almost curated, the motes drifting equidistantly from one another. 2D was the kind of person who had arranged her walk-in closets so the clothes didn't touch. No silken sleeve brushed up sensually against a gown's cinched waist. No skirt hem ever grazed a pressed pant leg. Even the individual units of a pair of shoes were denied intimacy, not jumbled up but placed in a line at the closet's entrance with half an inch between heels. It was as if 2D's mission was to safeguard the personal space of each and every article of clothing.

Ruby reached out and touched the long soft sleeve of a cashmere sweater.

Those pits the Windex made in 2D's see-through table—they had actually been kind of low-key pretty, hadn't they? Beautiful, really. Like ice that had been chipped at by children on skates. Like a new constellation of stars born to a blank and glassy sky. Although she had damaged the table (plus maybe destroyed her friendship with Caroline), Ruby felt the rush of energy she usually associated with creating something or looking at art, the same rush she had felt as a kid, painting the back of a shoebox so that it looked like Central Park, the same rush she had felt in art history classes in college as some new style of stillness was projected onto the screen: a Vermeer, an Ellsworth Kelly, an Alice Neel.

She moved farther into the walk-in closet. Long black dresses that were swoopy and dramatic. Short red dresses trying their damnedest to seem effortless enough. At the very back of the closet hung a silk chiffon dress in dark blue—the color probably had a name like "dark cove"—with a beaded illusion neckline, pleats in the skirt, and on-seam pockets similar to the ones on the dress Caroline had worn this morning. The dress, hemmed to just above knee-length, seemed too young for 2D. Had she ever even worn it?

Ruby took her hair out of its ponytail and unbuttoned her blouse and removed her professional skirt and her tights. After another moment she removed her bra and her underwear, just so she could have the experience of standing naked right there in 2D's walk-in closet. Another painting plunged back into her brain: an Edward Hopper, with a woman standing naked, her curvy body lit by the sturdy linear rays of light let in by a rectangular pane of glass. He had done a few paintings of naked women alone in their rooms, but this one had hung out an especially long time in Ruby's mind. Everything in the painting that should have seemed soft—the woman's body, the morning light, the olive greens of the room and of the woman's skin—seemed strong and hard. Some of the students in class said the woman looked lost and lonely and passive. To Ruby, the woman's loneliness looked like strength, like she could step out of that morning light and, in an Edward-Hopper-meets-Godzilla moment, rip down a skyscraper with her bare hands.

Her skin still felt far too hot.

She closed her eyes, tried to keep that Hopper woman in her head. Except as soon as Ruby attempted to pin her there, she vanished. Instead what floated up was the Alaska brown bear diorama in the Museum of Natural History. In the diorama, there were two bears, one on all fours, one standing on its hind legs. But Ruby really only ever noticed the one standing up. That bear stared like it was seeing past the glass, trying to figure out what the penumbral shapes on the other side might be—predators or prey? There were almost always people gathered in front of this display, but the people looked more like shadows than the bears did, the way they were silhouetted by all the diorama's bright faux-Alaskan light.

Naked in front of 2D's closet, Ruby felt not like the Hopper woman, but like that bear standing up. Outside her diorama space, through the glass that sealed off this moment, she could make out the silhouettes of younger selves, Rubys of all ages. They watched her from the other side of the pane. They were hushed and observant and all such good girls, all so grateful for what they had been given, eager to learn, eager to laugh in the right way at the right things.

She put on her bra and underwear again. Then she grabbed the dark blue dress and stepped back from the closet, as if edging away from an incoming tide. At last she put on 2D's blue dress, which fit perfectly.

And what about shoes? She couldn't wear her own dirty, ugly flats with this clean, lovely garment. That wouldn't do for the party tonight. Yes, now she wanted to go to Caroline's stupid party, just to show John she was okay, just to show Andy that he could not scare her away, just to show Caroline what a grand gesture really looked like.

She crouched down and looked at 2D's shoes, lined up at the bottom of the closet. She pulled out a pair of sparkly ballet flats, a scalloped pattern of glittering rhinestones. She took some experimental steps back out to 2D's living room. She walked over to the table and examined the pits again. She didn't feel guilty but closer to exhilarated. There was the sign of Ruby's exhalation, now preserved in something like glass. Her error hadn't been in breathing on 2D's table, but in trying to erase her breath. She didn't want to fix the table now. Still, she could conceal the damage she'd caused for at least a little while. She moved the vintage pool balls over slightly to the left. They covered up the pits. Ruby stepped back from the table and examined her work. She squeezed her toes in. The sparkly shoes were a bit small, yes, but she'd keep them on. They didn't hurt much at all.

11 GINKGO TREE WITH GARBAGE BIRD

Martin was never completely off work—the building's demands didn't follow a normal schedule—but at five every day, if he could, he liked to go for a walk in Central Park and look at birds and trees and stuff that it wasn't his job to manage. He was in the apartment grabbing his binoculars when Ruby came home at last, her coat over her arm. She was decked out in some Academy Awards–ish silky blue dress and glittering shoes, as though she had just won something, like in one of Martin's dreams. Ruby looked at the binoculars in Martin's hands. She was glowing, but in a way that reminded him of a child about to come down with the flu. He wanted to ask her where she got that dress and those shoes, but he wasn't sure he really wanted to know, and he wanted to ask her what had happened with the job interview, but he already knew the answer.

Maybe between parents and their grown children this was normal—this little shared universe of unsaid things, largely made up of what you didn't want to talk about and what you guessed you shouldn't ask. The dark matter of familial bonds. Ruby tugged at the right sleeve of her dress, her face reddening. *Martin comforts his daughter in distress.* The Lily voice. *He has advice! He has ideas!*

Martin said, "Ruby. Breathe."

She said, "I know about the stone."

He sat down heavily on the couch, the sad cow faces on the sad cow print elongating from his weight.

"Caroline told me."

"It was an accident." He looked down at the cushion, at the curve of a windmill. "Can you tell that to Caroline?"

"She didn't make it sound like an accident."

"Has Caroline told anyone else about the stone? Other than you?"

"I don't know. She told me she wouldn't say anything to her dad."

Martin put the binoculars around his neck.

"Do you think you'd be in big trouble if she said something?" Ruby asked. "Would you get fired?"

Earlier in the day, he would have wanted to change her voice, take that wobble out, but now he was glad to hear it. It helped his own voice regain its paternal qualities, to become strong and powerful again, re-fathered. "We'll be fine," Martin said. "There's nothing to worry about." But this voice maybe was too strong, *too* paternal, and the exchange sounded less real, more like acting.

"I need to get out of here," Ruby said.

"You want to look for this owl in the park with me?"

"An owl in the park?"

"I told you about it this morning. Remember? It's supposed to be nearby."

She tilted her head to the side. Like a robin listening for worms, for disruption in the dirt. He waited. The Lily voice stayed silent, too. And then Ruby nodded. "Okay."

"Okay?"

"What am I doing otherwise? I'd just be hanging out in the basement, waiting for Caroline's party to start."

"Looking for the owl is better."

"Yes," Ruby said graciously, in a dream-come-true, winning-all-the-awards way. "You're so right, Dad. Let's go."

They headed toward the main path of the park, winding down Terrace Drive. Cold out, but not freezing, the sky gauzy with purple-blue clouds and the sun just starting to sink. According to the people on the birding e-group, the owl should be near the Ramble, an especially woodsy area of the park, where the rarer birds and crazier people often went to sing to themselves. The owl had last been spotted just past the Bow Bridge. But Martin and Ruby didn't head right for the bridge. First Martin leaned in to look at the hedges near the perimeter of the park. He raised his binoculars to his eyes. The chill pricked at his fingertips, exposed in his fingerless canvas gloves. "There's a white-throated sparrow," he said. "By those two trees? You can tell by the yellow marking around the eye."

"So why don't they call it a yellow-eyed sparrow?"

"Ha ha. Can you see the bird?"

"Yeah."

"Can you see the marking?"

"Not really."

He held out the binoculars to Ruby.

"That's okay," she said. "I believe you. About the marking being there."

Of course, they both knew it wasn't a matter of believing, it was a matter of *seeing*, of spotting the specificity for your own damn self. But Martin let her comment go and they stayed motionless together, watching the sparrow. Sparrows found homes all over the city, of course, not just in the park. They turned street signs into perches, built nests in the tubing of traffic lights. Still Martin found himself watching the more common birds—the pigeons, the sparrows—as if they were rare. With the rarer birds there was a pressure to appreciate their presence in that moment. The sparrows and the pigeons were not just abundantly beautiful but abundant. It was easier to look on them and to feel real soaring awe as opposed to the heavier, guilt-tinged am-I-supposed-to-be-feeling-something-more awe.

Still, how much would it rule to see that owl? It would redeem this shit day, somehow. Stupid Frank from Sycamore and his stupid Frankian threats. He wished he'd farted way harder on Neilson's pillow. He wished he'd eaten those pigeon eggs that Ruby destroyed and farted the gas from the pigeon fetuses on the most golden pillow Neilson owned.

Compassion! Okay! Empathy extended to all life in this moment of time! He cleared his throat. "I'm sorry about the internship."

Ruby crunched her sparkly shoes on the dry leaves.

"What about working at a coffee shop again?" Martin asked. "A different coffee shop? Or a restaurant? At least temporarily?"

"Everything I do is always temporary. I guess I'm looking for something a little more serious, maybe." Her phone buzzed in her bag. She swallowed. She said, all loud like she was talking to someone hiding behind a tree, "I want a job that's more real. John was always telling me the coffee shop thing wasn't real."

Martin started to speak, then stopped himself.

"What?" Ruby asked. "Are you going to tell me something passive-aggressively Zen? Are you going to say that nothing is real? That the temporary is the only constant? That coffee is as real as anything else?"

Martin lifted the binoculars to cover his face. Actually, he had been going to ask her if she thought what *he* did was real. But the words got snagged up in his windpipe and he coughed. He pretended to spot movement low down in the leaf litter. "See that?" he said. "Some sort of thrush, I think."

"Can we keep walking?"

It was so quiet out. Later, in the warmer part of spring, noisy warblers filled the yellow forsythia bushes lining this path. Nothing like that now. In the silence that descended between Martin and Ruby, Martin wished for warblers and their calls. He wished for the Lily voice, even—but she never showed up when he was outside the building.

When they reached the pond, Ruby saw something in the reeds and said, "Look." The bird just feet from them. A black crown with long white plumes extending from the back of its head. It was the first bird she'd spotted before him in a while. A surprise upwelling of paternal pride like a barometric pressure shift inside his lungs. A change in the atmosphere created by his own deep, joyful exhalation.

"It's a black-crowned night heron," Martin said.

Having in his head the exactness of the name somehow made the bird itself seem more exact. Easier to notice its markings, the place where the feathers turned purple gray, the green muck from the pond on the webs of its feet. The night heron began to extend its neck toward the water. Martin reached for the binoculars, intending to hand them to Ruby, but the bird must have noticed the movement of his arm. It took off.

"Cool," Martin said in a happy, hushed way. Ruby put her hands in her coat pockets. In the reeds in front of them floated a pair of mallards. A rustling sound from the bushes. A bird, a rat, a mugger?

Nothing emerged, but Martin said, "Let's keep moving." The street-lights had switched on and were reflecting in the dark water behind them, like glowing columns from a ruined temple lodged in the bottom of the man-made pond. Or like the streak of white on the great horned owl's throat.

No owl yet.

They passed benches and birch trees and very few people and kept walking until they reached the much-filmed Bethesda Fountain with the bronze angel statue in the center. "I saw a bunch of starlings here the other day," he said. "Screaming at each other over a hot dog. They're my least favorite bird. They're not even native."

"Nothing is native to the park," Ruby said. "It's man-made. They razed one of New York's first middle-class black communities to build Central Park. Lily told me that."

"What do you mean, she told you that?" Martin looked up hope-fully. "Like, recently?"

"Well. Not super-recently. Obviously. Maybe a couple of years ago?"

He scratched the back of his neck.

"What is it?" Ruby asked. "What's wrong?"

"Sometimes I hear Lily's voice," he said. "In my head."

"You hear her voice?"

"Just in my head."

"Like, a grief thing?"

"I guess." Martin looked away. "Her voice is really clear."

"I wish I could hear her voice like that," Ruby said.

"No," Martin said. "You don't." A group of tourists passed them, holding their phones up in the dimming light. As they got farther away, their silhouettes faded, until only the glow of their phones could be seen.

"Dad," Ruby said. Then, very gently: "You were telling me about the starlings."

"Right. So, the starlings were released in the nineteenth century by the American Acclimatization Society." Martin tried to speak a little more loudly, like a tour guide. "I learned all about this from the birding e-group. Basically, these people decided they wanted Central Park to contain every bird mentioned in Shakespeare's plays. And starlings show up in one of the plays as some metaphor for mimicking abilities. So it's this beautiful plan, right?"

Ruby's phone buzzed again.

"Except then the starlings spread across the U.S., taking over all the tree cavities where other birds had nested."

"Let's keep moving, Dad."

"Am I being too Dadly, with my facts?"

"No, no. You're allowed to be Dadly. You're my dad."

He wanted to hug her. He was her dad.

"I see something!" Ruby cried. She pointed to a tree. A still and hulking shape. The owl? The breeze blew and the shape moved. Not an owl at all. Just a black plastic bag caught in a tall ginkgo. Featherless but flapping hard as the wind picked up. He thought Ruby would look disappointed, but she smiled. She said, "Lily used to call those garbage birds."

Lily. Something about the way she said the name, the childish nostalgia, made Martin suddenly angry at and worried for Ruby. What gave her the confidence to cry out like that, to be so sure she'd spied something alive and special? Her phone buzzed once more.

"You can check your phone," Martin said. "I don't care."

"You sure? I thought this was some sort of sacred father-daughter bonding endeavor."

"We're not at the movies or anything."

Ruby looked at her new messages. Her breathing went so deliberate, so regular, it was almost as if she were rearranging her own respiration, figuring out a pattern of breathing that would best display calmness. It seemed fake to Martin, this calmness, like a mask for some new horror.

He could be Dadly. He had her permission. He reached for her hand and took the phone from her. "Stop," she said sharply.

Too late. He'd turned the phone around so that he could see its screen.

The last message she'd received was a photograph. Of him.

Of Martin.

Of Martin alone in front of his building, his beard in pixel form a little burlier than in mind's eye, more grizzled. No pedestrians obscured him. It was a clear, clean shot, as if the photographer had lined up the phone so that the other people walking down the street were relegated to the sides of the photo, forming its borders. A pile of garbage bags clumped in the background. The innards of Lily's apartment. Martin was hosing off the sidewalk around the garbage bags. His arm, moving, a partway blur. His back was stooped, but he held his shoulders like he was trying to hide that hunch, an undercover Quasimodo. His eyes unfocused, sad. The photographer had zoomed in so much, Martin could make out the streak of plaster on his hat.

Beneath the photo, a series of messages. He scrolled down.

This your dad, right?

The super at the building where Caroline grew up?

has your eyes.

He was nice. I asked him if there were open apartments in your building.

Think I might use this pic for my next show . . . Good composition, right?

What do you think of the composition, R?

No words from Ruby, not on the screen, not in person. He scrolled up to the photograph again. Why was he always so worried about his translucent chest? He looked old and crusty, like his whole self had been filmed over with layers of dust and grime and shit.

"Dad," Ruby said. "Give me back my phone."

"What is this?"

"It's you."

"You know what I mean. What *is* this? Who sent you a photo of me?"

She switched her weight from one foot to the other.

"Who sent you a photo of me?" he asked again.

"This boy I kind of know. He takes pictures of homeless people. Addicts. Fringe people, he calls them. He puts the pictures in galleries."

"Do I look like that? Like a fringe person?"

"No," Ruby said, very quickly. "He only took this photo of you to screw with me. He thinks I stole something from him."

A fringe person. It did not take much. A hurt back. A plaster-streaked baseball cap. If he threw the phone down, would it break? Would Ruby cry out?

"He's just a stupid boy," Ruby said. "He's trying to intimidate me. Forget it. It has nothing to do with you."

Martin shook his head. "This is exactly why I didn't want you to move home. I've got enough adult babies in my life with the tenants."

"You're being a jerk, Dad."

"I'm being honest, finally, is all. You're a grown child, Ruby. This is embarrassing."

Ruby turned away. No face to her, just tangled hair and voice. She said, "I'm glad I let her in." She paused. In that stupid dress, in those stupid shoes, it seemed she paused for theatrical effect, not fear, not shame. "The woman. I buzzed her in and I'm not sorry at all."

"Who?" Hoo, hoo, hoo. He tried to think about the owl.

"Lily's cousin."

The woman from this morning.

"She clearly left the building pretty soon after I let her in, so don't get all pissy at me." Ruby looked up at the garbage bird. "I just didn't think it was right. You were like, oh, Lily's cousin, great, back to the gutter with you. It was disrespectful, Dad, what you did. It was gross. To the woman and to Lily, too."

There was a rat in the bushes. A rat like any of the rats in the building, but outdoors, so it was fine, it wasn't Martin's problem. Still, as it scuffled nearer, he thought of its scent trails. He'd read about them in the rodent-trapping how-to book. Rats produced little bursts of urine to remember where they had been, where they had safely traveled. It would feel good to put traps down now. He wanted to catch this rat, to bring down his foot right here, to end its trail of piss and memory.

Finally Martin looked at his daughter. "Well, great work." He clapped his hands, the sound dulled by the canvas gloves. "What a hero you are."

"I wasn't trying to be a hero," Ruby said. "I was just trying to do the right thing. I was trying to behave like a human being. Unlike you."

It was ridiculous the way a *feeling* now could look expensive. A certain kind of righteousness was like wearing diamonds. But he saw it for what it was, the morality she was parading around in, thinking she was being fancy, while no, nope, she was dressed in something cheap, something worthless.

"I was wrong before," Martin said. "You're not acting like a child. It's worse. You're acting like a tenant. You're acting like an entitled trustfundian fucktard."

Which was ranked number one in Martin's worst insults for a person. Definitely his chest was translucent now. Pure glass.

"Dad." Ruby's voice cracked.

He said in as measured a tone as he could manage, "Go." He handed her back her phone. "I need you to leave me alone right now. Go play with your friend Caroline."

Ruby's face went dark, then seemed to empty out entirely. She walked away, back up the path they'd come from. Martin did not allow himself to follow her. He did not allow himself to move at all.

NIGHT

12 THE CIRCADIAN RHYTHMS OF THE STREETLAMP

Hahaha ok I get what you are doing
   you not responding Ruby . . . ???
   wanna hear where I will put this picture in the show?
   yr dad will be placed next to this guy I took photo of this guy named
dennis
   wanna hear about what dennis did Ruby to end up without a place
to live
   where is rhino head
   also look please understand
   it is My invaluable heirloom
   when I say heirloom not just some diamond loony tunes shit that the
evil guys steal
   and it's seen as like a caper
   it's not like that it has emotional weight to me
   Ruby?
   I know you are there
   it's not like that listen
   it is from my grandfather he left it to me

my grandfather was the only one in my whole family w any goodness
was v kind to me encouraged me to pursue art
said it was brave and not being a pussy at all but the opposite
ask Caroline she knows this story too and what the rhino head
means
to me
he was a good man, Ruby. surely someone you love has been lost
right
and left you something
even just memories
then imagine if you let someone into your home and then that some-
one takes that thing/memories and won't tell you where it is hidden
soOoOoo
where is it.
come on that was a fucking moving metaphor thing right.
haha
I know you see this.
here's what dennis did.
let me tell you about the man your dad's photo will be next to

When Ruby left Central Park, she planned to return to 2D. She intended to rip the blue dress off her body and hang it back in the closet. It would look, dangling there, like a thing that had never been touched. She would kick off the shoes and put on her own shoes once again. She'd watch the fish for a while. Then Ruby would take her cell phone and drop it in the fish tank. And see what happened next.

But when she got to her father's building—the specialty bulb she'd installed was glowing—she found herself strolling right past it, as if she didn't grow up there, as if it were just a building like any other.

She needed to keep moving forward.

She walked past corner delis and shoe stores and Fairway, past a concrescence of brown bananas in a crate. She walked past a woman looking for bottles, a black trash bag tied like an apron around her waist. She walked past brownstone after brownstone with basements housing who knew what animals. Where was she headed? She began to realize it in her thoughts after she'd already begun to realize it in her feet. The Hudson River.

On her way to the river, she passed a church doorway where a thin guy with dreadlocks slept beside a pit bull terrier. All of a sudden the pit bull snorted and the skinny guy turned over. Ruby was sure he was going to see her standing there, gawking at him, she was sure he was going to say something to her, curse at her.

But when he turned over she saw that he was wearing a black sleep mask.

Lily had a collection of sleep masks, even though she never flew anywhere and the shades on her windows were thick. One of the sleep masks was just plain black silk. One was covered in paisley. One had the elongated orange tubes of an owl's eyes. One of the sleep masks was bright pink and had *NAP QUEEN* written across it in a floral cursive. When Lily napped, she snored. Her snore sounded like a voice, a high and nasal whine.

Her father had been hearing Lily's voice in his head.

Ruby walked faster.

A streetlamp shone through a garbage can's crosshatched gridding so that its pattern was projected onto the sidewalk. On a lobby window, a bright yellow sign advertised Mandarin lessons for pre-k students in the neighborhood. Every Monday, Wednesday, and Friday, from ten in the morning to twelve thirty in the afternoon, right near where Ruby was walking, the temporal lobes in a bunch of new brains would be endeavoring to distinguish tones. She could almost sense the residue of that cerebral striving in the air.

Ahead of her was Riverside Park. The Hudson's salty-muddy stink gave her a small rush of joy. She wanted to get as close as she could to the river's stench. Once, when they were in high school, she and Caroline had walked down to the Hudson to have a picnic on the pier. It had begun to storm and the girls had taken their container of hummus and their soggy sandwiches and their pita chips and thrown them into the river. The food hit the Hudson with a fwap-fwap-fwap. "A sacrifice to the stinking river gods!" Caroline had hollered to the Hudson. She and Ruby had held on to each other, bent over with laughter, soaked.

Ruby imagined dropping herself into the water now—not exactly in a suicidal way, but just in an effort to get closer to that wonderfully awful smell. The river would be so cool. Its water would taste like sewage and soaked-through pita chips. Its fish would sweetly drift. There would be no pane of glass or fish tank separating Ruby from them. They would nibble at her toes, maybe. Try to swim inside her head to get at all the juice in there. Her own thoughts and organs would go diorama-still and the fish would be the only life left moving.

Her father had looked at her in Central Park like she was nobody he'd want to know.

Ruby walked down the pier. In the summer, this place was full of people talking, dancing, fishing. In March, it was pretty quiet. Her legs felt like they were about to give out. Near the end of the pier, a bench had been placed beside a streetlamp that hadn't

turned on, even though it was dark out. Its sensor system was probably broken, its streetlamp circadian rhythms were off, or maybe its
bulb had just burned out.

She plopped down on the bench. From out here the George
Washington Bridge looked not like a powerful pathway, but like
lights on a string. At an adjacent bench, a jogger stretched.

Then the top of the streetlamp started to move.

What had seemed like part of the streetlamp, like structural or-
namentation, was actually darkly iridescent feathers: a perched
starling. Disturbed out of its nest, maybe, and awake. Ruby envisioned flocks of roosting birds that looked like the material stuff of
blue scaffolding or torn garbage bags or oxidizing scrap metal. What
if everything that she'd dismissed as inanimate was alive in this sort
of way?

She kept looking intently at the starling. Her stare caused the
jogger to look intently, too, to seek out what she saw. A woman
walking her poodle saw the jogger, paused, and glanced over at the
streetlamp.

A chain of close looking could start here with Ruby. They might
bring the whole city to a standstill if they looked hard enough at
what was thought to be a common bird. They might, all together,
change the way people saw.

The bird called out, and then it went very still again, and Ruby
wanted to make something. A sound or a sculpture or a diorama.
After a few more moments, the bird flew away. Then the dog-
walker departed and the jogger jogged past, and Ruby looked down
at her own empty hands.

A new feeling buzzed in her. She had made that woman with the
dog stop and look, too. Ruby had done that. The sense that she had

figured something out about the city, or at least something about staring at things in the city, lured her into fearlessness. She took out her phone. Many new messages from Andy.

All i want is my property back ruby.

I can go to great lengths to get my property back.

But! I don't want to go to great lengths.

I knoooow you are there . . .

I know where you live ruby, and your dad

She scrolled back up to the photo he had taken of her father looking sick and old, like a man lost. Like a man without family.

So compassionate, the people in the gallery would murmur. Her father's image a part of Andy's spectacle of empathy. *So tenderly wrought.*

No. She could still have the last word. She had untapped power. She had just changed the way a group of strangers saw the world around them! True, she had only changed their perceptions for a moment, but a moment could be everything. People lived inside nothing but moments.

Her father had taught her that.

She texted Andy back: *I'll see you at Caroline's party and we shall talk!!*

He wrote back: *Great!!!*

13 AN EIGHT-FOOT JUMP

After he'd told Ruby to leave him alone, Martin spent several hours walking park paths lit by streetlamps. There was a time not so long ago when walking alone in the park at night would have been extremely stupid. Now it was only mildly stupid. He walked all the way over to the east side of the park, to the Conservatory Water, where in a month or so New Yorkers would begin racing intricate model boats. For her eighth birthday, after reading *Stuart Little*, Ruby had begged for a model sailboat. "We don't have the money right now for a model sailboat," Debra had said, "but this building has plenty of approachable rats for you to befriend."

"Stuart Little isn't a rat, he's a mouse," Ruby had said, and began to cry.

He kept walking, past the Alice in Wonderland statue, the Met, the Great Lawn. He told himself he was looking for the owl, but mostly he was thinking about how the branches above his head teemed with hidden inhabitants. Mites and sleeping squirrels, and the squirming, ever-wakeful fungi that ate through the heart space of trees, creating cavities where other things could live. When he reached the Reservoir, he leaned against the fence and looked out at the dark water. Although it was almost eight, joggers ran past him. Was Debra at her banquet now? He called her. She picked up right away. "How was the panel?" he asked.

"It's tomorrow. Where are you?"

"I'm in the park."

"Did you take Ruby out for dinner like I suggested?"

"Not yet." He couldn't imagine eating food. His stomach hurt.

"Go take her somewhere."

"Where?"

"I mean nowhere fancy but somewhere."

"The Chinese place she liked shut down. It's baby clothes now. It's boutique baby clothes now."

"You'll figure it out. I've got to run to dinner myself."

"We're kind of fighting. Ruby and me."

"God. Martin. I said just for today, could you try—"

"She let the woman from this morning into the building."

"She did what?"

"She just told me. She let the woman into the building. Lily's cousin."

"Are you serious? Is she still in the building?"

"No," Martin said. "Ruby said the woman left pretty soon after." But Debra's question gave him pause. Suddenly he wasn't sure. Ruby had said the woman had left, but what did Ruby know? When Debra hung up, he walked for a while longer. "Do you have any change?" a voice near him said, only it felt less speechlike than like a scrabbling against his inner ear. Martin didn't turn to look at the person, but the voice chucked him out of his trance. It was night, and yet still, still, he wasn't off work. He had to play hide-and-seek.

The intruder might possibly be gone, as Ruby had suggested. But now something told him she was still around, and Martin had learned to trust his instincts when it came to building issues. The building wasn't alive, exactly, but after twenty-plus years taking care of it, Martin had become half convinced that even brick and drywall and marble tile had their own patterns of respiration, their own heartbeats. It sounded romantic, put like that, but it wasn't. It was scary as fuck—this idea that the structure he lived inside, watched over, was sentient and that maybe in certain ways it watched over *him*. Maybe in certain ways it spoke out.

Especially when something was off.

And something in the building was off. Ruby had thought the woman had left, but even after a childhood there, Ruby didn't understand how many nooks the building held. This whole day, the intruder had probably been so close, roaming around, cursing Martin under her breath. And in some respects, the idea of her possible presence was a huge relief—it might explain away Martin's anger today at Caroline, at Neilson, at Ruby. The vibrations in the building had gone awry because someone who wasn't supposed to be there had snuck inside. Now that same person could get away with all sorts of mischief—theft, assault, who knew what—and Martin's daughter would be blamed. Which meant Martin would be blamed. How was this possibility not clear to Ruby?

Martin was not a jogger. But a new urgency filled him and, although his legs were already tired from the long walk, he began a sort of jog across the park. By the time he had reached the building, he was sweaty and stinky and his knee was twanging and his heart was going crazy in all the ways he'd been trying to prevent. Still, he did not even stop for water. He began his search. He looked for the intruder first in the basement, starting with the laundry room. No humans in there, but plenty of clothes moving around in the dryers, sweater sleeves flailing outward, trying to escape the centripetal force. He went next to the storage room, which was filled with open metal cages that apartment owners rented. They kept their skis there, their papers, their piles of legal stuff in clear plastic bins. Some of the cages were taller than others. Sometimes tenants became very upset if they got assigned an eighty-one-inch cage instead of an eighty-four-inch one.

When Martin stepped into the storage space, the lights were off, but his entrance had unnerved some darkness-loving life. A rustling sound. Human? Rat? Scared, whatever it was. "Hello?" he said into the specific storage-room quiet, a wistful silence produced by unused skis dreaming of packed snow. "Hello?" So stupid. Skis did not dream! Skis were not wistful! They were wood. Or whatever. They were like the floorboards of 5A—dreamless, long dead, and oh, shit, he was letting himself think in the same dangerously sentimental way that had caused all those rich men to release starlings into the park leading to the death and displacement of songbird after songbird. The same dangerously sentimental way that had caused Ruby to buzz the intruder into the building in the first place. He wanted to hang up her plan for a diorama of Lily's apartment, the one that had TOOOOO SENTIMENTAL O WELL scrawled across its borders. Those poor displaced songbirds. They must have gotten hungry. *He* was hungry. Some dizziness, a fuzziness to this darkness. He hadn't had dinner. Power through. He'd find the intruder, he'd kick her out, and then he'd eat.

He flipped the light switch defiantly. Fluorescent beams flickered. Just clutter in the room. He walked down the line of cages, peering around large piles of papers. The Lily voice was silent, but the rustling sound was back. Then he saw it. A rat, just a rat, which scurried from one wall to the next and disappeared.

The intruder was not there.

Next, Martin went to the small closet-like room given to Rafael, where he kept spare brooms and mops and floor cleaners. Theoretically, the intruder could have slipped in there at some point in the day—Rafael often left the door unlocked. The door opened with no resistance when Martin pushed. He hadn't been in this room in some time, and when he stepped inside and switched on the light, he gasped. His first thought upon seeing the cluttered desk, the tower of books, the phalanx of lamps, was that Rafael had converted this place from what had been an extra-large utility closet into a scholar's den, a room redesigned for intense pondering and to-be-or-not-to-be-ing.

But the closer he looked the more he saw something bigger at play. This was not just a study: It was a gallery space for garbage that Rafael had found and morphed into something grander than itself. To Martin's right, a series of broken umbrellas had been arranged on the wall like spokes in a color wheel, red umbrellas fading to orange umbrellas changing to green umbrellas to blue and to violet and black. Tiny miniature cars and dinosaurs moved between a series of textbooks that had been stacked on a shelf into a skyline of buildings with spines advertising statistics lessons, beginner biology. An ancient basketball hoop hung over this book city, its net yellowed like a sagging sun. Several cutting boards were mounted to the wall and served as picture frames. Onto each one had been pasted a photo of Rafael's baby and wife.

But no intruder.

No intruder except Martin. He wanted to sit down on the floor of Rafael's storage space. It would have been nice to spend time in the universe of trash Rafael had given order to. He ran his hand over one of the cutting boards with a photograph of Rafael's baby beaming out and holding a stuffed rabbit. Ruby had beamed out at Martin like that once. But he shouldn't think of her, or of their fight. He was not done looking for the intruder yet.

Martin took the elevator up to the ninth floor. Once, a few years back, on a cold day, a very skinny man had snuck in and made it past the foyer. He had gone to the ninth floor and fallen asleep on the stairs that led to two doors. One of the doors went to the penthouse apartment, though Kenneth rarely used the stairway entrance since the elevator that opened into the penthouse was so much more convenient. The other door went to the roof. Martin probably would have gone a long time without discovering this intruder if he hadn't been delivering newspapers that had arrived late in the morning. His shoulders had jumped when he saw the skinny man, wrapped in a Little Mermaid beach towel. The man had gotten up, rushed past Martin, and left the building without another word.

He called into the ninth-floor stairway, "Hello there?" A twang to his hello, like he was trying to be folksy. Folksiness wouldn't scare the intruder, nor would it draw her out. He tried again, a little gruffer. "Hello?"

No response.

He climbed the stairs until he stood between the two doors. Caroline's party had started. The music through the door to the penthouse sounded like thumps and nothing more. He stepped up to the door that led to the roof, the door he would open tomorrow when it was time to clean up the bottles. Through its glass window, he saw a girl with green hair climbing the water tower. Although it couldn't be long past the beginning of the party, Caroline's guests were already crawling around the roof. They weren't supposed to be doing that, but they always did. They wandered around drinking, taking photos, doling out their truth-or-dares.

Martin entered the code that turned off the alarm, opened the security door, and stepped out into the cool of the evening. "You aren't supposed to be here," he shouted. "Get back in the penthouse or get out."

The green-haired girl, halfway up the water tower ladder, scuttled down again. "Sorry!" she called. "Oh, *sir*, I am so sorry! I thought this was Caroline's property!"

"It's the building's property. Get back inside."

Laughing—at Martin, at each other?—the group wandered toward the glow of the penthouse. Martin walked under the water tower. No intruder. He scooted behind the penthouse's walls, trying not to get tangled up in cable wires. The adjoining building wasn't as tall as Martin's building, and so he peered down to that lower roof, just in case the intruder had somehow made the crazy leap and hurt herself. What was it, an eight-foot, ten-foot jump?

Just black tar. Nobody down there. For a second, Martin thought about leaping himself. How amazing it would be to bound from roof to roof, mountain goat of a man, a basement dweller defying gravity to do his own dance across the skyline. But even an eight-foot jump could kill him, or mess up his back for good. He was far too old for this kind of thing—not just too old for jumping, but too old to fantasize about jumping, or skyline-dancing, or any of it. Oh, that dangerous sentimentality was back again.

Still, could he be blamed for a little sentimentality right now, a little lyricism? The lights of the city were glowing like a dream. The bright windows like electric stitches, forming a seam that turned the night into a sewn-up thing. *The super on the rooftop turns into a bad poet, searching for a seam in the sky when he is supposed to be searching for an intruder.*

But she was not up there. And he had looked everywhere.

Maybe his instincts were off after all. Maybe it was just as Ruby had suggested. The woman had made her way to 5A, seen the mess of demolition and dust, and simply wandered outside once more, into the chill of the day.

Back to the basement. The apartment was empty again. Post-park, where had Ruby gone? He checked his cell. Nothing. But his answering machine was blinking.

Another message from Sycamore, could be. Maybe Caroline had gone ahead and said something to her father. Maybe Martin was fired. He brought his hand close to the little arrow of green on the answering machine. Go forward, play, play.

He stepped back. There was still one place he hadn't looked. He dreaded searching that room more than he dreaded searching even the ninth-floor stairwell. A whole host of memories and terrible imaginings got kicked up every time he went in there. But he had to do it.

Martin left the apartment and walked to the elevator-motor room.

The motor room, all these years later, still felt like the most haunted part of the building, more so even than 5A. What if the girls had touched the machines at the wrong instant, or what if they hadn't sung "I Am the Cute One" loudly enough? Martin, in his nightmares, had pictured it many times. Putting in the code, opening the door, finding the hurt or lifeless bodies of Ruby and Caroline. Was it unhealthy to be haunted by an almost-loss? An almost-loss left space for the imagination, which was usually more terrifying than reality.

He entered the code into the number panel on the motor-room door.

Nobody.

But as Martin watched the wheels spinning in there, he felt like maybe someone was pulling them, like it wasn't electricity that moved the elevators, but invisible spirits yanking on pulleys, pushing forward complicated gears. He called Debra but she didn't pick up. She was at her banquet now, a party not exactly like Caroline's party, but not all the way different. He needed to hear her voice, to see her face and to feel he was in the presence of a beloved clock, something by which he might properly measure time. His legs felt like stilts, sticks of bone and flesh that Martin could hardly balance on. How had he been stupid enough to run across the park? He managed to stumble out of the elevator-motor room, into the garbage room again.

Could be what he feared most was not that Ruby would never move out of the basement, but that in staying the odds increased that she would one day find Martin, find him the way he had found Lily—dead and disgusting. Then she would have to go around for the rest of her days with this soul-knowledge of what her father looked like in death. The dark mess of his failing heart. To carry that image around like a painting hung off the ribs, always. He tried to breathe and couldn't. His throat was parched. No rhythm of wet/dry now. Despite the rain earlier, the air seemed scorched, brittle. He sat down between two garbage cans. He breathed in deeply, tried to summon the image of himself full of strength, leaping between rooftops, bouncing back from even an eight-foot leap. But he was so, so tired. He closed his eyes, as though about to begin some brand-new meditation.

Lily's voice filled the garbage room. *Martin, stand up. Martin Martin stand stand stand.*

He was supposed to be looking for the intruder. She was near, he could tell she was so near. The walls between himself and the intruder were thinning, close to dissolution. Between the apartments, too, the boundaries between one person's home and the next—all seemed to waver. The walls in the place where he worked and lived were vanishing.

14 RHINO HEAD

Ruby spent a while in Riverside Park after texting Andy, watching joggers go past, and then, since she didn't want to wait at home for the party to start and risk interaction with her father, she had gone to a Starbucks. If money wasn't an issue, she would have gone to a neighborhood diner, but it was better not to spend what she didn't have. So she let the gift cards guide her. She bought the largest and most sugary latte she could find on the menu, and a gigantic cookie, making fast work of one and a half gift cards. After waiting on line for the bathroom, she found herself a spot by the window and read Lily's diorama book again—she had wanted it close by even after the non-interview, and still hadn't taken it out of her bag. Then she fielded a few crazy texts from her mother. *Dad said YOU LET WOMAN FROM MORNING IN??? R we will need to talk tomorrow but your dad works hard and you are making his life harder.*

I'm sorry, Ruby wrote, *I'm sorry, I'm sorry.*

Mostly she looked out the window and tried to work up her courage. She was wearing a dress that didn't belong to her, and shoes that didn't belong to her. She had transformed herself into someone who could own her anger. This was not a grand gesture. She would see this act all the way through. She would make sure Andy deleted the photograph of her father. She ordered another latte. Some of the people around her were working on their laptops, but some, like Ruby, were clearly waiting for something to open up in the night, waiting for the dark to become more cavernous. At last, around nine thirty, when she decided she would be fashionably late, she slurped down the sugary dregs of her drink and headed back to her father's building.

There was nobody in the foyer. In the lobby, a couple of tenants were exiting the elevator, on their way out for the night, new people she didn't recognize. They didn't give a glance to Ruby. She stepped inside the empty elevator and pressed *PH*. The doors closed and as she rose to the penthouse, she practiced what she'd say to Andy when she confronted him. Under her breath she said, over and over, "Delete the photograph of my father or I will tell everyone what you tried to do. Make that photo vanish, or else." She attempted a fierce smile in the elevator's mirror. The smile seemed too stretchy, too tight, like dental floss. She put her hair into a ponytail to see if a stretchier-looking forehead might help balance out the smile's proportions. It was no good. Only two floors before Caroline's, she decided to take her hair out again, to let it fall down her back.

Better. Looser. She unbuttoned her coat so the illusion neckline of 2D's dress could be seen. The elevator rose up, up, up. Then the doors juddered open and Ruby was at Caroline's party.

Music was playing, or an almost-music that sounded like a group of monks stuck in a computer and desperately trying to Gregorian chant their way out—deep male voices punctuated by electronic beeps and trills and clicks and sometimes whistles. A clot of girls in gauzy dresses stood by the elevator, their fingers crooked around wineglass stems. Nobody she recognized. Ruby had to say "Excuse me" for them to part and let her step onto the apartment's wood floors. She hated the first few moments of any party, when familiar faces had yet to register and her lungs struggled to adjust to the party's altitude. She didn't see Caroline.

After hanging her coat on top of another coat, and her tote bag on top of another tote bag, she craned her neck and scanned the room, listening for the jangle of Andy's tinny voice through the other voices striking her ears. "The screenplay," said a girl, "parallels the perils of hookup culture with the economic recession." Some guy rambled about the killing to be had in patent portfolios and some girl discussed job placement statistics and some other guy impersonated Werner Herzog or maybe that was just how he spoke. Ruby found the table with the wine and poured a glass of red.

At the far end of the living room there was a table full of snacks—and John. He wore his usual: dark jeans, a button-down shirt. Leaning against him, muttering something into his ear, must have been his new girlfriend, the one in public health. She was cute, polished, pixie-cutted.

Ruby did not want to talk to John or Miss Public Health, but she was suddenly so hungry that the migration to the other side of the room seemed worth it. Keeping her head down, she was able to reach the snack table without John noticing her. There was a stack of white paper plates on the table. At first she thought maybe they only looked like paper plates and that when she lifted one up, it would prove to be made of marble, part of Caroline's *Expendables* series. But nope, the paper plate was just a paper plate. She avoided the snack table's slices of apples, the healthy-looking crackers, the pomegranate seeds, and instead gathered up cheese cubes and cookies. Ruby ate the cookies first—they were incredible, crumbly with the weight of their chocolate chips—and by the time she started on the cheese cubes, the elevator doors had opened and shut and there he was. Andy had arrived.

He immediately began talking with the dress-clot, but his eyes darted around with the frantic to-and-fro of a clown fish. This suggested, perhaps, that he was afraid. If she got close to him, she'd smell his fear, and some prehistoric limbic-system sense of dominance would be activated in her. Maybe Ruby, on inhaling those fear pheromones, would really become strong and powerful and alpha.

So Ruby walked right up to Andy, who separated himself a little from the dress-clot when he saw her. Around his neck was his camera. She inhaled in a nonmeditative way, and said, "We need to talk. Outside."

"You're here," Andy said.

He did look a little scared, a little sweaty. She made herself as tall as she could. "Duh, I'm here. Thanks for letting me know, Captain Obvious."

Captain Obvious? She sounded like a preteen girl trying to figure out how to be just-toeing-the-line sassy to her mother. She didn't sound confident or breezy or brave or fierce. Stupid, stupid, stupid. She could feel herself deflate. Andy seemed less unnerved now. His eyes stopped darting, settled on Ruby's face. "Where would you like to talk?" he asked.

"Outside."

"You said that already, Captain Obvious." He smiled, disguising the contempt between them as a game, a flirtation. "But outside where? Outside the building? On the terrace?"

"Yes. The terrace." She had to gain back her edge. "Here. Hold these." She handed Andy her wine and plate of snacks before he could protest. Then she walked to the hooks and shrugged on her coat. She took the snack plate and the wineglass back from Andy, tossed her hair over her shoulders, and slid open the terrace door. A gust of wind blew up the skirt of 2D's dress, not in a completely Marilyn Monroe–ish way, but enough to shock and expose her a little. Ruby smoothed the dress down quickly. On the left corner of the terrace two women were smoking. Most of the guests were inside because of the cold, but the temperature drop somehow made the view more spectacular than she had remembered. A ribbon of bright lights.

Andy stepped outside, too.

Another gust blew past and Ruby's hair flew behind her. She recalled what Andy had said the last time they were at Caroline's party together, when they first met—how the wind out here sounded like all the female opera singers in this city belting out arias. Ruby took a sip of wine, then put her glass and snack plate on the ground. She thrummed her fingertips against the terrace railing, listening for those arias. "Well," she began. But she'd forgotten what she had planned to tell him, all the operatics of her furious commands and threats.

Andy said, "I'm honestly a little shocked that you would agree to meet me here."

"I'm not scared of you." Another not-great comeback. *I'm not scared of you* made her sound like a deep-down terrified schoolkid in a horror movie. She tried the stretchy-fierce smile again. The two smokers glanced over at them.

"Ruby," Andy said, "I think we need more privacy."

"Don't mind us," one of the smokers said, and winked. But Andy hopped over the terrace railing, clambered down onto the roof.

"I want to talk here," Ruby called after him.

"Well, I want to explore. Come on. You just said you weren't scared of me, right?"

The smokers both laughed. The woman with green hair said to Ruby, "He's not *un*-cute."

Andy was already walking away from Ruby on the roof, circling toward the water tower. Ruby bent down, picked up her glass, and finished her wine in a few gulps. She put the empty glass back on the ground and picked up her snack plate.

"You should go with him," said Green Hair. "It's really beautiful and quiet out there. Explore the roof."

"Go have yourself an *adventure*," said the other girl, and the two laughed again, as if the word *adventure* was an inside joke they lived in together, some shared home where they could retreat to cackle.

It would be nice to stay there and try to live inside a laugh with those women. Instead Ruby lifted the skirt of her dress up with one hand, holding her snack plate full of cheese with the other, hopped the railing, and followed the bop-bop-bopping motion of Andy's puny head. He was moving toward the edge of the building. When Ruby caught up to him, Andy said, "It's a view, I guess." He gestured to the skyline, the lights blurred with mist. Then he put a hand on her shoulder. "Here's the deal. The deal is I won't press charges, despite the fact that you assaulted and robbed me after I invited you into my home."

Ruby stepped back so he wasn't touching her. She placed her snack plate on the ground again and glanced back at the terrace. The smokers had gone inside. She said quietly, "You attempted—"

"What? What exactly are you saying I attempted? Do you have a bruise? Any sign of damages? I've got a large welt on the side of my head."

"Because you attacked me."

"No. Because you threw an heirloom at me and then stole that heirloom. I can show you the welt if you'd like. Also I have lawyers on retainer. Do you have lawyers on retainer?"

The tiny headlights in the distance moved very slowly. For a moment, she imagined herself in jail, her mother sadly lending her books. More of Ruby's new boldness and resolve floated away.

"You do not have lawyers," Andy said. "But you have a nice dress, I see. And better shoes than earlier. Did you steal your outfit, too? Are you on some kind of spree?"

"Where's Caroline? If Caroline could hear how you're threatening me—"

"If you bring me the rhino head back, I won't make any phone calls," Andy said. "Not to law enforcement. Not to any members of any boards of any buildings. And I'll delete the photographs I took of your father. I won't use them in my shows or sell them, even though I *could* sell them. There's a lot of pathos in those images, you know?"

Something in Ruby felt knifed. Maybe *this* was what John had called a hate boner.

"We can forget we ever knew each other," Andy said. "We can forget each other's names. Just get me the head of the rhino."

Get me the head of the rhino. Like some fairy-tale task issued by a despotic ogre. Which would make Ruby what? A hero. Or a beautiful and resourceful peasant. A secret princess.

"I can't get you back the rhino head," she said.

"Why not?"

It began to drizzle. The silky skirt of 2D's dress and the sparkly surface of 2D's shoes became speckled with raindrops. She bit her lower lip. "The rhino head is gone, is why. It's art. It's evolved. It's part of a piece I did today." Her words didn't seem to be changing his mind at all. He stepped close to her again.

"It's not art," he said. "It's property. I don't know what dry-macaroni project you're using the head for, but my grandfather left it to me and it's mine."

Property. The word clarified things for Ruby again. What she had experienced in Andy's basement was supposed to have been an exchange. He was here threatening her, and yet they'd had a deal! "How about me?" she said. "I mean, how about my money?"

"Your money?"

"You said it was an artistic collaboration. You said you'd pay me if you took my photograph. Well, you took my photograph. Over and over again. And you took a photograph of my father, too. So where's my money? That money is *my* property."

Andy walked away from her and looked over the edge of the roof. They were on the side of the building that shared its wall with another, shorter building. The fall was long enough to seriously hurt. He turned to face her again and said, "You are not a model, Ruby. And you are definitely not an artist. I don't need to give you anything, because you are a thief."

The wind picked up. Anger had warmed everything but her toes, which felt frozen in the sparkly shoes. Was she an artist or a thief? Could she be both? Tonight, at least, those questions seemed like part of someone else's agenda. She didn't care about the answers. She cared about the way the wind was growing stronger. She cared about how, when she lifted her hand to brush her hair out of her eyes, Andy flinched.

As if she might be raising her hand to hit him.

An astonishing thing to realize—that he truly was a little afraid of her.

She took a step forward. "I want to get out of here," she said. "I really, really, really want to leave Caroline's party. But I'm not going to leave without being paid for my work and I'm not going to leave without a guarantee that you will delete that photograph you took and not bother my father or me again."

"Are you actually trying to bargain with me?"

She took another step forward. Their bodies were very close.

"Or are you throwing yourself at me again?" Andy said. In a high-pitched voice: "'Oh, I'd just love to see your basement!'"

"I never said that. And I'm not throwing myself at you."

"So what are you doing?"

She thought about it for a minute before she reached for his left pocket. She said, "I'm taking your wallet."

"Right."

"I'm taking the money you owe me. You said you'd pay me if you took my photograph."

"You need a mint," he said. "Your breath smells like cheese."

Why had she been worrying he'd push her? She could easily push *him* off the building here. He would fall onto the lower roof, hard and fast. He was little. She was taller and stronger than he was. She could lift him up. If he fell right, if he fell just the right way the ten feet down on that little neck—

Wow. Yes. Definitely a hate boner. It felt good, powerful.

Andy reached forward and gripped her wrist. She ripped her hand away, groped around in his left pocket, found nothing but some old rolling papers, a receipt. He stopped resisting, but kept his eyes trained on her. She pinned his left hand behind his back. He said, "Go right on ahead. Go on and steal my wallet. And see what happens next."

"Here is what happens next," Ruby said.

He put up no resistance when she tried the right pocket. "You know I can't fight back," he said. "Physically, I mean, I won't fight you. I don't hit girls."

"You're such a gentleman," Ruby said. "You're a prince among men."

He was shaking now. It was not just the cold. It was the way she had pushed him. The camera around his neck moved up and down, he was breathing so fast. She had the funny feeling that if she unscrewed the lens cap, his heart would be right there, pulsing behind glass. He would not test his strength against her, she realized. He would make this decision not for chivalry's sake, but for fear of failure. Here Ruby had an advantage on him. Over the course of this day, she had become an expert at failure, had grown so skilled at self-made disasters that she had lost some of her dread of them. She had failed as a daughter today. She had failed as a candidate for a job. She had failed as a house sitter. And she had failed as an oldest friend.

There was nothing in his right pocket either.

"Go right ahead," Andy said, and though he was still shaking, he spoke as though unfazed, like his steady voice didn't belong to his quivery body. "I won't tell anyone. Confirm everything I've said about you. Prove me right. Thief."

She put her hand down the back pocket of Andy's jeans. Because his wrists and arms were so bony, she was surprised to realize he had a butt, a dorsal softness. She shoved her hand down the other back pocket of his jeans and found the wallet there, as well as his phone.

"Think about what you're doing here, Ruby. Think about who you're stealing from."

She opened his wallet.

Now Andy's eyelids blinked: Click, click. Ruby's dolls had

blinked that way if their eyelids got a little stuck. When that happened, the key was to give the dolls a good shake. But before she
could do such a thing, Andy's nose began to bleed for the second
time that day, even though she hadn't hurled a thing at his face up
here. She stepped back and opened his wallet, removing the cash, a
whole bunch of bills. She didn't even glance at the IDs or credit
cards. He would cancel them as soon as she was out of sight. She
ripped them free of the wallet and tossed them off the roof. It
would have been more dramatic if they had fallen the ten stories.
Instead they fell onto the adjacent roof.

"Jump down there," Andy said. Blood had beaded at the groove
beneath his nose. "Jump down there immediately and get those
cards, Ruby."

She held out the locked phone to him. "Delete the photograph
of my father."

"That photograph has nothing to do with you. It's my art. It's not
yours. Just like the rhino head isn't yours."

She leaned back and hurled his phone off the roof. Even just
falling to the next roof down was enough. The phone broke with a
crack.

"Wow," Andy said. "Nice work. It's going to be so much easier
now to convince Caroline that you've been behaving like an insane
woman. There's the proof."

"You know I'm not insane. You tried earlier—"

"I was just trying to make you feel better, Ruby. If you had been
clearer about what *you* wanted . . . I was just trying to make you feel
desired, and you repaid me by stealing from me."

"Bullshit." She shoved the cash from the wallet into the little
blue pocket on the dress. Then she threw the wallet at Andy's feet.
She leaned in close. "You won't tell anyone about me taking this

money or tossing your phone," she said, "not just because I told you not to tell, but because you'll be too embarrassed by your actions. Okay? You'll be too embarrassed by how you treated me." She leaned down and picked up her snack plate, which was now slightly wet from the drizzle of rain. She put all the remaining cheese cubes in her mouth, chewed loudly, swallowed, and breathed hard into his face, trying not to look at the red line beneath his right nostril. "And you should be embarrassed. You should be ashamed. Besides, it's my money anyway. You owe me so bad."

Andy didn't say anything. He cupped his bleeding nose with one hand.

"Stay here." She tried to think about robberies she'd seen in the movies. "Don't go inside until you count to, I don't know, five hundred."

"I don't want to be in that apartment with you anyway. You better be gone by the time I go back inside."

She started to walk away.

"You're an idiot!" Andy crowed after her. "This wallet is worth a hundred times the cash you took!" He lifted the empty wallet up and waved it in the air. "It's made out of genuine shell cordovan leather!"

She called over her shoulder, "Count to five hundred, okay?" And then she thought of asking Lily to count to five hundred the time she took Caroline to the motor room. She shivered a little and began to walk more quickly away from Andy. When she hopped over the terrace railing, the skirt of the dress caught. She pulled at it hard. Now there was just the littlest tear in the fabric, but she didn't mind. Let the dress rip. She refused to spend her night trying to protect 2D's dress from harm.

Back in the penthouse, Ruby ate three crackers very quickly. She glanced around. No sign of Caroline. Maybe she was in the bathroom. Maybe she was out getting more snacks. Maybe she decided to ditch her own party. Yet this was still Caroline's party, whether or not she deigned to show up.

That was the beauty of being Caroline.

A glutinous glob of cracker had gotten trapped near the top of Ruby's gum. She swung her tongue up there, got the glob, swallowed as hard as she could. Then, just as she grabbed her tote bag, John sidled up to her, like she was a horse he was afraid to spook. "Ruby," he said. "Can we talk?"

The last time she'd seen John after spending time with Andy, she'd been struck by how superhero-ish he'd appeared in comparison. Tonight she didn't see much of a difference. John was taller, that was all, and his face was redder. But he and Andy looked at her the same way. Like she owed them more than she would ever realize. Oh, maybe she wasn't being fair to John.

Or maybe she should go through his wallet, too.

He stood between her and the elevator. "We can talk for about three hundred seconds," Ruby said.

John, in his most infuriatingly calm tone: "We're going to talk for however long we need to talk. Caroline called me today."

"She called *you?*"

"She said you're spinning out. I thought maybe I could help."

"You thought you could help."

"Well. Caroline suggested I could help. If I said something. And I do feel slightly responsible."

"Whatever Caroline thinks is going on with me, it has almost nothing to do with you."

He looked a little insulted. "I can't help but think I gave you a lot of support during our relationship, Ruby. And now that support is gone. That would destabilize anyone. It's totally understandable. It doesn't make you weak."

"Aren't you seeing someone now?"

"Kind of. But I still don't want to see you lose your mind."

"It's been at least three hundred seconds."

"Caroline told me about the whole internship-job-confusion thing."

"Oh, great. Do you have professional advice for me, too?"

"Yes. I think you should take the position." He crossed his arms over his chest, like he was issuing a command. "Is it too late to tell them you've changed your mind?"

"You're not my career counselor." 2D's dress seemed to be regressing into some older version of a dress, its bodice becoming lined with whalebones, constricting Ruby's breath. "All through our relationship," she gasped, "you acted like my career counselor."

"I just wanted better things for you."

"That's exactly it. It's like you were always wanting *for* me, never just wanting me."

"Just because something sounds pithy, Ruby, doesn't mean it's true."

"You're being dismissive."

"*You're* being dismissive."

He would not be able to see her point. And was it really her job to educate him on her feelings now that they'd broken up? No. She didn't have to do that any longer. Their relationship had been like one long mutual unpaid internship. They had each felt slightly exploited, but they'd also each hoped the experience would help them achieve something greater in the future. "John," Ruby said, "I need to go." And, to her surprise, she reached for his hand and she shook it. "Tell Caroline I'm not spinning out," she said, and then she walked around him toward the elevator.

She was done. She had shaken John's hand and now she should shake herself loose of this place and these people for good. She should find people who looked at her and didn't see all her past debts to them, nor her future potential. She should find people who looked at her and saw what was there, present, before them. She hit the call button and tucked her hand into the dress's blue skirt pocket to make sure the cash was still there. It was. The elevator doors opened and she stepped on. She had eaten so much good cheese, she had scared Andy, and she had money now. The doors closed on Caroline's party. Ruby, descending, felt just a little rich.

15   PLASTIC BAG

"Martin's dead!" A darkness all around. "Martin, are you dead? Ohgodohgod. Martin?"

At first Martin thought it was Lily's voice informing him he had passed on. But no, too nasal. He opened his eyes. Neilson towered over him, the handle of a plastic shopping bag around his wrist. Martin was slumped between two trash cans in the garbage room.

"I'm okay," he said. He took a moment to process his own weight, to make sure he wasn't himself a ghost. "I'm okay."

"Holy crap, Martin. What happened?"

"I passed out, I think. Or fell asleep. Maybe I forgot to eat enough today."

"Here," Neilson said, "here." He reached into his sweater pocket and pulled out a power bar. The bar seemed to be made of cardboard and granola clusters. Martin ate it all.

"I'm so glad you're okay," Neilson said. "Is the food helping?"

Martin nodded. He at last began to stand. Neilson rushed forward. But Martin did not take his outstretched hand. He got up on his own.

"I heard you called Frank about me," Martin said.

Neilson's forehead shone. "I should apologize, my brother." He smelled like he'd been drinking. "I don't know why I called. It had something to do with when you said . . . Well, you implied . . ."

"That I purposefully farted on your meditation pillow."

"Right. That. Something inside me got out of alignment." Neilson shook his head. "No. That's being too polite. I was pissed. That you would do something like that, just to make me uncomfortable. So I called and complained about the drain." He moved the shopping bag from his right hand to his left. "The farting was a triggering thing. Karla and I lived together ten years and never farted in front of each other. It's bizarre. You can cohabitate side by side with each other and not . . . share this thing with each other. This smell. Isn't that weird?"

"That is weird."

"Do you and Debra—"

"Yeah, sometimes. It happens. You eat a fatty meal. Or gluten, on accident. And it happens."

"If it hadn't seemed so deliberate, what you did, I wouldn't have made that call."

"I understand," Martin said, because Neilson was a tenant, because he must seem understanding.

"But still. I shouldn't have said anything to Sycamore. I act rashly. Karla always used to say that. Too rash. That's why I've been trying to get back into the meditation thing."

"You have the right to complain." Martin rubbed his temples. "Everyone in this city has the right to complain. That's why so many people come here."

"Are you in real trouble?"

Two strikes, Frank from Sycamore had said. Martin had not

listened to the message that had been left for him while he and Ruby were in the park. The message was about the second strike, maybe. If Caroline had said something to her father, well, then. Then.

Another wave of dizziness.

But this was what he had been training for, right? He breathed with as much intent as he could muster. He tried to experience the moment, the texture of the rising dark, and as soon as he attempted to watch it, feel it, the darkness vanished and the world around him became crisp and clear. He didn't collapse this time.

"I'll be fine," he told Neilson. "Don't worry." When he saw Neilson's shoulders relaxing, Martin found his shoulders doing the same. Moving his shoulders downward felt, at first, a little like pushing a heavy rock. Only there, yes, they were sinking. Both men breathed out.

That was when Martin noticed the plastic shopping bag handles cutting into Neilson's wrist. Neilson's eyes followed Martin's, moved to the plastic bag. "I came down here originally to throw this out. There's a rat in it." He looked up at Martin again. "There was a rat in my apartment."

Martin nodded. "With all the construction going on in the neighborhood, I'm not surprised. But you got it?"

"I wanted to call you," Neilson said, "but I thought you'd be mad because I called Sycamore. It was under the fridge. I heard it. So I got glue traps like I've seen you do. I've learned from you, man. And I caught it. But I couldn't . . ."

"Take the final step," Martin said. And then, trying to make it sound like a joke, "Literally the final step. Right? The fun ole squishy punch line."

"I couldn't do it." And now Neilson focused his gaze on the floor.

"So I kicked the glue trap and the rat into this bag." He jostled the bag a little. "And I tied it."

The air stank. Not from Martin. From all the garbage. He wanted to step outside into the courtyard, to leave. *Martin escapes into the cool March air.* But he didn't move. He stood there.

"You let it suffocate." Martin spoke as neutrally as possible. Neilson nodded.

"It suffers more that way."

Little red spiders inside the whites of Neilson's eyes. He plopped down on the floor of the garbage room, the very spot where Martin had passed out. "I fucked up so bad today, brother."

"No, no." Martin squatted down next to Neilson. "Get up, okay?"

"I ratted you out and then I killed this rat so slow, so slow. God. It's like this karmic pun. And I pretend I'm . . . Like that I'm mindful of . . . Here." He dug his wallet out of his back pocket. He tried to give Martin a hundred-dollar bill. "How I acted today was just so shitty. Just take the money, okay? Take your wife and kid out for a nice dinner. Karla liked the Thai place on the corner. Karla used to say . . ." And Neilson was sobbing, his chest heaving, his shoulders scrunched nearly around his ears.

"Here." Martin reached for the plastic bag. "I'll throw this away."

But Neilson shook his head. "The more I think about it, man," he told Martin, "the more I don't think it was right. I suffocated this creature and now it's going to be left to rot with all the garbage of the building? No, no, I've already fucked up by this rat. I need to do better, Martin, man. There's a mantra for this, something to do with karma and the creatures of the universe big and small, the ecosystem of the karmic forces, it has to do with—"

"Okay," Martin said. "Chill. Breathe. We gotta throw the rat out.

Let go of the bag. That's the first step. Neilson, listen, what else would we do with it, man, but throw it in the trash?"

"Burn it," Neilson muttered into his kneecaps.

"Burn it?"

"In the boiler room. Toss it in there. That's more respectful, Martin."

Toss it in there. Martin tilted his head. His legs hurt. He could stop squatting and sit down on the garbage room floor with Neilson. Or he could stand up and look down at the top of Neilson's head.

He stood up. His knees cracked like the pop-pop of bubble wrap. "You've never been to the boiler room, Neilson."

"No."

"What do you imagine it's like? You think there's some big incinerator?"

Neilson didn't speak.

But Martin knew. Neilson was picturing some kind of hellscape, a pit of fire. He thought that was what the basement must contain. Neilson probably imagined himself stepping into the boiler room and tossing the rat bag into a smoldering, sulfuric vat as easily as tossing bread crumbs to a group of ducks.

"Come with me, Neilson," Martin said. "Bring the rat bag."

He hadn't searched for the intruder in the boiler room. Martin knew no one would sleep in there, hide in there. As he expected, when he'd opened the door to the boiler room—nobody. But the room sounded like it was mobbed with people. All sorts of machines were running and roaring: The house pumps, the bladder tank, the blower on the boiler and the burner on the boiler, a motor pumping oil, a motor pumping air, the sump pump going *errrrr*. The room itself was a big hollow place, all bricked up, so everything echoed until it was nearly orchestral. The sounds muffled Martin's own thoughts, his intentions, which made him so mad. He was tired of Lily putting her voice over his thoughts, and of the building putting its sounds over his thoughts, and of listening so hard all day long, translating the demands and anxieties of one tenant to the contractors, then having to express the contractors' demands and anxieties back to the tenant. He was tired of Neilson and the way Neilson was in charge of generating their mantras, shaping their meditation sessions, while Martin was simply the quiet student.

Now here he was, in the bowels of the building, or in its heart, or *somewhere* important. And he wanted his own voice to be louder than the machine music around him.

He and Neilson walked past the water pumps, and down a few steps, until they reached the boiler. Through a small window in the boiler's side, Martin saw the fire leaping up within. "Where's the door on the boiler?" Neilson asked. "Can you unlock it?" A swift urge to strike Neilson. No, not strike. *Make contact*, the meditation teacher had said. What if Martin turned his own voice into a kind of singing bowl, changing the vibratory frequencies in the air? He cleared his throat. He said, "There was a flood in the boiler room a few years back."

"Martin," Neilson said, jostling the plastic bag, "where's the door?"

"The sewage had backed up and there were at least six inches of wastewater," Martin said. "The plumbers told me they'd try to fix it but they didn't show up, so I called the fire department who came by and the fire department said what the hell, that all piss water in there? Said they'd like to pump it out but they weren't allowed, and eventually the plumbing company sent Fred, the Jamaican guy, and he fixed it."

When Neilson tried to respond, Martin cleared his throat again and asked, loudly, if Neilson had noticed that big old rusty steel beam near the tank, and before Neilson could reply, Martin said, "That was the framework from the old days when they used coal to heat the building. The coal would get shoved down a chute into the tank room, a lot of ash you'd put on the hoist, and haul up onto the street, and the boiler itself, maybe you noticed this, but the boiler itself is connected to really big steam pipes, the steam pipes have been in the building since 1911 when it was a coal boiler, which builds a fire slow, they have really big pipes, and the pipes are really too big for this oil boiler that the building has now, but the coal boiler pipes are used anyway, and if they were constructing this building today, they'd put in much smaller pipes."

"Martin—"

"Once a week," Martin said, "I come in here to clean the oil burner filter, or sometimes more than once a week when the heat is going heavy. We use heavy oil, number four oil, tar, real thick. So thick that in the filter, you get chunks of tar. To scrape the filter clean, I use this chopstick I got ten years ago from China Fun. You remember China Fun? It's boutique baby clothes now. That's fine. China Fun's food wasn't great, gave me the runs once, bad lo mein. But right, so, oil and wood are interesting. For years I used a China Fun chopstick to scrape out the tar chunks. The chopstick has turned from white cheap wood into this beautiful dark and burnished pretty thing. From years of using it on the oil filter. I think the oil must be good for it, because otherwise you think it'd break.

I'd show you the chopstick but it's in my office. I keep it in a coffee can, with a brass brush and a little thing of WD-40."

"Martin—"

"The filter itself is smaller than a coffee can. There's a clamp on the top that you spin and a small round lid you unclamp and you reach in there, right, and there's a little brass basket with a handle on it, you pull out the basket and let the oil drip back into the container and then you take it to the garbage can and clean it out. It's pretty, too, the filter is, because brass is pretty. Everything else down there in the oil tank is black and dirty and then you take this filter, it's all full of junk, but you clean it out and hold it up to the light to make sure the holes are clear, and it's old, too, the filter, it's the same one that we've always used, for decades, but when you hold it to the light after it's cleaned, it's really beautiful."

"What's your point, Martin?"

Martin walked Neilson to the back of the boiler, where there were two metal plates, each about two feet by one. "You see those plates?"

Neilson nodded.

"You'd take off the lower plate on the back of the boiler. There are about twenty bolts on it, so you need to remove each of those bolts. Which would take a while. You need tools. That would give you access to the fire chamber and you'd throw your rat in there."

"Okay," Neilson said. "I get it. The boiler room isn't as simple as it seems. I can't just toss the rat in there."

"No."

"Why couldn't you just say that?"

Why couldn't he?

Because he wanted his voice to reverberate a little longer in Neilson's mind. Because the boiler room was not a simple mantra.

Because his life, his daily routines, were not as uncomplicated as they seemed to Neilson. Because the boiler room wasn't a hell, or at least it wasn't *only* a hell. There could be beauty in it and stories to tell.

Neilson fidgeted with the plastic bag. Its handles were wrapped around his fingers and the tips had turned white. Suddenly Martin remembered the time he had just returned from Montauk with Debra, their anniversary, and one of his rare trips away from the building, at Debra's insistence. Ruby had been messing around in the garbage room while he was away, stealing from Rafael's pile. When he returned and took her to the front of the building where the bottle pickers lined up—a probably overdone effort to show her why messing around in the garbage room wasn't her place here in the building's cycle of trash—she'd been carrying a plastic bag, like Neilson, gingerly, nervously, as if she did not want Martin to notice. Which of course made him want to ask what was in the bag. But he didn't, he had respected her space, just like Debra would have asked him to do, just like a respectful paternal figure should.

But now he wondered if she, too, had asphyxiated a rat that day, and had been ashamed to tell him because she'd realized the suffering she had caused. Oh, Ruby. He was hit by a wave of love for his daughter, who had been mortified, who had carried a bag with a dead rat all the way upstairs and said nothing while her father lectured her. She was, in her humiliated foolishness, behaving not like a child that day (as he'd believed then), but like an adult. Aware of the suffering she caused.

Martin took out his phone. Reception in the boiler room wasn't great. Still, he got a weak signal, and he texted Ruby. *I'm sorry. I was harsh in park. dumb ole dad. come home soon.*

After he sent the message he looked at Neilson.

"What?" Neilson said.

"I think we should meditate."

"Here in the boiler room, Martin?"

"Here in the boiler room, Neilson." Martin sat down. And to his surprise, Neilson sat down, too, on the floor, which was dirty and hard. Martin was leading their meditation session! "Stay present," he said, over the sound of the machines. "Stay present." They closed their eyes. They breathed in and they breathed out. Lily said not a word. Somehow, he'd silenced her.

Ruby had said Caroline wouldn't tell about the stone, but Martin knew better. Of course Caroline would say something to Kenneth. She wouldn't be able to help herself. When Caroline's father called to check in, when she heard the familiar tenor of his general concern, she would feel the need to speak specifically, to share the distress Martin had put her through with the coffee, with the stone, and she would say, "Dad, here's what happened." Martin did not blame Caroline for wanting to tell her father about her day.

Soon, he would go back to the basement apartment. He would check the message he'd neglected on his machine. Maybe the message had nothing to do with the stone in the coffee. Or maybe the message was exactly what he feared. It didn't matter. His action would be the same. He'd press play. He'd let a voice out of the answering machine and into his mind.

He breathed in. He breathed out.

He wondered where Neilson would end up dumping the dead rat and then he wondered where Ruby was. As quietly as he could, he took out his phone again. Neilson did not even open his eyes. His eyelids were veined and paper thin, about as veined and paper thin as Martin's. Why had Martin convinced himself that Neilson's eyelids were so much smoother?

He texted Ruby: *But really it is getting very late. Where did you go after our dramatic park fight haha. Did you go to the party? Are you ok? did you get food today bc I forgot until very late and got dizzy and almost fell but I am ok.*

16 UTOPIA

Ruby sat in Utopia diner near the subway station. It was well after eleven at night and she was eating strawberry pancakes with Andy's money. No, her money now. Each pancake bite tasted better than the last. Her mouth stung from the syrup's sweetness. She ate everything in front of her and then she ordered more pancakes, with blueberries and a scoop of ice cream this time, and a coffee refill. There was a man reading a newspaper at the counter, and a middle-aged couple talking in a booth near the back. "I just didn't think it'd be *that* crowded," the woman said. The sky was dark enough that Ruby's own face reflected in the window, a pink swatch of forehead mirrored back at her, dimming her view of passersby.

When Lily took Ruby to Utopia as a kid, they played a game where they'd look at the people on the street and give them names. She looks like a Jody, he looks like a Daniel, that kid looks like a Sue. A game of classification, really. When her second round of pancakes arrived, Ruby had the impulse to name all three of the pancakes, too. But instead she looked up at the waiter—an old man with a dark brown spot in the white of his right eye, Angelo she would name him—and asked for extra butter. He put three small packets of butter before her. Then he looked at her harder and put two more packets down. She slathered the butter across the pancakes' soft warm faces. She watched the butter and the ice cream scoop melt.

Her phone buzzed and buzzed. All of a sudden, like a Greek chorus of concern, the non-Carolines were texting her en masse. There was a party here, a brunch thing tomorrow, a new coffee shop opening up and looking to hire, wasn't Ruby still searching for a job, didn't she want to grab a drink soon?

She couldn't bring herself to respond.

And after pancake number five, she realized why.

Because she was leaving them.

There had been more in Andy's wallet than she had initially guessed—several hundred dollars—enough cash to get on a bus and go somewhere else. She wasn't sure where she was going, but what seemed clear was that she needed to get out of the city. She would go somewhere with cheaper rents and work off her debt and she would be okay.

The man at the counter rolled up his newspaper. When he left, Angelo looked at Ruby and said, "We're closing soon." He gave her the check.

"I'm almost done." She pointed to the remaining scraggles of pancake.

"You're too young and cute to be here alone," Angelo said. "I mean that not in a creepy way. I mean, are you doing okay?"

"I'm doing great," Ruby said.

"Me, I'm very old, so it makes sense that I'm still here." Angelo gestured out the window. "You know that park? By the subway? What would you call that place?"

"Verdi Square," Ruby said.

"Good for you. So you know its name. But I knew it when it was called Needle Park. Crime, crime, crime. They made a movie about it with Al Pacino! You know him or are you too young? *The Panic in Needle Park*. Amazing, right? When you look now?"

"Amazing," said Ruby.

"Amazing! Needle Park! Right there. Then they open this diner and call it Utopia. The only Utopia in all of New York City. That is what I heard. The only Utopia in all of New York City, right next to Needle Park. Now, every other hair salon, it's called Utopia Hair Salon. Utopias everywhere. But we were the first in this city."

"Is that really true?" Ruby asked.

"Now there are no needles in Verdi." The waiter did not seem to hear anything other than his own voice. "Now there are just butter-cream cupcakes with one bite taken out of them, yes, no needles, only cupcakes and Utopias all over." The waiter shook his head slowly back and forth. "Crazy! Well! Are you ready for the check? Because we're closing. You ready?"

"I'll be ready in a minute," Ruby told him.

Ghost stories of gentrification. What people here said to spook each other. *You or your favorite bagel place could be next.* To spook each other or, sometimes, to connect. She wanted neither to be afraid nor connected right now. She simply wanted to leave.

She would go to Port Authority first thing in the morning and figure it out. Maybe she hadn't even wanted to work on dioramas. Maybe she hadn't cared about building or restoring them. This whole time maybe she'd just wanted to live inside them, to make her home in frozen moments. In her tote, still, was the book she'd stolen from Lily. She took it out to see if examining the images might change her mind, cause her to want to stay. But instead of paging through it, she looked out the window again at Verdi Square.

When Ruby was a young girl, her mother had instructed her not to make eye contact with strangers passing by. Watching people from the window relieved her of this anxiety—pedestrians usually didn't stare back through the glass at you. They were entranced by their own momentum.

The neighborhood didn't look too dirty now, but it also didn't look too clean. Probably there were still quite a few needles in Verdi Square. Definitely there was still trash. A grocery bag tumbled past. A man hulked next to the M7 bus stop with an expression that suggested he was somewhere else entirely and wouldn't be getting on any bus anytime soon.

"It's after midnight," Angelo said. "Officially. We're closing."

The couple in the back got up and left, the man saying to the woman, "What I didn't understand was the ending."

"I told you. It was too crowded."

They left. "Miss," Angelo said. "Are you listening?"

Her father had texted her a little while back. He forgave her. A little show of benevolence. Now, with Angelo standing over her, she replied to her father's text with a smiley face. After midnight. She should go pack her things so she could get an early bus out of Port Authority. She paid for her meal and she headed home.

But when she neared her father's building, she paused, and then, for the second time that day, she veered. Not westward to the river's stink. She walked uptown instead, watched the numbers of the city streets climb, still dizzy with her theft, with the money in her pocket. The shoes of 2D clacked loudly down the street, rubbed part of her right heel shiny and raw. The pain didn't feel bad, was just a different kind of heat to warm the bones. Yes, there was a new openness inside—some part of her seemed as if it had been excavated to make room for a different horizon. As if the moment she'd taken Andy's money, she'd paid for a secret lobotomy and now her brain had a view. She'd given the waiter at Utopia what she thought of as not a big tip, but a handsome tip. *Old man, bearer of pancakes, I shall reward ye handsomely.* Yes, she was a secret princess, a concealed heroine this whole time.

When she reached the steps of the Museum of Natural History, the cart and the rhino head were nowhere in sight. She had not expected they would still be out here, but it was good to know for sure. She could not return the rhino head to Andy now even if she'd wanted to. Which was fine, because she didn't want to.

At the top of the museum stairs was a guard, a young woman with short hair, smoking and checking her phone. She would keep out visitors. If Ruby went up to her now, she would say, *Come back during the day. We're closed.* A powerful person in her way. She put out her cigarette under her shoe. Ruby stared at the guard, hoping she'd start a chain of looking again, like she had at the pier. But nobody else passing on the street looked at the guard and the guard didn't even grant a glance to gawking Ruby.

That weight in her bag. The diorama book. *Behind the Glass: A Chronicle of Habitat Dioramas.* She'd been carrying it all damn day.

She walked a couple of avenues west to the St. Agnes Library branch, and she pitched the book into the gleaming metal return box, where it dropped like, what, a stone? No, like exactly what it was: like an old book. A large stubble-faced man on the street whistled to her. "I'll stamp your library card tonight," he said, which didn't even make any sense, and Ruby said to the man, "That doesn't even make any sense." She added, "Fuck off," and was surprised she had said all the words not under her breath, but loudly, with eye contact. "Cunt," the man said, in an almost sweet way, like she was a pancake he was naming.

She turned and began to walk south again, and the man didn't follow. She wanted to be in pajamas, out of this dress and out of these shoes. She wanted a few hours of heavy sleep before she left first thing in the morning.

When she got back to the apartment, her father was standing in the middle of the living room. At first she thought he was staring at a small cockroach making its way across the wall. But no, he was staring at the answering machine. It was blinking red.

"Hi, Ruby," Martin said, not moving.

"Dad. I'm sorry. About everything."

"It's okay. It's fine." He pointed to the answering machine. "There's a new message. Well. Not that new. It's been here for a few hours, I guess."

"You don't want to listen to it?"

He shook his head. He said he and Neilson had meditated together for a long while and he was feeling too Zenned out for bad news. Also, the rats were for sure back, infesting the building again, and he'd have to figure that out, he'd definitely have to deal with the situation, but he hated killing rats. "I never told you that before, did I?" her father said. "How much I hated killing rats?" Then he sat down on his meditation bench.

Ruby lifted her hand. "I'm going to play the message. Okay?"

"I already know what it is."

"How do you know?"

"I just know, I'm in tune with the energy of this place, and I *know*, and I'm feeling good, like, except for the rat thing I'm grooving. I led the meditation session, Ruby! And I don't want to ruin how I'm feeling quite yet."

"You think Caroline said something? I told you she wouldn't."

"You did tell me that." He sighed. "You're right. The message is probably just about a package."

"Or it might be the exterminator."

"Or it might be a wrong number."

The light kept blinking. She stepped forward and she pressed play.

The message was from Frank at Sycamore Management. Frank was half screaming into the phone. He had, yes, received a call from Kenneth, who was on vacation but who had talked to Caroline, and Kenneth was outraged, so outraged that he'd contacted Sycamore right away. Kenneth had said something about Martin threatening Caroline with a rock, throwing the rock at her, and did Martin actually want charges to be pressed, could Martin call Frank back immediately, did Martin know what all this meant?

The blinking light earlier had seemed almost like a sound, a pulse designed to keep time to their day, but now there was just an unmoving red light, no new messages, no blinking.

"But she said—" Ruby bit her lip.

"Don't worry."

"She told on you, and she said she wouldn't."

"She didn't *tell* on me. I'm not a kid, Ruby. She just told her father what she experienced. Which she should have done."

"The cunt."

"Shh. Don't use that language."

"It's better if I call her a trustfundian fucktard?"

"Yes," Martin said. "It's better. Calm down." His eyes moved to the cockroach on the wall. "It's fine, it's fine."

"It's not fine."

Adjacent to his meditation bench lay what looked like a conductor's baton. He picked it up.

"What's that?" Ruby asked.

"This is a striker," he said. "For a singing bowl."

"A singing bowl?"

"I stole it," he said. "But by accident." Then he stood up very fast and raised the baton-like object and slammed it against the cockroach on the wall. The cockroach fell. Her father took the striker and walked to the kitchen. She heard the trash can opening, shutting. He came back to the living room empty-handed and sat down, not on the meditation bench, but on the couch.

"Oh," Ruby said. "Oh, Dad."

"I'm fine," he said. "Honest."

Caroline had hurt her father. She felt so strange. If stealing from Andy had excavated a space in her brain, now that space seemed to be widening. Her very bones would go hollow, birdlike. She needed to act before she felt so weightless. Next to the answering machine was the toolbox. She opened it.

"What are you doing?" he asked.

"I'm going to talk to Caroline."

She took out the two pieces of turquoise cloth. The shoe covers. She pulled them over 2D's sparkly shoes. She wanted to make Caroline think about Ruby's father. To bring that sign of respect upstairs, so that Caroline had to recognize all the ways she'd disrespected Ruby and Ruby's family. These shoe covers were her final disguise. At least for today.

"Ruby," her father said. "Stop. It's okay."

She turned away. She began to walk out of the apartment. The covers over her shoes made a sound like shush shush shush. She felt very focused. She felt very, very in the moment, like her every stride forward was a meditation. Her father followed her out the door. "Ruby," he said, "stay here. I'm your father. I'm telling you to stay here."

She jabbed her index finger against the call button. Her father was too old to chase after her, too old to tell her what to do. When the elevator doors opened on the basement, she stepped on and he did not follow. He said, "Ruby, just relax. Stay here." And he said some more words she didn't hear, because the doors closed and she was ascending.

Another game she'd played with Caroline as a child: In the moment before the elevator began to go down, they'd jump up. The elevator would sink just as they would rise and they would drop farther down than they had ascended. Every time. It was thrilling, like pulling one over on gravity. The elevator-jumping game was one of the few games Ruby was better at than Caroline. Ruby always dropped farther than Caroline because she was more skilled at recognizing the moment before the elevator descended, the perfect moment to jump. The trick was in the timing.

The penthouse had not been locked. The elevator doors opened onto the party, or at least onto what remained of it. There were wine-glasses out, plates of different gunked-together cheeses, but no people. The party had not been so exciting, then, or perhaps there was a better one elsewhere. So the guests were all gone. But was Caroline gone, too? She must still be here, or she wouldn't have left the place unlocked. Ruby should call out. *Hello, O Caroline, I am here to confront you. I am here to challenge you to a duel. I am here, I am here.*

But she said nothing. Instead she took a few steps forward. The shoe covers made their shush sound. A cold breeze hit her. The terrace door had been left partway open. Someone was out there.

She stepped onto the terrace. Nobody in sight, but Caroline's keening laughter was being carried on the wind. Caroline was somewhere on the roof.

Again, Ruby hopped over the railing. She walked along the edge of the building, trying not to splash her feet in puddles, toeing aside stray cables, beer bottles.

Then she saw them. Andy and Caroline standing in the same spot where, hours before, Ruby had stolen Andy's wallet. And next to Caroline: Lily's cousin.

Lily's cousin, off the intercom screen, live and in color, in three dimensions, in a puffy pink coat, on the roof near the penthouse, chewing on cheese, while Andy adjusted a tripod.

They hadn't noticed Ruby yet. She could hardly breathe. She stepped back into the shadow of the water tower. Caroline hovered at Andy's shoulder, muttered something to him. Andy crouched down, his face covered by the camera. They were, Ruby realized, collaborating.

Now Andy seemed to be taking the woman's photo. He said, "No, no, it's better . . . Better you don't look away. Look right at the camera. Okay? Like, look hard. Glare! Okay. And at the very last minute, let your eyes just sort of *soften*. No, no, *not* so soft that they close. Just imagine you're looking thousands of miles into the distance—"

"Let her do what she wants," Caroline said. Caroline had not worn a dress for her party. She had instead changed into an oversize sweater and a long spandex skirt with a plaid print. She looked *frumpier*. She looked like how Ruby must have looked in her interview outfit, except Caroline was wearing this outfit because she had a choice. She was demonstrating to the world all the ways she was empowered in her rejection of the feminine norm. Or something. Abruptly, Ruby felt the ridiculousness of the dress she had taken from 2D, its silken swaths calling attention to their own excess, the beadwork on the illusion neckline, the pleats on the skirt making her look like some giant blue, dimpled Smurf, smiling stupidly out at the world. Why had she ever put on 2D's dress? Here she was playing at being Caroline (and getting it all wrong) while Caroline was playing at being Ruby. Truly? Could the exchange be so simple?

"Keep going with your story, Evie." Caroline held up a small recording device. "You were talking about what it was like, stepping into 5A."

"It was dusty," the woman said. "Really dusty."

Her eyes, her mouth, her forehead's blocky frankness—all of that was so familiar. The resemblance to Lily had come through on the video screen on the intercom this morning, but now, here, it was like part of Lily had risen up again to greet Ruby.

Caroline held her recorder a little closer to the woman's face. "That must have been very hard, to walk in and see just dust. Do you have a lot of nice memories of your cousin?"

The clicking of Andy's camera. A weight on Ruby's chest.

"Nice memories?" said the woman. "Oh, she was fine. A nice full fridge. Sometimes she could be a real riot. But sometimes a little bit exhausting to talk to. Always blaming my problems on *systems*. When sometimes people are just shitheads, you know?" At this, Caroline laughed a little, and the woman said, "It's no damn joke, little girl. Lily thought she knew more about my problems than I did. But then she said to me one day, she said they're eyeing my apartment, they're waiting for my death, and she said . . ." The woman pulled proudly on the sleeves of her puffy coat. "She said if I was ever in a bad way, I should come and move in, and since I was technically family, she could get me on the lease. If things with Hal got bad again, she said . . ." Now the woman's eyes rolled upward to the sky. "She said it would kill them if I wound up on the lease and that would be funny, the way it would kill them. So I came. But I didn't come soon enough. It's not so funny now. She's the one killed."

"She wasn't killed," Caroline said. "She died of natural causes."

"Same difference for someone like Lily," the woman said. For a second she covered her face with her hands, forming a kind of carapace with her thick-nailed fingers.

"I'm so sorry, Evie," Caroline said. "That all sounds really hard."

"Thank god you found me this morning. Thank god you let me stay with you." She turned to Andy, releasing her face from her finger cage. "This one"—and the woman pointed at Caroline—"this one is a real true angel. Letting me stay here in this mansion all day."

All day. Ruby understood it now. She had been here all day. In the penthouse, inside one of the empty rooms. Caroline must have gone to 5A right after Ruby had admitted to letting Lily's cousin into the building. Before Ruby had gone to check 5A herself, Caroline had found the woman in the remains of the apartment, taken her upstairs, and kept her there until Andy had come over to take her picture against the city skyline at night. When Ruby's father was in the penthouse, fixing the door, the woman was hidden. During the party, she had been secreted away in Caroline's room with Caroline keeping her company. A kind of hide-and-seek.

Caroline must have been worried Ruby would have told her father. Or maybe she did not want to share the mantle of "real true angel" with Ruby. The woman had become Caroline's project. Caroline's doll.

She wanted to run at Caroline now, to push her over the wall, just as she'd wanted to do with Andy before taking his wallet. The wall was low enough here. A quick hard push. But no, that was the move of a villain. Or at least the move of a deranged psycho Dickensian urchin with a vendetta. Which was who she would be in Andy's stories to Caroline, probably. But she was not inside Andy's stories. Thank god. Instead, she was inside her own life, inside whatever story made the most sense to her. A secret princess. A secret heroine. A secret real true angel. Now was the time for her to reveal her truest self.

"I was the one who let you in," Ruby said. She stepped forward and Caroline's shoulders jumped and Andy's shoulders tightened and the woman cocked her head and, down below, a car horn screamed. In the silence that followed, Ruby stood up straighter. "Yes," she went on. "I'm the reason you're here, right now, on the roof outside this penthouse apartment."

The woman, wearing Lily's squint, looked back at Ruby. Caroline squealed. She ran to Ruby, hugged her close. "Oh my god!" she said. "See, Andy, I told you. I *told* him, Ruby, that you were just kidding."

"Kidding?"

"Joking. I told him you would be back here to say so."

"To say . . . ?"

"That you were joking," Andy said. He had put his face close to his camera, the lens pointed at the intruder. "But you weren't joking when you stole from me, Ruby. I know that. Caroline just sees the best in people. It's cute. But it's delusional."

"Oh, shut up," Caroline said, beaming.

"Who is that one?" asked the woman.

"Nobody," Andy said. "No, don't do *that* with your face, please."

Caroline clung to Ruby's arm, her chin tilted so she could look Ruby in the eye. That little ruffle of skin, where the potentially cancerous beauty mark had been removed, seemed to smile up at Ruby. "Listen, babe, Andy told me this story, this crazy story, and I said it was a joke. Or, like, a kind of you-version of performance art. Right?" Then Caroline looked down. "What's on your feet?"

"Shoe covers," Ruby said.

"Shoe covers?"

"Like my dad wears. When he visits an apartment. It's a symbol." She turned to Lily's cousin again and spoke up. "I was the one who let you in."

"Ruby," Caroline said, "you *are* here to return Andy's money, right?"

"Look at me, please," Andy said to Lily's cousin. "Right here. Not at the new person. Good." He paused. "She's not here to return anything, Caroline."

"Ruby." Caroline's breath had the new-upholstery smell of too many drinks. "Kiddo, kiddo, kiddo. Explain to me. What is going on?"

"You told about my dad," Ruby said.

"Well, *my* dad called and I just mentioned it. I'd had a shot or two of tequila before the party . . . I didn't exactly mean to tell my dad. But it came up, and it kind of slipped out."

The stone caught in Ruby's throat. If she pushed Caroline off this building and onto the roof next door, it would have to be quick. But no, what she needed to do was use her words. She tried again to gather up the nobility of the secret princess heroine angel star. She said, "I'm really angry at you, Caroline."

Caroline tilted her head. "Do you know, I don't think you're actually angry, Ruby, not really. I don't think you've actually been truly angry at me once today. You've just been playing pretend. I think you're angry at yourself. And embarrassed."

The stone inside her throat was sweating somehow. Her whole face was hot.

"Rube. Look, your dad won't be in any real trouble. He's been working here so long. I know things have been weird today. But see what we're doing?" Caroline moved her arms in a Vanna White sweep toward Lily's cousin, like she was a costly vowel newly revealed. "I found the woman you mentioned! Her name is Evie. We're going to make her image iconic and we're going to tell her story. Andy has this concept where she's standing against the skyline at night, like she herself is one of the buildings! Can you see it? It'll be gorgeous. Andy is going to do a whole series of photographs on her, and we'll get her truth out there and we're going to find her a forever home." The wind rose, cool and steady. "It's poignant, Ruby, it's this really exquisite thing that you've been a part of today, by buzzing this woman in, don't you see that? Don't you see what you've helped us create? You're like . . . the precipitating force." Caroline was drunk, she was excited, she was thrilled, she was buzzing with her own goodness. She had not thought about what she had done, what she might do, in reporting to Kenneth on Ruby's father. She reached forward and hugged Ruby so hard that they swayed back and forth together. Caroline said, "It's fine. Do you know? It's all going to be fine. Do you know that?"

Do you know, do you know.

"You weren't at your party," Ruby managed at last. "At your own party. I didn't see you."

"I came out a few times and said hi. But mostly I was with Evie."

Caroline smiled at the woman. "Getting her psychologically ready for talking to Andy."

"We got psychologically ready by drinking tequila!" sang Evie, and Andy said, "Okay, good, keep your face like that for a second, happy but not, like, *too* happy."

"We drank lots of tequila," said Evie, "so I'd be honest and go viral."

Andy said something about the shots being very powerful, that there was a kind of cross formed between the horizontal skyline and the intense verticality of Evie's stance, and if she actually could slouch just a bit more, right, so the cross shape and the Christlike echoes were implied but not overly obvious, yes, like that—it would be an important statement, going alongside her story, and the loss of her affordable apartment, the specter of Hal's anger, right, and domestic violence, wasn't Hal the boyfriend's name, plus the death of her sister—

"Cousin," said Evie.

But Andy's eyes were now trained on Ruby. "Caroline," he said, "why don't you get in some of these photographs."

"Me?" Caroline's mouth fluttered open.

"You should be in some shots with Evie, right?" Andy said. "You took her in, you kept her safe all day, you're part of her story now."

At Andy's words, Caroline blushed a little, said she didn't want to intrude, but Evie clapped her hands and said, "Come on, you cutie, come right in here, let's take some pictures together. A very kind individual, this lady," Evie said, and now, oh, oh, that tone. The playful slinking quality in the voice. She sounded so much like Lily, but a Lily who was declaring approval for Caroline, at last, while Ruby went unmentioned.

Caroline pushed back the wisps of her hair, tucking them behind her ears. "How do I look, Andy? Is this right? Am I supposed to smile?"

He picked up the camera and got closer to their faces. "Just in your eyes a little. Keep your mouth stern but smile inside."

Sweat seeped into the silk of 2D's dress despite the chill; Ruby's mouth felt stoppered by some inner humidity, as if her body's eco-system was shifting into a rain forest. Caroline gawked at the cam-era like a lost baby deer, a fragile cervine creature in an oversize sweater. Next to her, the intruder. Evie. Caroline had known her name first. What was Ruby's own to know first, to name? It was not fair. *Do you know*, Caroline had said. *Do you know, I don't think you're actually angry.* The way Caroline had tried to un-truth Ru-by's rage, to steal that rage away, the way even now she pretended she knew what Ruby was thinking. Caroline had found the woman in Lily's old apartment. She had walked through the demolition debris and seen the woman there, kneeling, maybe, in the dust that had been Lily's walls. She had found her before the workers arrived and asked the intruder her name and offered help so easily because help was always hers to give, and then she had talked to her father and told him about Ruby's father, told him maybe that he seemed unstable, erratic, unfit.

She could give and take, just like that, without even thinking about what her gifts and thefts might do.

"You're too far away from her, Caroline," Andy said. "Get closer to Evie. No, no, move a little. We want the skyline to show up be-hind you."

"Should I step forward?" Caroline asked. "Back?"

And now, at this moment, the stone in Ruby's throat seemed to dissolve. She eyed the sloping wall and called to Caroline, "You should definitely step back a little."

Ruby had meant it sarcastically. She'd tell herself later, for her own sake, that she had meant it sarcastically, or at least that she had never guessed she'd at last be taken seriously. The words were only designed to show Caroline that Ruby's anger was real and present and solid. She'd assumed, just as she had in the motor room, that Caroline knew where she stood. That Caroline was aware of the dangers around her.

But Caroline's face lit up. She smiled graciously and stepped backward. It was slippery up on the roof, because it had rained, and she cried out in surprise as she lost her balance and fell backward.

Later, when Ruby remembered Caroline's fall, she could swear she had heard Lily's voice starting to count. "One, two, three, four." Like a new game of hide-and-seek had begun. Ruby, standing there on the roof, had not closed her eyes but had covered her ears.

A LATER DAY

17 RUBY'S MUSEUM

M artin migrated.

It was not so hard. A few difficult weeks. Caroline was in a bad place. A broken ankle and shoulder, plus some spinal issues. An intense regimen of physical therapy. He and Debra left New York, and Martin knew he would not see Caroline again in his life. "I'll visit maybe," Neilson in 3C said, but Neilson in 3C would not visit. Still, Martin said, "That will be nice."

They went south, which was strange, but Debra was able to get a job at a library in a college town in Georgia, where a close friend of hers from high school, who could no longer afford New York's rent, had moved. She helped supervise college volunteers for a new adult literacy program. And Martin found a gig repairing things on the campus. There was a lot to fix. The hotter weather seemed to break stuff down faster. And there were different pests. Brown recluses. Spiders that could kill. Once, possums in a roof, with possum babies. Rent was not free, but because of his maintenance work for the university, Martin was able to take several free classes there every year. He took a biology class and dissected a rat. Its heart was smaller than he might have guessed. He took a drawing class and drew birds. Their eyes, he realized in sketching them, were even bigger than he'd thought.

He had fought so hard against what would happen if they lost their apartment, against the threat of his own life turning to dust, but they were not fringe people, as he had feared. That was what was surprising. Now he saw how much of his fear was a trick of faulty comparison, how he hadn't been able to see the full context of their situation. They were okay. "Middle class." Thanks mostly to Debra, of course, and her education. He had been fortunate there and fortunate that she was so flexible. Martin had begged Debra to leave the city with him after Caroline fell off the roof and onto the next building's. She could have died if she'd been angled a little differently. That almost-death, on top of Lily's actual death, was too much. The whole city felt haunted.

"The whole city," Debra said, "what whole city? You barely leave the neighborhood. We could just move to Queens and you'd think you were in a whole new cosmos."

"I want to leave," he said. "Please, Deb. What about how burned out you feel?"

"Well," she said. And she closed her eyes. Maybe she was thinking about her panel, about how she'd done just what she'd feared— shared the anecdote about the Dungeons & Dragons questions from prisoners, and joined in the crowd's laughter because she was too tired to do anything else.

"Please, Deb," Martin said. "Let's leave."

"Okay," she said.

After Caroline's fall, Martin had stopped hearing Lily. She did not voice-over his day or intrude into his mind. She was gone.

This was good from a long-term consider-your-sanity standpoint.

But also sad.

In addition to free classes every semester, Martin got a staff discount for membership to the college gym. Meditation classes, led by one of the gym's yoga instructors, took place every Wednesday night in a room covered with blue mats. The meditation classes had only a few regular attendees: two biology PhD students, one undergraduate Martin had never heard speak, and Martin himself. There were no singing bowls, and the yoga instructor used a daily calendar called "Enlightenment Hacks" as inspiration for her opening remarks. "Carpe diem," the instructor said once. "Seize the day." Martin no longer felt the same solace in these mantras. A single day nested a great many dangerous things. You never seemed to seize on to the right ones. Or at least Martin didn't. Maybe in his old age he would learn better what to seize, what to let drop. Some stuff was already dropping from him without his realizing. One night, when he couldn't sleep, he tried to take out the map in his mind, to link up as many of the tenants in the old building as he could. But now he found it was impossible. 7A had once seen the Yorkies of 3D pissing into the flower bed of impatiens she loved, although 5C felt impatiens were rather populist, or was it 8A who thought that, or was it 6C . . . Everything unraveled very quickly, seemed unsubstantial and silly as fuck, and in the end he could only repeat in his mind, like a new mantra, *landfills landfills landfills*, until he felt there was no solid ground beneath him.

They lived on the second floor of a condominium building.

It was a bit unnerving.

Sometimes after dinner Martin would call Ruby, who still lived in New York City and worked nights. It was always good to hear her voice and now, when they talked, he never worried about his heart. One afternoon, a couple of years after he and Debra left New York, she called him. He was with some guys trying to get a bat out of the engineering building. He stepped aside to take Ruby's call.

She said, "He has a new show coming up, Dad. Of his photos."

"Oh," Martin said.

"The first since the accident."

"Yeah?"

"He got my address somehow, and he sent me an invitation."

A show. With the photograph of himself in it, maybe?

"Are you okay, Dad?"

Martin looked at his reflection in a window and he stood up as straight as he could and remembered how he had hollered his stories in the boiler room, hollered over the sounds of the machines, and he said to Ruby, "I don't care. Just don't tell me any more about it. Not a word." But then he said, "Are you going?"

"To his show? No, of course not. I'm not even curious."

"Oh, come on, Ruby."

"I should get ready for work," she said. "I'll call you later, okay?"

"Tomorrow afternoon?"

"I promise."

After she spoke to her father, Ruby got on the subway, closed her eyes, and thought about Andy's show. Of course she wondered if he would display the photographs from that day. Photographs of her father, maybe, or photographs of her, her face shielded by the rhino head. But she especially wondered if there would be a photograph of Caroline moments before her fall, standing next to Lily's cousin, who had disappeared during the chaos that followed the accident and whose "story," as captured by Caroline, remained untold.

But now they might all be in the show together, frozen on film, Lily's cousin and Caroline and her father and Ruby and the rhino head. A kind of family portrait that nobody but Ruby would recognize as such.

Her stop. She got off the train, climbed the stairs to the surface. She was meeting friends for dinner before work. But she had a little time.

Even though she worked on the Upper West Side now, commuting most evenings from her apartment in Astoria, it had been years since she had walked past what had once been her father's building. She avoided the street. But when she'd heard about Andy's show, something in her had shifted. She wanted to test the limits of her own guilt, or maybe the limits of her own ghosts. She walked right up to the entrance of the building. A new awning now, this one navy blue and lit by the same wrought-iron lantern. They were no impatiens in the tree pit, but big-petaled flowers she didn't recognize. New shrubs out front by the door, chained down in their pots. The street smelled the same—like a wet towel. Like some secret spore-ish life might start growing across its surface at any second.

She walked into the foyer.

Under her feet, beneath her sneakers, was the place where she'd been raised. She tried to envision the basement. Her room with the steam pipe going through it. The couch with its windmills and cows. The laundry room. The garbage room and the boiler room and the elevator-motor room.

But all she could imagine now were those familiar spaces turned dark and fantastical, full of sleeping birds, overrun with pigeons and pigeon shit, with mice and rats. She imagined stepping into the basement apartment and finding the floor thick and soft, carpeted with guano. Would it smell like shit? Or old orange peels? An owl. Maybe there would be an owl nested in the dark of the motor room and a whole flock of pigeons gathered in her room, and rats moving freely all over, darting between the motor room's wheels, which would be webbed through with the homes of busy spiders bursting silken threads out of the microscopic spigots in their asses. How intricate those webs would be.

If she wanted, she could stand here and wait to see the new super, emerging to hose down the sidewalk. The new super would look at Ruby and see a stranger, someone who did not belong there. Or maybe it would be Rafael who would come upstairs. He had stayed at the building as a porter the last she'd heard. Perhaps his daughter came from New Jersey sometimes to visit him at work. Perhaps she sliced vegetables on the cutting boards her father had rescued from the garbage room.

Or 2D would emerge. Ruby had never returned the dress or the shoes, and just as she had guessed, 2D had never noticed they were missing. Nor had she reached out about any damage to the table. Ruby had given the dress to Goodwill, but she kept the shoes. She never wore them but she was glad that they existed in her closet, like shiny napping beasts.

Kenneth still lived in the penthouse apartment, even though Caroline now refused to set foot in the building, said she had flashbacks of falling whenever she stepped inside. John had told Ruby this when she'd run into him on the subway some months back. Caroline no longer spoke to Ruby. After Caroline's grandmother had died, Ruby had texted her. *I am so sorry, Caroline*, she wrote. *I saw the obituary. Very beautiful.* Caroline never replied. Well, what had Ruby expected? A sad-face emoji? A *thanks*?

Ruby waited a minute longer inside the foyer. Someone pushed open the door from the lobby. A nanny with a double-decker stroller, two little kids inside. "Oh," Ruby said. "Let me help." She held open the lobby door and the nanny smiled her thanks.

The lobby door was open. If Ruby wanted, she could slip inside. It would be easy.

But she stepped back. She took a breath. She went outside. It was supposed to storm. She hurried on to meet her friends.

Her father thought she should get out of the city. He said it was bad for her stress levels to take two subway lines to the Upper West Side every damn day and move around all those memories. He said she should just leave. She could even stay with them for a while. "Your mother would be happy to see you more," he said, "and I would, too."

His idea of the order of things had shifted around. What it meant to make your own home, what it meant to show the world you could stand on your own two feet—all of that had loosened. He just wanted Ruby to live closer. But she couldn't leave, she told her father. She did not mind her roommates, at least not most of the time. And she liked both of her jobs.

"You can get jobs like those anywhere," he said, and she had to tell him, trying not to sound condescending, that he simply did not understand the true nature of the work.

At night, she had the Museum of Natural History all to herself. Of course there were other guards, maintenance staff, scientists. But when she was given a designated area, that area, from late at night until morning, was her own.

"Is it like those *Night at the Museum* movies?" her mother asked. "With haunted mummies and the dinosaurs come to life and whatnot?"

"Have you heard voices?" her father asked.

It was not like those movies. It was not haunted or very cinematic. The museum at night was the most peaceful place Ruby had ever been. What she liked best about it was the way it shut out all the nocturnal city noise. She could not hear the nightlife or the parties or the homeless people crying for change from church doorways. She just heard her own breath.

There was a lot to guard in the museum of course, a lot that someone might want to steal. Gems and ancient farming artifacts and the rib bones of dinosaurs and meteoric bits. But of greater concern to museum officials was the risk that something might go wrong in the building, damaging the objects within. A leak might damage the hide of a significant beast. A mouse might chew on a wire, causing a short circuit, a fire. A big part of Ruby's job was to keep an eye out for signs of breakdown.

Often, though, nothing much was going on. Then she would think about Caroline and Lily and it was like they were right there, standing before her again. In the museum at night, memory was revealed to be nothing more than a feat of mental taxidermy. The salvaged skins of long-gone moments were draped over the structure provided by the present. The hours were weird. Her sense of time and of debt sometimes became scrambled.

"Is it your dream job?" her father asked her once. Ruby had laughed at the stilted way her father said *dream job*, like he was switching into a different language. Her dream job? No. But the job gave her the mental space to dream.

Of course, that didn't change the fact that this job was not what she had fantasized about when she thought about working at the museum. She was not restoring the dioramas or strategizing content for new educational exhibits. Her roommates sometimes asked if she was hoping to work in the museum in another capacity one day, was there mobility, and she'd say, "Oh, yeah, I'm hoping it might open some doors for me higher up." But she said this only because it was an easier story to share than the truth—that she was not looking to open doors in her career quite yet. She was looking only to open the doors inside her own self, to see what she might be hiding, what she might have to state or make.

Well, maybe that wasn't all the way true. Shortly after she'd run into John on the subway, he had sent her an e-mail. He said a friend of his, an art therapist, had seriously injured her arm while snowboarding and needed an assistant a couple of afternoons to help with the slide projector and art supplies, and yeah, he most certainly remembered Ruby telling him she didn't want him to be her career counselor, and he most certainly respected her decision to spend hours gazing into the belly button of the blue whale or whatever, but maybe this was something she could do on top of that, during the day, and couldn't they maybe be pals again? She ignored his e-mail for a little while. Then she asked for his friend's contact info. Now, a couple of days a week during the late afternoons, she helped conduct "dialogue-based lectures" about art at a few different seniors' centers. "Dialogue-based lectures" turned out to mean getting very old people—mostly very old women—to look at slides of paintings and talk about their memories and sometimes to collage or draw pictures of those memories. Ruby was a contract worker, assisting the art therapist who was some years older than Ruby and who wore beautiful shawls and who was also a contract worker. Ruby would set up the slide projector and then cast images onto a white wall. Mostly, the art therapist was in charge. She stuck with the Impressionists, those luminous crowd-pleasers. But sometimes she let Ruby choose slides and lead the discussion. Whenever Ruby put up an image from a Hopper painting of a naked woman alone in a room, all the old women had much to say. "I once had a room like that!" "I once had boobs like that!"

No matter what paintings they showed and discussed, at the end of the session some of the women would clasp Ruby's wrist on their way out the door and thank her. They did not remind her of Lily, although she wanted them to. Still, the more the women clasped her wrist, the more aware she became of the weight of her own tenderness on the earth. Afterward, she always wanted to go back to her room to work a little before her night shift. One of her roommates had a job at a shoe store and, vaguely aware of Ruby's "diorama thing," now brought Ruby old shoeboxes for shoes she could never afford. Ruby had begun to paint the backs of these shoeboxes. The Bethesda Fountain. The garbage room. The roof. She wanted to begin putting something three-dimensional inside the boxes, but she wasn't there yet. And anyway, they seemed too small for what she imagined. She was trying to think of them as prototypes or sketches, plans for something bigger when she was ready. She didn't want to rush herself.

The guard job offered her the fuel and the quiet she needed to think. Something about wandering around all sorts of extinct and endangered animals made her stop worrying too much about whether her own dioramas would look or sound stupid to other human beings. At night, in a half dream, she still could plan her own large-scale exhibits, which she would sketch out during her breaks. She would imagine each of the displays populated with a moment from her past. She had a vision every now and again of the end of the world. Some sort of apocalypse, but a gentle one. There would no longer be any documentation of debt. Everyone would have to move away from New York. But she would stay, manage to survive alone in the city, in the museum. She would use the material she found there to build, finally, her dioramas.

It would be a kind of meditation, a kind of art, a kind of naturalism, a kind of scientific record.

As she paced through the Hall of North American Mammals that night, she thought about how the nanny had smiled at her exiting the building where Ruby had grown up, how she had held open the door. Then Ruby shook the moment loose and began to plan a diorama to capture the day in the elevator-motor room with Caroline. This diorama she'd call *Behind Elevators*. On the other side of the display glass would stand three-dimensional remodelings of two girls, surrounded by cables and wheels. Ruby would indicate the griminess of the motor room with three-dimensional mice and water bugs, even though they had seen no mice or water bugs that day. The two girls would stand in the middle of the space. The taller, slightly pudgy girl on the right would have pissed all over her pants. How to indicate the urine? In the book on dioramas she'd taken from Lily, there was a line about an artist adding a streak of motor oil to make it look like a salmon had been dragged to shore by an otter. Would motor oil work for urine?

More important: The skinny girl on the left, the re-creation of Caroline, would have scrunched her nose up. The re-creation of Ruby would be looking to the side, ashamed. The re-creation of Ruby would not be a cute little girl at all. She would look young, yes, and feral. But in no way cute.

In the middle ground she'd place the elevator machine and many ropes going round and round. A motor generator that turned the alternative current into direct current. The two-dimensional background would be nothing but gray paint. No fake horizon. Just the sense of an indestructible wall.

As far as those diorama girls knew, they would be trapped together in the elevator room forever. They would starve listening to the sounds of the machinery that allowed the elevators to rise and fall and rise again. The display would have a lost-in-the-woods watching-out-for-the-witch atmosphere, coded with the wild, weird morality of fairy tales. A space of powerful whirring created by machines the girls couldn't name because they hadn't yet been taught.

Ruby took a deep breath.

She might not be a thief. She might not be an artist. Definitely, though, she was a guard. And what artifacts was she protecting?

Her shoulders jumped. An unexpected sound. A slow drip-drip. Perhaps the storm had started in earnest? And now there was a leak somewhere in her hall. She must find the water and report it, get word out before serious damage occurred, before a display got mucked up, before a piece of ceiling crumbled down on her own head—or, worse, on the head of some unsuspecting future visitor who had traveled great distances, come to the museum from a far-away state, seeking only a sense of wonder.

Acknowledgments

Thank you to Scott Moyers, my editor, for your wisdom, steadiness, and for really seeing and believing in this book. I'm so grateful to you, to Mia Council, and to everyone at Penguin Press. To my agent, Sarah Burnes, for her big-heartedness and fierce intelligence. To the Tennessee Arts Commission, the Scholastic Art & Writing Awards Alumni Micro-Grant program, and to Vanderbilt University for funding and support.

I owe so much to many people at SUNY New Paltz, Sewanee: the University of the South, and Vanderbilt University. Special thanks to Lorraine López, for creating a space where I could start to write this even though I was a little terrified. To Marysa LaRowe, Kevin Wilson, Lorrie Moore, Nancy Reisman, Tony Earley, Justin Quarry, Rachel Teukolsky, Claire Jimenez, Cara Dees, Anna Silverstein, Simon Han, Sara Renberg, and Emily Jacobson. Thank you all for your humor, your encouragement, and for being there for me at various stages of flailing during the writing process. It's meant more than you know.

To Hedy in remembrance.

To Garrett Warren—well, obviously.

Most of all, to my mother and father.